The Boundaries of Their Dwelling

Iowa Short Fiction Award

For David

For Jason B.

University of Iowa Press, Iowa City 52242
Copyright © 2021 by Blake Sanz
uipress.uiowa.edu
Printed in the United States of America

Cover design by Derek 'Thornton, Notch Design·
Text design and typesetting by Sara T. Sauers
Printed on acid-free paper

This is a work of fiction. Names, characters, places, and incidents are the product of the author's imagination. Any resemblance to actual persons, living or dead, is entirely coincidental

Library of Congress Cataloging-in-Publication Data
Names: Sanz, Blake, 1977– author.
Title: The Boundaries of Their Dwelling / Blake Sanz.
Description: Iowa City: University of Iowa Press, [2021] |
    Series: Iowa Short Fiction Award
Identifiers: LCCN 2021008815 (print) | LCCN 2021008816 (ebook) |
    ISBN 9781609388072 (paperback; acid-free paper) |
    ISBN 9781609388089 (ebook)
Subjects: LCGFT: Short stories.
Classification: LCC PS3619.A627 B68 2021 (print) |
    LCC PS3619.A627 (ebook) | DDC 813/.6—dc23
LC record available at https://lccn.loc.gov/2021008815
LC ebook record available at https://lccn.loc.gov/2021008816

The Boundaries of Their Dwelling

Blake Sanz

University of Iowa Press · Iowa City

Vida Loca," and Emi and Frida, her best friend, sang it aloud on the flight from Mexico City. They mimed dancing girls from the video as Frida belted out the silly words—*SHE WILL WEAR YOU OUT!* The panzón beside them pretended not to be bothered. Emi wasn't surprised to notice how Frida's perfect freaking figure undercut his annoyance.

An airport shuttle picked them up and ushered them along the Dolphin Expressway, past downtown, and over the MacArthur Causeway to South Beach. As it eased along a main drag, skyscraper glass angled the sun down at them with a fierceness the smog of Mexico City never allowed. Gaps between buildings provided snippets of ocean views where tanned men on Jet Skis carved out sea foam from the green Atlantic. Lines of yachts floated in perfect rows behind them. A boardwalk teemed with half-naked white people desperate to be brown.

They mocked this excess casually, much as they'd always mocked Americans from afar. As kids growing up in Frida's house in DF, after Emi's dad left and her mother died, they'd seen *Miami Vice* reruns and wondered how anyone could possibly say those sorts of things, act those crazy ways. Did Miami cops really take a full five minutes to watch a girl in a bikini oil herself up? Was a saxophone always playing in the background while it happened? Well, no, it turned out, but almost.

The show had bought their plane tickets and reserved them a suite at the Grand Marriott. They offered to comp room service too, and the first thing—the first thing!—they did on arrival was order a single hot dog. Frida's idea, of course. Just for the fun of it. A bellhop brought it to the room on a silver platter, yellow mustard pretentiously dolloped onto a porcelain saucer. Already down to bare feet and boy shorts, Frida thanked the bellhop with a Marilyn Monroe knee-bend and blown kiss, which turned the boy red. Emi slipped him a bill and nodded in sincere thanks to make sure he didn't get the wrong idea.

Frida squealed when the door shut, clapping at the sight of the hot dog. She grabbed it and jumped onto the bed, laughing. Emi followed suit. Crumbs fell as Frida tossed the sheets in the air. Outside, the sun scattered diamonds across the ocean. Emi reached for the hot dog, but

¡Hablamos!

THE FIRST TIME Emi and Frida traveled to the US, it was to appear as paid participants on a Jerry Springer–style, Spanish-language talk show filmed in Miami. *¡Hablamos!*, Univision called it. Emi hadn't known anything about it until one day when Frida came screaming into their shared bedroom.

"We won!" she yelled.

"Won what?" Emi replied.

On a lark, Frida had entered them both into a contest, the grand prize being an all-expenses paid, three-day trip to film an episode of *¡Hablamos!*.

"Wow," Emi said. "Okay."

That summer, Americans listened like classic gringos to "Livin' la

PART I
Lives of the Saints

And He has made from one blood every nation

of men to dwell on all the face of the earth, and

has determined their pre-appointed times,

and the boundaries of their dwellings.

—ACTS 17:26

I returned to my existence, the existence I had

chosen instead of you.

—JHUMPA LAHIRI, *Unaccustomed Earth*

Contents

Frida gobbled down the whole thing. Emi yielded to the playfulness of the moment. "Puta!" she yelled.

"Who, meeee?" Frida said, going into her character for *¡Hablamos!*. According to a treatment sent to them by Hugh, an assistant producer for the show, Emi and Frida were to be disgruntled sisters vying for the attention of their father, a copy shop employee of modest means named Rodrigo. This was ironic, given Frida's family's wealth. Hugh included a photo of the man cast to play the father. He could've played a part in *Ángel Rebelde*, the telenovela on Univision, though in fact he'd lived the whole of his blue-collar life in Miami, in Florida City. Emi's estranged father had worked a similar job as a copy shop clerk long ago, but this man bore no resemblance to Manuel.

In the role of disaffected daughter Conchita, Emi was to be sleeved with gang tattoos and wear a studded vest to show them off. Meanwhile, Frida—or rather, María—would wear a pink cardigan with a white collared blouse and designer jeans, so as to play the dutiful daughter who would try to bring her wayward sister back into the family's fold. Maria was to be frustrated at how much time their father spent trying to save her sister, while she herself had always been such a princesita perfectita.

But, of course, Frida was no Virgen de Guadalupe. That irony unsettled Emi, for it reminded her of something she wished she didn't know. At thirteen, as they gossiped in their bunk beds late one night, Frida had casually admitted to sleeping with her own cousin earlier that year. He had been twenty at the time. "It was just for, como, three seconds. Then Mom came in. He pulled out, y ya. Nunca hablamos de eso," she'd offered. *We never talked about it.* In the awkward silence that followed, Emi considered recounting her visit with her father in Veracruz when she was six, how one morning she'd walked into his bathroom and accidentally seen him getting out of the shower naked. But in the aftermath of Frida's scandalous revelation, that story seemed childish, and Emi decided to keep it to herself. She wished she could've responded with more empathy, but she didn't know how. Often, when Frida told stories about her recklessness—with boys, with her family, with herself—Emi could only think to nod. Wince. Blink. Breathe. In moments like these, she clung to Frida's nearness—that pungency of oversweet perfume, that familiar slackness of posture post-revelation—hoping her willingness to listen without judgment would maintain her access to this improbable friendship she otherwise imagined impossible.

That first night in Miami, they went out. Frida in heels and Emi in Converse All Stars, they roved the strip near the hotel, spry with mischief. They mocked the well-lit shops and clearly signed streets. The heart of Coyoacán near their prepa offered so much more interesting decrepitude, Emi thought. She had expected more from the States: more ads, more debauchery, more everything. In DF the capitalism was worn down, baldly omnipresent: a stray dog pooped on a fallen ad for Absolut; vagrants robbed businessmen beneath the tattered billboard gaze of a miniskirted flaca holding a bottle of Coca-Cola. Here, capitalism presented itself so *cleanly*. Sharp borders framed ads. Neon beer signs in bar windows burned bright. Despite what the white women they passed on the streets might've thought, Frida and Emi weren't from a village in the rain forest. Capitalism came naturally to them, and they approached it with the malaise and recklessness that DF required of its youth.

Under the mandarin-orange glow of a neon sign, they entered a club. Inside, purple strobes subdued pink walls. Steel tables shimmered in the glow of soft candles. No music played yet. This early, just a few souls lingered at the bar, and the paucity of conversation gave their low voices the illusion of importance. A dance floor spread out to the side, but no one braved it this soon after sundown.

Frida tried to order a drink, but the bartender asked for their IDs. Emi and Frida looked at each other. In DF, this never happened. They looked old enough, and it never mattered there anyway. When the bartender saw they were seventeen, he laughed. "Good job," Emi said, praising him like he'd passed a test, and then ordered two Shirley Temples. The bartender looked as though he might kick them out, but Frida flashed him a coy gaze, and instead he mixed their drinks.

Sprite, ginger ale, and grenadine: a drink Emi knew because of her father. On that childhood visit to Veracruz, he'd told her a story over Shirley Temples about the immigrant adventure of his youth, a decade before her birth. "We need to talk," he started. After crossing, he found his job at the copy shop, in a small Louisiana town. He met a Cajun girl there and they had a son, born in a trailer home by the Gulf of Mexico. "Last I heard," he added when Emi asked, "your brother is living in New Orleans." Her father gave her a black-and-white picture of him from a local daily in Louisiana. In it, he's playing basketball, jumping into the air, catching a ball, but his face is turned away from the camera. How she wished she could adjust the angle of the shot! It was the only photo of him she had, and she wondered about his eyes: Would she recognize them? Would they remind her of her father's? Of hers?

Mocktails in hand, Emi and Frida sat on leather couches by a cube sculpture illuminated by the multi-colored reflections of a disco ball. Soon, a boy entered, and Frida locked onto him. He wore a blue oxford shirt and gray pants lined with perfect creases and looked to be in his twenties. Black boots polished to a sheen. Blond crew cut, square jaw. Cold blue eyes that were, Emi imagined, not at all like her brother's. His teeth glowed as if under black light when he smiled. Frida bumped knees with Emi under the table, meaning either she couldn't wait to make fun of him, or else: *He's mine.*

For the first time, music permeated the bar: "Kangaroo" by This Mortal Coil. Emi knew it. It was the kind of weird, mopey song she'd sought out for herself, apart from Frida's influence, while browsing American music shops in the Zona Rosa alone, thinking of her brother and whether he was someone she could ever relate to. But maybe he was just some asshole basketball player. Anyway, in this bar, she found it an odd choice, strangely fitting for this time of the early evening. She knew that Frida would never have heard of it. Indeed, her friend ignored its melancholy, focused instead on the new boy.

"Hi," he said. "Mind if I take a seat?"

"Not at all," Frida said.

"You don't look like the typical trendy Cubans that come here."

"That's because we're Mexican," Emi deadpanned.

"You're from there?" he said.

"We live there, papi," Frida said. "Where are you from, the Land of Oz?"

He put his hands over his heart, miming fake hurt at the jab, and then laughed vaguely as if the gesture was charming. Frida giggled.

"What are you in town for?"

"Visiting our father," Frida said. "*She* doesn't like him, but *I* think he's great."

They could've told him about ¡Hablamos!, of course. But when they were out, Frida liked to play these kinds of games. And Emi, she liked watching them play out. Liked rehashing the blow by blow of these encounters with Frida later as a way of gleaning lessons on how to interact with boys, as a way of getting a better handle on Frida. And so, she played along with the deception.

"Yeah? Well, I don't like my dad either," he said.

"What about you?" Frida asked. "What are you here for?"

"I play ball at Florida International. It's a college around here. Name's Duke," he said, extending a hand to Frida.

"Call me Frida, if you want."

"And your friend?"

"That's Emi. Don't mind her. She's crazy." At that, Emi stifled a smirk. "What kind of ball do you play?"

So, Duke would be sticking around. Emi glared at her friend. Frida averted her eyes.

Duke didn't ask her age, and Frida didn't let on. When he finished his beer, he got up to get more for everyone.

"What are you drinking?" he asked.

"Vodka and cranberry," Frida said, and then winked at Emi as he walked away.

"Frida," Emi warned. But Frida, being Frida, simply kept her eyes fixed on her Shirley Temple. As with most nights, this one would play to her whim.

· · ·

Back at the hotel, while Duke and Frida banged the headboard against the wall in the bedroom, Emi folded out the sleeper sofa in the suite's living room and propped herself up. She changed into pajama pants and a worn-out T-shirt from grade school, and put her earbuds in (collected Ozomatli). She read from a Miami travel guide, but her eyes just passed over the words. Through the techno-Latin beats of "Cumbia," she felt the headboard thudding. She took off her headphones and walked to the bathroom to brush her teeth. There in the mirror, she looked at her face and tried to conjure her brother. He'd be about Duke's age now. Was he tall? Charming? Awkward? Did he look Mexican at all? Would she have somehow recognized him if he'd showed up tonight in the club? Of course, he probably still lived in Louisiana, so that wasn't likely. She'd tried to look him up many times before, but all she'd found was reference to an award he'd won in high school for perfect attendance.

Abruptly, the headboard stopped banging. "Asshole!" she heard Frida yell through the door. Duke's deep baritone came in, laughing. She couldn't make out his words, but they sounded harsh. She heard no movement through the door. Emi held the toothbrush still in her mouth, foam building at the back of her throat. That silence, awful. Then, talking again in muted tones. With a crack in the door, she might've made out the words, but even with the door firmly shut, she could hear the tension. She resumed brushing her teeth, scrubbing at her molars with her mouth open, making a point to pitch the sound outward. She turned on the faucet full force, spit, cleared her throat, and then sang the words to "Cumbia de los Muertos," about how there is no sadness in this place, only joy. She watched herself in the mirror, belting out the song. Focused on her body. The shaking of her hips in the reflection, the moving of her lips, they dampened those tense voices from the other room. She smiled at the sight of herself, and soon, no more sound filtered through the closed door. Emi decided she wouldn't knock.

...

Hugh had already arranged to meet them in the lobby at ten the next morning, and Emi woke up at nine to the sound of Duke closing the door behind him as he left. Frida came out of the bedroom in short shorts and a white top. "¿Quieres coffee?" she managed. Emi tried to measure out Frida's emotions, gauge the right response, but her friend was a brick wall. All Emi could offer was a tentative nod. When it came to Frida, she worried she'd never know how to act.

Down in the lobby, Frida donned her sunglasses and shuffled her sandals across the carpet. "¿Cómo fue Duke?" Emi asked. Frida shrugged. Emi let it go. Frida walked a step ahead, and Emi sized her up. Her shorts showed off her muscular legs. The spaghetti-strapped top accentuated her broad, slumped shoulders. She walked with her hands at her sides, uninterested in this new place. She took out a pack of Camels and went to light up beneath a No Smoking sign, but then saw Emi wince. Emi could tell, even with Frida hiding behind those sunglasses, that her friend was rolling her eyes as she put them back in her purse.

At a counter with a steaming coffee maker, the AC blasted so cold Emi swore she could see her own breath. Frida made herself a latte and Emi poured a water. They sat at a pair of plush chairs across from the hotel's main entryway. Frida took off her sunglasses, revealing dark and baggy eyes. The lobby was crowded with Americans coming and going. "Mira, Emi. Estas personas, qué horror," Frida said. Two middle-aged women with fake breasts wore triangle-top bikinis and sarongs that clung to their flat asses. Three men wore muscle shirts imprinted with the names of surfing companies, sunglasses atop their heads, their tanned faces etched into fake smiles that turned into leers for a young girl who walked by. "Is the whole country like this?" Frida asked.

"So many muscle men, so little time," Emi teased.

"Porfa," Frida pleaded. She rolled her eyes.

"Dukie Dukie!" Emi squealed, testing those waters.

Frida put her hands to her face. "Estaba loco," she said through her fingers.

"¿Cómo?"

"He kept talking about this plan he has. He wants to open a chicken restaurant in his hometown. Someplace que se llama Missouri. Patetiquísimo, Emi. I sucked his dick just to shut him up."

"A chicken restaurant? What the fuck is that? What were you fighting about?"

Frida traced an amorphous pattern on the tabletop with her finger. "Nada," she said. Emi thought to respond, but Frida glanced up at someone behind them. It was Hugh. He stood waiting, chic and stout, in a skinny tie, his beard well trimmed. "Ladies," he said. They stood to greet him, and he extended his hand to Emi. She took it limply, too entranced by his American confidence to shake back. "And you must be Frida," he said. Frida leaned in and offered her cheek. Amused, Hugh gave her a peck.

"We're excited you're here!" he said. "This production's a well-oiled machine, so we should get going. There's lots to do. I'm eager to introduce you to some people."

In the car Hugh played the role of a sprightly docent. "Now, don't be anxious, girls! We'll take good care of you. The show's format is pretty simple, so don't worry. More than anything, I'm here to make sure you have a good experience, okay? I mean that."

Emi noticed Frida watching Hugh as he gesticulated. "Do you think he's gay?" Frida whispered to Emi. Hugh gave them a glance in the rearview. Frida straightened up, a cut-up caught in the act. "Do you think we'll meet any celebrities?" she asked him.

"Well, nobody like Brad Pitt, if that's what you mean. But there'll be plenty of things you've never seen before."

At the studio, Hugh led them to a conference room with a long table where a group of interns sat. An older man looked out of place. Emi recognized him from photos as the man who would play their father. So she thought. She wondered how long he'd lived in Miami. He didn't look like Manuel. He was shorter, rougher looking, less roguishly handsome than her father. More the family man, though he wore no wedding ring. Hugh closed the door and the room fell silent. Emi caught the father's eye. He smiled, revealing crow's feet and yellow teeth.

"Everybody, Frida and Emi," said Hugh. "Frida and Emi, everybody." The interns chirped back hellos. The father approached Emi, extended his hand. She was taller than him, and he looked up at her with kind eyes. "Rodrigo," he said, and bowed. "Encantada de conocerle." His look didn't surprise her, but his voice. Emi had never met anyone besides Manuel who skimmed over their rolled *r*'s that way, exaggerated and extended their *e*'s and *a*'s like that. Emi wondered if that's how she would sound if she grew up in Veracruz.

"Everyone," Hugh started. "Let's go over the basics of tomorrow's taping. Before we start, has everyone seen the show? You're all big fans, am I right?"

Frida and Emi had seen it a thousand times. A hybrid of Springer and Oprah, it boasted a melodramatic Univision flair. Meaning, in part, that it held absolutely no obligation to real life, even though it was supposed to be a real-life talk show. The host, Susana Desertiados—what kind of name was that, anyway?—wore pastel pantsuits and blouses that exposed her balloonish breasts. Blond highlights streaked her light brown hair, which waved like Farrah Fawcett's in old episodes of *Charlie's Angels* they'd seen, and she outlined her lips a shade darker than her lipstick. She bugged her eyes out when she turned from her guests to the camera to ask a rhetorical question to get the audience riled.

It was like Oprah because, for certain segments, Susana tinged her questions with empathy. Still, the audience rarely seemed to care about the guests' lives, instead biding time like circling vultures, waiting to erupt in disgust. By the show's penultimate segment, the Springer in Susana would emerge. She'd ask judgmental questions to match the audience's budding contempt. And how they pounced! Snarls, jeers, pointing. But in the final segment, she'd reveal something cheaply sympathetic about her guests. The camera would show audience members bursting into tears, their rabid thirst for the blood of the stagebound swept up into a sea of melodramatic shows of pained empathy, matched only by La Virgen herself.

Hugh called them to attention to go over the third act: the segment of the show between the second and third commercials, where the action would crescendo. "Tell me what you think, Emi. Maybe you could take off your belt and throw it at Frida in a fit."

"That could work," an intern offered. "Rodrigo, you could start crying."

"And Frida," another interjected, "you could break character, go full crazy, and, like, come at Emi full force with a roundhouse to the face."

"Don't worry if we do it that way, Frida," Hugh said. "You won't have to strike her. Our security guys will break it up before anything happens. What do you say?"

In a shared glance of mischief, Emi and Frida exchanged a thought: it would be impossible not to laugh through all this. "Sounds great!" said Frida, answering for both of them.

As Hugh walked the interns through the choreography of that exchange, Susana walked in, wearing tight jeans, a blouse with a matching headscarf, and a pair of sunglasses. She looked like Cher on a sidewalk trying to avoid the paparazzi. A hush fell over the interns as she said hello. She took off her glasses, sat down at the head of the table, and smiled a prefab smile. Hugh introduced Emi, Frida, and Rodrigo. "Bienvenidos, dulces," Susana intoned with import. "Tomorrow, you will be stars. But today, you must listen to Hugh!"

Frida bumped Emi's knee under the table. "¿Puedes creerlo?" Frida whispered.

• • •

When Frida said she didn't want to go out that night, Emi conjured dramatic scenes taking place behind those locked doors from the night before. "That's okay," Emi said, trying to hide her eagerness to simply stay in and talk. "We have to tape the show early tomorrow anyway." After getting bags of chips and bottles of Coke from the vending machine, they turned on the TV and settled in to watch *The Godfather* on HBO. Snuggled together on the bed, they snacked and watched like they would've at home. "I believe in America," the old family friend said to Marlon Brando in his study. The camera panned back as he continued his story of coming to this country, slowly revealing the back of Brando's head as he gestured for his assistant to the get the sad storyteller a drink. Beneath the quiet words, Emi could hear Cheetos crunching in Frida's mouth. She took a sip of her Coke and turned up the volume.

Somewhere around when Michael Corleone retrieved the gun from the bathroom, Frida started snoring. Her head fell against Emi's shoulder, and gradually, she slumped down onto Emi's lap. She'd always been such a heavy sleeper, Emi knew, but this slumber seemed like something else. Emi hoped that, one day, Frida would feel close enough to her to tell her what was really on her mind. Whatever that was.

As she had so many nights back in DF, Emi undertook her solemn routine. She shifted open her knees beneath Frida's slumped body—slow, so that she wouldn't wake her, knees open so that there was a space through which she could slip her hands beneath her friend. In the time it took Michael to flee to Italy, Emi slid her fingers under Frida's head. By Michael's marriage to the Italian beauty, she'd painstakingly moved her lap out from under Frida's body. She spent another few minutes sliding a pillow beneath her head. Throughout the process, each time Emi sensed the slightest change in Frida's breathing, she froze until the tenuous moment passed. By the time Michael had shut the door on his new American wife and the credits ran, Emi had laid Frida in her favorite position (the fetal) and had moved far enough away from the bed that she could resume a natural disposition. She let out a controlled sigh, feeding the air slowly out of her body so as not to negate the meticulous work with any noise.

Though she'd never smoked, Emi grabbed Frida's pack of Camels from the nightstand and went out onto the balcony. She looked over the ledge, down to the neon of Ocean Drive. She lit one and tried to inhale, but the smoke caught in her throat and she stifled a cough. She'd always figured that one day Frida would teach her, but now she decided that she might as well teach herself.

She surprised herself with how quickly she picked it up. Within a few puffs, she'd mastered a deep inhale that put her in mind of mysterious characters on American TV dramas that ran on syndication in DF. She practiced her smoking expressions in the reflection of the sliding door's glass. Here is how to be pensive. Here is how to be pained. Here is how to be secretly satisfied. Here, one day, is how you will look after anonymous sex. She morphed through her new expressions to the faraway *oontz* beats of the neon-saturated clubs below, the single light of a ship blinking on the dark sea near the horizon.

Reaching for another cigarette, her fingers grazed the top of a piece of paper rolled up beside the remaining Camels. She took it out and unfurled it. It was an unsigned affidavit from a court in Mexico City. In an impersonal Spanish, it read: "Personally came and appeared before me, the undersigned Notary, the within, named *Nenetl Frida Coaxoch*, who is a resident of Distrito Federal, México, and makes this his/her statement of and General Affidavit upon oath and affirmation of belief and personal knowledge that the following matters, facts, and things set forth are true and correct to the best of his/her knowledge..." There was a gap then, and in that space, Frida had written out a small paragraph. Emi read, caught Frida's cousin's name. It appeared that the cousin had been charged recently with rape, that Frida was being subpoenaed to provide information about her incident with him.

She peered back inside the room through the balcony's sliding door. Frida lay asleep, fetal and dreaming. A burst of lightning and thunder destroyed the moment. Frida shifted positions. She opened her eyes and seemed surprised to find her head on the pillow. In how Frida looked at her, Emi imagined herself a dark and ominous figure standing here at the entrance to the bedroom. She inhaled, thinking of what the orange ember glowing bright at her lips would look like to Frida in the dark.

"¿Que hora es?" Frida asked. Her eyes were squinty. She put her hand to her face and touched the imprint of wrinkles from the sheet on her cheek.

Emi exhaled, tried on her new mysterious face. "Morning's a long way off," she said.

"You don't smoke," Frida replied.

Emi didn't say anything.

"Ya no estoy cansada," Frida said.

"¿Qué quieres hacer?" The ash on Emi's cigarette grew long.

Frida got up and brought her an ashtray. *The Godfather* had been perfect to fall asleep to, but now the calm of the turned-off TV left them with only each other and the quiet. Frida slinked back down onto the bed. Her languid arm stretched out over a pillow beside her head. A constant rain fell outside, and Emi watched it with her.

"This is a strange place," Frida said.

"Quién sabe."

"Los Estados. Los Yunaites. Los Yanquis."

Emi hesitated, unsure what to say. "I wonder where my brother is," she offered.

"You have a brother?" Frida looked at her, mouth open, like the betrayed.

"He lives here, in the States. He's from here."

"Why didn't you ever tell me?"

"I've never known what I should and shouldn't say."

"To me?"

"To anyone." Emi took a drag, exhaled. Tried on her pained face. Then the nausea of smoking for the first time set in, and the pained face became real.

Frida observed her and smiled. "Mi Emi," she cooed. "You can tell me anything."

"Can I?"

"Listen to you. My little Emi. Of course you can. You know what? Maybe we could stay here. You know, after the show is over. Or, fuck it. Forget the show. In the morning, we could just pack our things and hitchhike to—where is your brother?"

"New Orleans."

"Yeah. New Orleans. Forget *¡Hablamos!*. What do you say?"

"Just like that." Emi snorted. She moved from the sliding door to the bedside. Frida cast a casual wrist in her direction. Emi's own hand fell down on top of it.

"We could be our own gang," Frida said, in English. "Not on *¡Hablamos!*, but in real life."

Was it a sincere plea? Emi wondered. So little between them ever seemed to be.

To stay, Emi thought. To search out her brother. To find him and tell him all of the things, whatever they were. And for Frida, lying there in all her cultivated whimsy, why would she stay? Her friend's expression was something between a promise and a wink. By the bed, Emi plucked another cigarette out of Frida's stash and laid the carton on the nightstand, making sure the rolled up affidavit remained flush against the base of the cardboard. She put the cigarette to her lips, lit it—a clear violation of hotel policy—and inhaled with a cough. Frida laughed. "Seriously, puta," she said. "Tomorrow? We don't even have to show up for the taping."

The phone rang. Frida answered. It was Hugh.

"You girls ready for your big day tomorrow?"

"We've got just the right outfits," Frida said, smirking at Emi. *Habla Hugh,* she mouthed across the room. "Just the right makeup, too."

Hugh asked officious questions about their familiarity with the episode's premise. Frida placated him with that mischievous smile. "Don't worry, Hugh," she concluded, "everything will be perfect."

After she hung up, the two girls raised eyebrows at each other. "¿Qué piensas, chica?" asked Frida.

The moment was ripe—anything could happen—but their practiced rapport muted the drama, and Emi chose to envision this moment as being like so many other similar ones: the silky comfort of their meaningless words. Late-night proposals. Banalities as numberless as the stars. This, their way: gentle mm-hmms and clearings of the throat, sighs of comfort and cackles of laughter, playful interjections of *ay chingón* and *a la chingada*. No actual things being sorted out, just this lingering: there was relief in it. Emi closed the lid on the cigarette carton and placed it on the nightstand. In the wake of the question, she said nothing, only shrugged, and that, for now, was that.

. . .

Before sunrise, Emi ironed the black vest she'd brought for the show, the one she'd called ahead to Hugh to have approved. Frida stripped down to her lingerie and looked at her modest outfit laid out on the bed: her cardigan and blouse, faux-designer jeans from Forever 21. The clothes looked so unlike her.

"But, then, look at your panties," Emi noted: a green silk thong. Frida also sported an underwire bra from Frederick's of Hollywood, a trashy number she'd bought on a whim during a night out in La Zona Rosa, back when they were too young and flat to worry about bras. Frida filled it out now. Emi was pretty, but she didn't have those curves. Frida zipped up her jeans over the thong with a smile.

"They'll never know," she said with a wink. She pulled her blouse over her head, down to her waist. Her curves disappeared in its loose folds. When her head popped out with her hair messed up, she looked at Emi, pregnant with silliness.

"Now let's see *you*, Miss Hot Pants," Frida said.

Emi made tough faces as she pulled on her ripped-up jeans. She couldn't quite pull off the coked-up gang-girl look yet, partly because she needed fake tattoos to complete the façade. She wondered what tattoo designs the show would have. Skull and crossbones? The giant lips of the Rolling Stones? Che Guevara?

At the studio Hugh led them to a greenroom. There, Frida joshed Emi about what ridiculous nightclubs she hoped to go to later. Makeup girls arrived and sat them in chairs like marionettes. Emi and Frida faced a mirrored dresser flooded with harsh light. These girls were themselves made up for a night out, and they commanded the room with their airy gossip, indifferent to Frida and Emi's presence.

As one of them brushed and blushed Emi, she watched her transformation in the mirror. First, the eyeliner, black and thick. Then the pop-orange lipstick and purple lip liner. Next, the hair: flat-ironed and lowlighted to make her look brooding. She turned to Frida, who looked back and exploded in laughter, the way Emi had seen her laugh at hapless boys before.

"Emi!" Frida said, pointing.

Emi shrugged. She wanted to imagine they were getting ready for a costume party. In that case, she would laugh at how she looked, too. But this wasn't like that, for now she knew she was supposed to act like someone real. "Are we done yet?" she asked the makeup lady.

"No," she replied. "Jenny!"

A henna artist entered with a binder of designs. "Who do we have today? Oh, right. Druggie bitch gang whore." She flipped through the binder. Emi took her in. Orange and green Pippi Longstocking–style tights. Four-inch black heels. Stud through her nose and an eyebrow ring. Jenny assessed Emi's arms and shoulders.

"Let's see, hon," she said. "How's about an AK on your forearm and some Neruda poetry on your bicep? A little cartel cross on your shoulder. Maybe some letters on your knuckles could spell out C-U-N-T or something. That sound about right? For Conchita, I mean?" Jenny took Emi's silence as assent and applied the stamps to her bare arms.

Meanwhile, the makeup artist put on Frida's face. As she did, she muttered under her breath, "Let's see if we can lighten up those cheekbones, sweetie." Frida was Nahuatl, and she owed her beauty, Emi had always thought, largely to the severity of her jawline, the darkness of her skin contrasting with the arched angle of her thick brow, what the light-skinned of Mexico City often called her exotic features. And to have these things noted in any kind of negative light? By a beauty professional? Well, Emi could bet that this was something Frida had never before encountered. The makeup girl looked at Frida's face as if it were a puzzle. "I wonder how we can soften that jaw," she said. Frida acted like she didn't understand. Of course, Emi knew that she did. She knew she should say something—cut off this gringa's arrogant mumbles—but once again, Emi was at a loss.

"Thirty minutes to air," someone said from the hall.

The henna artist escorted the two girls to the side of the set, out of the cameras' view. Through a sliver in a curtain, they saw the audience gathering. Women in the front row gabbed in Spanish. Bored souls in the back tried to start the wave. Most of the audience was Latina, though a few white faces clustered in spots. Emi and Frida each felt a hand on their shoulders and turned to see Susana.

"Don't be nervous," she said. "These people, they won't ever know who you really are. Hugh prepared you, right?"

They nodded.

"So, this is nothing! This is show business!" She motioned to the booms and wires and lights and dollies surrounding them. Between the stage and the audience stood a bank of cameras as big as cars. On set, grips moved a love seat and repositioned a folding chair. Opposite a coffee table stood a highbacked throne of a chair for Susana. Maria and Rodrigo would take the love seat, and the folding chair by itself was for Emi—Conchita, the outcast.

"Trust in the magic of the show, little ones," Susana opined. "Wait for your cue, and join me on set when Hugh gives the word. You will be unforgettable!"

With that, Susana left them alone. The lights came down and the theme music played. Lights on set blazed up. Hugh cued Susana, and the girls watched her posture change as she walked into the cameras' view. The microphone she held tunneled her voice away from Emi and Frida, toward the audience, which stood in applause, hoping a camera might glimpse them. Some flailed their arms like concertgoers. Others wore expressions of bemused calm and golf-clapped.

Susana took it all as her due, bowing deep as a Beatle when she reached the X marked on the floor. Emi guessed that in these moments, Susana felt most like herself: those assured gestures, that confident expression. The crowd's rapt attention reaffirmed her every word. She opened with a canned line about the good show in store for them all. In a lilting Puerto Rican Spanish that dropped in tone to reflect the pending drama, she summarized Rodrigo and Maria's sad predicament: the Conchita problem. At the mention of Conchita's affiliation with a drug cartel, the crowd booed. Frida jabbed Emi in the ribs.

At the first commercial break, the cameras' green lights went red. The audience buzzed with excitement. An assistant fetched Frida, who kissed Emi on the cheek, and then whisked her onto the stage. "Here we go, sister!" she called back. On set, Frida sat beside Rodrigo on the love seat. Frida practiced crossing her legs primly, trying to become Maria. It didn't come naturally. She looked up at Emi offstage and shrugged her shoulders.

The director motioned for the audience to stand, and they did. When an APPLAUSE sign lit up, they complied. Lights shone on Susana, who held her microphone and stood in the bleachers chatting insincerely with audience members. As the director fed volume to her mic, she looked up at the camera and acted like she was emerging out of a real conversation and was only now getting back to moderating the show. As she recapped the Conchita problem facing Rodrigo and Maria, she sauntered to the stage, ending her summary standing next to them. She introduced them to the audience. The crowd applauded moral approval at their sad plight. She sat down, hands folded on her lap, and asked them about Conchita.

Behind the curtain, Emi waited. Hugh joined her silently and she felt his gaze. "When she calls your name," he whispered, "wait a bit before you walk out." Live on air, Maria answered Susana's questions about Conchita. At first, Frida's gestures seemed playful, actress-like. She just couldn't help worrying about poor Chita, she was saying.

At a certain point, Frida's expression changed.

When Susana asked her about Conchita's reckless dalliances with dangerous men, Frida nearly started crying. Susana pressed, interjecting with an anecdote about Conchita's indiscretions with their aunt's husband. The crowd exhaled exasperated sighs of disbelief. Frida's anxiety mounted like a wave about to crest.

Emi looked out into the audience. A single face jolted her. Resting his hand on his crotch, with an indifferent lean and his shoulders hiply unsquare, sat Duke. With a friend. Two white faces in the brown crowd. Emi looked back at Frida, who was stone-still, petrified.

"Let's bring out Conchita," Susana said.

It wasn't Hugh's imploring that caused Emi to wait a dramatic moment before going out. Quickly enough to prevent alarm, she composed herself and walked on set. To a chorus of boos, she flexed her bicep to show off her tattoos. She couldn't help but know that Duke was looking right at her. She ran through the faces she'd tried on the night before, and then decided to egg on the crowd by raising her clenched fists in a bring-it-on gesture. They responded with jeers and hisses, just like Hugh had said they would. She tried not to focus on Duke, worried this would break the spell of the show. She sat in the lone chair and folded her arms. She snarled. Hoping her raised upper lip was convincing, she stared at the floor as sullenly as she could muster.

In her mediator's voice, Susana implored her to recognize her faults. Only when she beckoned "Conchita" for the third time did Emi turn. At that, Susana relaxed her posture in the way of a ten-cent therapist, as if relieved to have brought Conchita back into the present. Emi saw the makeup cheaply faded at the base of Susana's neck, how the blush didn't hide the creases in her smile lines.

"My dear," Susana asked, "do you see the hurt you are causing your father and your sister?"

Emi looked at Rodrigo. He was trying and failing to feign his disappointment with her. Really, he just looked like he had to fart. Beside him, Frida kept her hands tensed in her lap, legs crossed tightly at the knee.

Emi had memorized an immature introductory line, and she recited it now. The audience burst into a thousand varieties of vitriol. Some stood up and pointed. Others shouted insults with a rage she hadn't anticipated. Others simply shook their heads in disbelief. She dared not look in Duke's direction, though she imagined he and his friend cackling, their white faces filled with casual disdain.

Meanwhile, Frida was buckling. Susana seemed to notice it but let the scene play.

"Maria," Susana said. "Do you have anything you want to say to Conchita?"

Frida snapped out of it. She looked at Emi. Emi returned the gaze with a prescribed look of rage, but as they found each other's eyes for the first time on set, they couldn't maintain the charade. Rodrigo put his hand on Frida's knee and patted it like a father. After a beat, she spoke.

"I wish I could talk to you," she said to Emi. She placed her hands between her legs. Emi wondered: Was this movement real? It didn't seem like Frida, and yet the sincerity in that gesture was unmistakable. The crowd quieted. They waited for the show to turn from Springer blowout to Oprah catharsis. Emi caught sight of Duke. He sat with his legs open. As Emi was about to deliver the saccharine line she'd rehearsed, Duke's friend stood up and yelled out, "The Aztec-looking chick's the real whore!"

The camera's light went red. The director commanded the cameraman to resume taping. The camera went green again. Emi felt the tension in the audience. Backstage, Hugh made a beeline for security. Duke didn't say anything, just slouched with his hand to his mouth like he had nothing to do with it. Two security guards walked up to Duke's friend. "What?" he protested. They grabbed him by the arms. "What the fuck is this? I'm being thrown *out*? What about *them*? They're the fucking liars, not me! That Aztec chick is a whore!"

The audience watched, stone-faced. A whiff of violence filled the air. When the friend was gone, a nervous applause rose up. The sharpness of the boy's words about Frida rang in Emi's ears. Frida was still trying to hold a prim posture, like Maria would. She refused to look up in the stands at Duke, who continued to gesticulate like the self-righteous asshole he was. Rodrigo only watched onstage, just like everyone else. He was no father. Duke leaned back in his seat. He scratched his chin and smirked like Skeet Ulrich in *Scream*. Glaring at Emi, he raised his arms as if to absolve himself of all recrimination.

Emi wanted then to become Conchita, to call on her drug cartel friends to fucking smoke him. Instead, she did the only thing she could think of. She got up and walked around the stage clucking like a chicken. The audience sat dumbfounded. Emi looked right at Duke and said, in her best redneck English accent (which wasn't very good), "Fry me up and serve me hot! I could make you a million dollars!" Frida's mouth morphed from a quivering tilde to a perfect O, and then she machine-gunned a staccato laugh that split the silence. There she is, Emi thought. Everyone looked stunned. "This gringo thinks he's gonna run a chicken shack one day!" Emi continued in Spanish. Duke rose, face flushed, squinting his eyes. He smiled as he looked Frida up and down, then scowled at Emi as he walked to the exit. Someone in the crowd yelled an obscenity at him, but he held his glare. Others yelled out their frustrations at Susana. "¡Qué chafa!" some screamed. "¿Quiénes son esas putas?" one yelled. "Fuck these girls!" another offered. As Duke walked out, he pointed at the last heckler in approval. Emi mock-waved. "Goodbyyyyyyyyeeeeeeee!" she taunted. Her show of bravado might have looked credible, but inside, she was shaking and her heart was thumping like a frightened rabbit's. Some burst into applause at her gesture. Others booed.

They taped the rest of the show, but Frida and Emi didn't fake it well. They were too in need of each other's affections to play prescribed parts. The story line unfolded unconvincingly, and Emi could sense Susana's anger beneath her rote, Oprah-like advice. Afterward, the two friends walked off set alone. Nobody talked to them. They stood outside the greenroom, not sure whether to leave or even how to get back to the Marriott. Frida stood with her arms folded around herself. Emi had never seen her friend so clearly at the center of such scorn. Such vitriolic rage. And these people, this audience of Latinos, they were supposed to be allies. This was supposed to be fun. And then, Duke. That fucker. This whole thing, it was supposed to be a lark. Frida's eyes were gone. A silent tear trailed down her cheek. Emi knew from experience that a hug wouldn't help.

Eventually Hugh and Susana found them. Susana cursed them out, yelling how they'd fucked everything up. After she stormed off, Hugh remained. "Oh, brother," he mumbled. "Don't worry about that," he told them. "She's just really particular about the plotlines. She was really hoping y'all could pull off the rivalry, you know?" He patted them on the back, seeming to have done this before. He affected the sincere manner he'd shown when they'd arrived. Rubbed their shoulders. Feeling empathy for his plight, they let him, their hands awkwardly at their sides. With what grace he could muster, he escorted them back to the hotel, never once apologizing, never once admonishing.

Aware of being alone together for the first time since watching *The Godfather*, Frida and Emi packed their things. Their flight would leave that night, and a couple hours remained before the shuttle would arrive to take them to the airport. Emi watched as Frida took the cigarette pack from the nightstand and threw it into her purse.

"Espera," Emi said. *Wait.*

Frida looked up. "¿Qué?" she asked.

"Un cigarillo."

"¿En serio?" Frida asked.

Emi nodded. Frida took the carton out of her purse and handed it to Emi. Emi looked to see if it made Frida nervous to see how close Emi's hands came to the affidavit in the carton, but her friend gave no sign. Emi lit a cigarette and put it to her lips. She conjured the faces of angst and melodrama she'd practiced the night before on the balcony.

"I think that I might love basketball," Emi said, "but I don't like Duke."

Frida smiled.

"Also, I don't love this country, but I do think that there is someone here that I might love."

"Emi!" Frida raised an eyebrow. "Who is he?! Should we stay?"

Emi sighed. *Not that kind of love, puta!* she thought. She took a long, dramatic drag. She tapped her cigarette against the nightstand. "Maybe," she said in English, "we could try to talk to each other. For real. Do you know what I mean?" And this time, it was like some kind of magic: they were different people when they spoke this other language.

Frida sighed. "There are some things I need to tell you," she allowed.

Emi let the silence hang for a moment. *To be loved. To love. To see. Truly, to be seen. This: our mortal coil. She breathed in. Exhaled.*

"Bueno," Emi said. "Hablemos."

Hurricane Gothic

A wedding! In the gnat-filled heat of a Louisiana backyard, a small-town couple jumped the broomstick. The modest ceremony took place at the newly built house of a family friend, a self-taught handyman who'd made a killing fixing up houses after Hurricane Audrey. The groom professed to love his little lady better than anyone could ever think to do, and the bride countered that he better, because her daddy would never let him live it down if he didn't! At eighteen, they were the first of the baby boomers in that town to get married. Ben: prone to raising a little hell, firstborn charmer of a local Pacific Theater vet. Anne: drum major for the Holden High Hornets and newly minted Avon girl of the Livingston Parish chapter.

A distant uncle had died that spring, and in his will, he left Ben a plot of land at the edge of the river. Ben didn't question his luck. These were the 60s! Anything was possible! He took the gift as his due and set to building his bride a house. The job would've daunted others, but behind his mischievous eyes, Ben possessed the will of a mule. He used old drawings of his father's childhood house as a blueprint. Before the flood of 1958 ravaged it, that old-timey cabin stood in the swell and sway of fertile land tucked in the gentle curve of Blood River. It was a hidden Eden: satsuma trees in a grove, blackberries on the vine, Katrina and Rita not yet even flutters of a butterfly's wing.

Like a penitent to Lourdes, Ben pilgrimaged to the abandoned flood site for salvageable wood. Hand-cut relics of oak and cypress lay half-buried beneath the tall grass—shutters and cabinets, hard-wood slats and varnished shelves, humble prisms of rural life. He sorted through the debris. Here, a cypress plank from an old kitchen shelf from which his father, the story went, nearly fell to his death at age six. There, a hand-carved post from his old man's childhood bed, notched with knife slits to mark his father's growth. From the homestead's muck and ruin, Ben gathered wooden talismans and imagined new purposes for each: this bedpost could become a stair rail on his porch, that kitchen shelf a floorboard in his new living room. Each slat became a story, every watermark a warning.

For wedding presents, he sweet-talked Anne into asking not for grapefruit spoons and cheese boards, or wine glasses and potholders, but instead for copper wiring, insulation, and panes of window glass, nails and glue. What he couldn't acquire that way, he bartered with local merchants to procure, promising work on their personal projects in exchange for the things he lacked. Even at that tender age, he'd garnered a reputation as a hard and honest worker, and so the materials came. By July 4, he'd finished prep work. As cement mix filled Ben's planked forms beside the river, the stack of found wood from his daddy's old place stood sentinel, awaiting its chance for rebirth.

. . .

THAT TUESDAY IN LATE SUMMER
OF 2009, 4:30 AM

Through the predawn, Judah carries his weight in cut wood from the loading docks to the lumber aisle. Other workers haul smaller amounts, but Judah's pride won't allow that. Washed in the blue-tinged light of the Home Depot parking lot, he carries boards inside: two-by-eights here, four-by-fours there. He lodges the bundles on his broad shoulders like boom boxes, slides the timber into marked stacks before returning to the docks until dawn emerges, misty-gray. Heavy-gaited, he escapes to the storefront and leans against the wall, the weight of the morning's work pulling him back against the brick.

As he lights a cigarette, a girl approaches. Hat on backward, she's dressed in cutoff jean shorts and a graphic tee: "Save a Horse, Ride a Cowboy." She recognizes him. She looks familiar. Who is she? Wait— Brennan's sister. Judah and Brennan used to get high together, throw parties, do tons of stupid shit. He can't remember this girl's name, but she was always there. She'd been a freshman then. At the parties, she meekly observed the wide array of illegal goings-on: lines snorted in the kitchen, sex in the bedrooms, who-knew-what outside in the woods. She never told Brennan's parents anything, never partook either. Once, cops raided the place, caught Judah in bed with this girl's friend, another 14-year-old. He was 19. This landed him, for the first time, in the parish prison.

It's been years since he's seen this girl, or Brennan, or anyone from those days. She must be in her twenties now. She looks so different: mischief in her eyes, an awareness of her body. She asks him for a light, and he obliges.

"You remember me?"

"You're Brennan's sister."

She smirks. "Come on, Judah. You don't remember my name?" She looks at his orange apron. "You work here?"

"Something like that."

"I just got fired from the truck stop on 1-12. So did Rachel."

Rachel. The one from the party. Judah gulps. "Yeah? How's she?"

"She never held that night against you, you know. It's all good."

"Well, I'm glad to hear y'all are doing well."

"Who said I'm doing well?"

"I just thought—"

"I'm just kidding, Judah. I mean, shit. I'm a grown woman now. Look at me."

He notices her black eyeliner, sunken cheeks. Her eyes are chlorinated pools of blue. Track marks line her arm.

"So, anyways, I'm here looking for that J-O-B"—this, a phrase Judah used to turn—"but I can't work anywhere they drug test. They do that here? It's like that crazy chick used to sing: 'They'll try to send me back to rehab.' Ha."

"You'll say, 'No, no, no'?"

"Super-gay comeback, dude. You sure you fit to work the floor?" She raises an eyebrow, takes a drag. Judah looks back, scratches his whiskers. The sky's lightened. "Give me your number," she says. "We could have some fun together. And by the way, dork, I'm Sylvie."

. . .

FALL 1999

The house's first disaster was a stealth affair. Through the births, baptisms, and graduations of Ben's six children, the steady push of Blood River softened the banks atop which he'd built. Then, one evening, a crash. He ran to check on Anne to find the living room floor caved in, down to the river. His wife stood at the precipice, mouth agape. Then Judah entered, a strapping kid of nineteen.

"Daddy?" he said. "What was that?"

It made sense, the appearance of his youngest at a moment of crisis. From Judah's birth, Ben learned to expect one with the other. As a preemie, Judah clawed for life in the NICU. The sight of him swaddled in his mother's arms in the hospital parking lot caused an old woman to stop and gush at the exact moment a car sped round the corner and knocked her down. The experience branded Judah. His siblings took to calling him names: troublemaker, whiny-baby, faggot. Faggot, as in prone to vanity. Spoiled. Likely to be raised soft. His older brothers took it upon themselves to harden him up. When he complained about doing work around the house, they called him a pussy; when he took up basketball, they called him part black; when he took to football, they smashed his head in the dirt on every backyard play, then said he'd never amount to shit if he didn't stop his bitch-ass whining.

Meanwhile, his sisters rolled their eyes at his arrogance. Shook their heads at his vanity. When he'd curse out their mother for moving his CDs, when he'd keep his hand on his crotch while watching a game instead of studying, when he'd speak crudely on the phone to girls for the perverse benefit of his sisters' ears, his eldest sister, Constance, would lash out: "That's not gonna fly in the real world, boy." He threw it back at them. Made a mantra out of "You'll see." Developed a penchant for explaining how things *could've* been, if only so-and-so hadn't done such-and-such. To his friends, he claimed to "hate all the drama," which was precisely how they knew he loved it.

And so, for Judah's face to be the first thing Ben saw as his wife cried "Holy Hell" and half the house hung down to the banks of Blood River? That didn't surprise him. Not one damn bit.

. . .

THAT TUESDAY IN LATE SUMMER
OF 2009, 6:02 AM

Sylvie gone, Judah flicks his Camel to the pavement, checks his watch. Store's open now. Inside, he recognizes an old stoop of a man who comes often to chitchat about projects, to solicit advice on whether he should buy this or that cut of wood, to otherwise shoot the proverbial handyman shit.

"What can I do you for?" Judah asks.

After a senile pause, the man smiles wide and rests his hand fondly on Judah's shoulder. "What you say, spoke?"

"Doing all right, sir. Any luck with that planter for your wife?"

"Well now. First, she wanted it just for her hydrangeas. Now, she wants it to fit her petunias, too. Just like that. Like it won't make any difference to how I go about framing it."

"Gotta keep the missus happy."

"She's all I got. We never had kids, you know. I imagine you might be about the right age to start thinking about that."

Judah guides him to Lumber, recalls how close he came once to fatherhood. After prison for the stat rape charge, during those cloudy years of meth and women, this girl, one of many, informed him she was two weeks late. She was a country knockout who never understood how little he'd cared beyond the physical. "I'm not pregnant," she'd whispered one night. "Word," he'd responded. He convened his boys at a bar, got drunk. They joked in crude hypotheticals about what such a sorry infant would've looked like. Judah absorbed the ribbing, threw back Coors like water. Not only was the girl not pregnant. Not only had his friends just picked up the tab, but also this: after a stint of probation for a second-offense DUI, he had just one week before his driving record would be wiped clean. Reveling in the thought of what havoc such freedom would allow him to wreak, he turned the key, pulled his truck onto the highway, and drove the thing into a ditch. Within minutes, the cops had arrived.

"Here we are, sir," he says to the old man. "Just brought in these bundles this morning."

. . .

SUMMER 2001

To anyone who'd listen, Ben told stories of the catastrophe. Of how the TV dangled from the edge of his den's ripped floor, hanging by its cord down to the river like one of his wife's peacock earrings. Of how a bed of water moccasins writhed out of the roots of a cypress near the foundation in the hours after the collapse. Of how the new place he had in mind to build? It was gonna be slicker than owl shit.

This tendency to hold court dated back to high school, when he'd snuck three gallons of Dawn into the town's fountain, and suds ran into the streets for hours. He spent the next week telling the tale, watching as his friends' eyes lit up at the story. Every time he told it, he added something: the number of gallons of detergent; the length of time he stayed watching people react; the nature of their incredulous responses. He saw that he was earning a reputation as a charmer, and with that came a certain unexpected brand of validation.

In his fifty-sixth year, he rebuilt the house. Or, rather, moved it stud by stud across the gravel road, away from the disintegrating riverbank. He enlisted his sons' help—all except Judah, who was locked up on yet another DUI. Ben's disappointment ran deep, but he revealed it only by complaining about the impact of Judah's absence on the rate of construction. Meanwhile, his other sons noted with helplessness the limits of their father's aging body. He could no longer whip out a wall's worth of framing in a single afternoon. Couldn't carry his toolbox without limping. Out of respect, they didn't say anything, but their silence was all the damnation he could bear.

To compensate, he worked longer days. As his days lengthened, his mood worsened. The sounds of resignation marked his habits. The whack of his hammer thudded more flatly. His grunts were tinged with a wheezy whine. That quiet sigh of knowing he'd have to redo what he'd just done: this, too, came more frequently—not only during the workday, but also at night as he looked over the site, aching, replaying the day's small failures in his head. Yes, the crown molding he detached from the old living room and reattached to the new brick *was* as perfectly flush as it'd been before; and yes, the hardwood boards *were* as painstakingly nailed down as he'd managed at eighteen. But the time it took this go-round! The energy it sapped! Thirty years ago, he'd insisted on triple-checking the work of those who'd volunteered to the cause. Now, he just claimed to trust their handicraft. Over months of this, he began to see that there were no more stories to tell, just things to get done.

Through the work, he stayed at his daughter Connie's house. He saw Anne only occasionally. What would their life look like when they moved back in? What could they look forward to? He was losing the gumption that had attracted her to him. His steel-glinted stare on the level. That saw blade's edge of corny country humor.

Truth was, their marriage had begun rotting before the house caved into the river. There'd been fights about Judah. At Anne's prodding, Ben had confronted the boy about his drinking and indiscretions the only way he knew how: with stewing silences that boiled over into violence. In the morning wash of one of his son's hangovers, he'd stormed into Judah's room, pulled the sheets off him, soaked them with turpentine, and made a bonfire on the carpet by the boy's bed. Anne acted like it never happened.

Then the house collapsed. Which had been good, in a sense, because it gave Ben something new to fix.

Now, every Sunday after work on the house, Ben drove to Judah's prison. On the highway, he entertained dire possibilities he didn't consider with others around. To hold those at bay, he'd switch on a conservative talk show and reflect beneath the doomsday chatter—on the uselessness of rebuilding, for example, given the region's propensity for disaster; on Anne's silence; on the wondrous mechanics of Judah's descent. In the prison parking lot, the radio's angry voices would come back into focus. He'd sit there listening for a full hour, staring at the prison gates, then turn the key and go back home.

· · ·

THAT TUESDAY IN LATE SUMMER
OF 2009, 10:38 AM

Judah clocks out, hops in his truck. Blows into the Breathalyzer wired to his ignition. The display registers a blood alcohol level of 0.0; the engine turns over. Between Home Depot and his gen-ed English class at the community college—one of a few credits that will let him transfer to LSU, part of the life plan his father demanded of him—there's no time for a shower. He changes out of his work shirt, brushes off his jeans, and puts the truck in gear.

This stretch of I-12 he's committed to memory. Someone could spin him around, lay him in the Tacoma's flatbed, and on this highway, he'd name their location by the shapes of the pines moving across his line of vision. Though he's driven this route a thousand times, the view's changed. A billboard that once advertised for a well-coiffed ambulance chaser now advertises for roof repair. A new exit ramp accommodates the population that's moved here since the famous storm. A clearing in a field boasts the foundation for what will become the governor's pet project, a private hospital. Mile markers appear in rhythm. Here is #22, Livingston, where Brennan used to throw parties. Here is #19, Satsuma, where his meth dealer lived. Here is #15, Walker, where Connie rented a studio through nursing school.

During his most recent spell in lockup, she visited. "What you say, boy," she'd offered.

"Just doing my thing. What's up with y'all?"

"You know Daddy. Working like a fiend. Overdoing it."

"Somebody needs to watch him."

She nodded. "What about you? You need anybody watching out for you?"

"Shit ain't like you hear on TV, Con. My ass is tight and dry, if that's what you mean."

"Judah, that's gross," she said. He smiled. She cut the silence with a complaint about their mother, how she wasted so much effort worrying about Daddy. They weren't doing so well, she let slip. "Maybe once this latest rebuild is done."

"I want to make it right, Connie. When I get out."

"Well, I'm glad to hear that, Judah."

"I don't know what to do."

"Now that Daddy's about to finish on the house yet again, they're gonna give you some thought. My guess? He's gonna see about getting you a job somewhere. Maybe Home Depot, since he knows everybody there. I bet Momma'll even try to convince him to let you live rent-free, help you get on your feet. But don't think for a second that—"

Judah took his sister's hand. Started crying.

"They're old, Judah. Especially Daddy. You can't imagine what all this work is doing to him."

"I just wish—"

"What I'm saying is, when you get out of here, you need to start flying right. Let them enjoy each other. Why else you think Daddy is going through all this trouble?"

Judah pictures his father as a young man. Young Daddy must've had no idea how the river was softening up that riverbank. In retrospect, the house collapsing was just the start. This most recent hurricane damage, it was much worse. As Judah drives into Baton Rouge where I-10 and I-12 merge, the interstate's exit numbers reset. He'll get off at #1. Here, near the community college, exit numbers are just numbers and the highways aren't conduits to the past, just things that get you from one place to another.

· · ·

SUMMER 2008

Another goddamn hurricane. Fourth in three years. Ben lay propped up in bed beside Anne, shaking his head at the howling wind. As the joints of the new house creaked, safety didn't enter his thinking, only frustration at his own shoddy work. He looked up at the skylight. Its frame was slightly askew, its facing not quite square to the glass. He noted the wide groove he'd cut into the wood, into which the beveled edge of the glass should've fit snug. This accounted for the vibrations he heard, the sense of uncertainty creeping through the skylight's thin veil of shelter. Beyond it, clouds swirled like milk in a coffee-colored sky.

Water oaks in the backyard groaned. Out the window, the wind moved through in solemn waves. It bent the trees so that the highest branches reached down to the eave of the new house and kissed it, as if the storm were a golfer lining up a drive. In a single, shearing burst, the ground exploded as roots tore through the earth, spraying mud and sand. An oak crashed through his skylight and landed beside the bed. The spray and roar of the rain flung them into chaos. Adrenaline pulsed through them as they jumped upright. Ben hurried Anne to the den in time to watch another oak pummel the roof and crush the sofa. He took her by the arm, hurried her to the garage, where the wind raged louder. Looking at the felled oaks lying atop his TV and fireplace, he thought with contempt of Judah, sitting safe at that moment in the well-constructed fortress of his prison cell.

. . .

THAT TUESDAY IN LATE SUMMER OF 2009, 11:12 AM

Judah enters the classroom late. Heads turn as the door clicks shut behind him. He slinks into a seat in the back. For today, the class has read "The Storm" by Kate Chopin. Discussion has begun. None of the characters, the professor says, seem to have acted out of anything but self-interest, but they all seem better off. The cheating wife sees her husband in a better light. The cheating husband fares the same. The husband is washed in the glow of his cheating wife's guilty ministrations. The storm has passed, and life has not only returned to normal, it has mysteriously made things better. Is it possible that good things can result from a series of randomly destructive and selfish acts? This is what the professor wants to know.

. . .

FALL 2008

Ben climbed over twice-destroyed walls and waterlogged furniture to inspect the damage. To salvage what he could. He gathered pieces and laid them on the wet grass in rows, careful to turn the nails face down. Kept an inventory of each board, labeling them by length and origin and story, by type of wood and functions served in this house and the one before that, and in his father's before that. By the light of an oil lamp, he drew thumbnail sketches of new bedrooms and bathrooms, porches and foyers. He taped them to the garage wall and looked out in the moonlight at stacks of wood soon to be on their fourth use, gazing back and forth from woodpile to sketch, imagining how one might become the other.

Over weeks, he leafed through books with pictures of rural houses. Photos of porches, vaulted ceilings, crown molding insets, inlays of hand-carved doors. When he saw a photo he liked, he noted the address and drove to inspect it. He'd study the curve of a porch post, pass his hand over the carving of a built-in bookshelf. He took photos. Asked questions. Measured the widths of bay window sills. Nodded at fluted baseboards. Balked at prefab track lighting. Thus prepared, he sketched plans. His own rebuild he envisioned in the Spanish Colonial style, with French doors and a porch across the front. A high-pitched roof with a central beam running the length of the home.

In this way, he swung into a manic phase that carried him through the tasks of rebuilding yet again with an ebullience that was not real but that would pay real dividends. Where the move across the road had been marred by his depression, the storm's destruction of the new house had jolted him into frenzied action. Awake at night beside Anne in the garage, which had been spared and where he insisted he and Anne stay together as he worked this time, Ben obsessed. What was he missing? How much would it cost? Where could he save? What would insurance pay for? Mornings after no sleep, he rose and took to the swamps to see what timber he could find.

· · ·

THAT TUESDAY IN LATE SUMMER
OF 2009, 1:04 PM

Class is dismissed. A shuffle of rustling bags fills the room. Judah wants to explain his lateness, but the professor's engaged with another student, so he gathers his books and leaves. Walking to his truck, a pretty girl strides up beside him.

"Hey, you're the guy who always comes in late," she says. She's blonde and tan, young.

He offers his hand. Hers is soft. The look in her eye as she squeezes it unsettles him.

"You worried about the midterm?" she asks.

"I reckon it'll be okay."

She complains about their class in the context of her larger workload. Segues into her plans to become a nurse. The readiness with which she shares her dreams fascinates him. He takes her in: mousy blonde, petite, the sort of submissive girl he's always gone for. She's organizing a study group. Would he be interested?

"Just think about it, okay? Let me give you my number," she says. "The more we band together on this thing, the better off we'll be."

Judah nods and considers saying something about himself—about his own plan for his future, the one his father's made for him—but decides against it. He looks at the girl's number, back up at her. She hugs him goodbye, and he knows she must smell the scent of lumber on him. "Thanks," he says. Heads for his truck.

. . .

FALL 2008

Ben drove I-12 away from his own rubble, toward the chaos beside the highway, where fallen pines lay like pickup sticks. The radio mumbled, aghast—talk of the aftermath—but he kept it turned low. North of the lake, he guided his truck beside swampland soaked with rainfall and exited on a ramp that descended into the muck. That road took him to a T, where he drove over the curb, over bumps and dips in the grass, between cypress and pine that somehow still stood. When he couldn't four-wheel it any farther, he killed the engine and walked on foot into the woods. Beside a fallen trunk, he knelt down to pass his hands over its soaked bark. He was looking for something, some sort of strength. This wasn't quite it, but close. The ground squeaked as he sank his boots into the squish. The sticky shade didn't feel like shade, and though no sign of the storm lingered in the sky, woody refuse everywhere marked its indifferent passing.

He gaped at how the wind had repositioned this backcountry. Why did this tree stand? Why did that one fall? Even puddles of still water dotting the forest looked to be created by the hand of a careless painter. The random arrangement, as arbitrary as his own suffering, held until he reached the lake's edge. There, he saw something seemingly placed for him alone to discover: a thick, imperfectly round trunk of cypress. Half in the water, half out. The muted gray of its grain. How it spanned the lake and the shore—this made it look like it was emerging out of the dark water for some new purpose. Ben felt a rush of hope. He sensed that no one else had yet witnessed its potential. This, he thought. This could hold the new house steady.

· · ·

THAT TUESDAY IN LATE SUMMER OF 2009, 2:30 PM

As part of Daddy's recovery plan, Judah drives home to cut his parents' lawn. Once inside the new house, he looks up at the vast, vaulted ceiling. The living and dining rooms stand together as one big, unwalled area encased in a throng of lumber his father had gathered from across the parish. Judah focuses on the beam supporting it all. He's been back from prison living in the garage a few months, and even after all the rest of what's happened since then, every time he enters, his father's creation overwhelms him, reminds him how he had no part in the work.

Before cutting the grass, Judah fixes a quick lunch. Everywhere, his father's hand is inescapable: getting plates from the cabinet (ash from Springfield); retrieving silverware out of the drawer (cherry from Ponchatoula); sitting at the dining room table (birch from Lake Maurepas). He passes a reverent hand over the sanded grain of a chair, sits down to eat.

Outside, he fills the mower's tank. He pulls the starter cable, the engine catches, and he pushes it into the naked sunlight, his own stink covered by the smell of gasoline. He walks the mower in a rhythm, snaking back and forth from road to house, house to road. Near the shoulder, he can see Blood River beyond, where the old house used to stand. The engine vibrates the handle, sending oscillations up through his arms. Dips in the lawn sharpen his attention. He tries not to burn the grass. On his final pass, his phone vibrates in his pocket. Sylvie: *Wanna party 2night?* 😊

Judah flips it shut, cuts the engine. He abandons the mower and rushes to the garage. He puts in earbuds and takes off his shirt, smelling of sweat and gas and wood. In his work pants, he gets into plank position and holds it for the duration of a Pantera song. It's a song from the old days with Brennan and Rachel. Sylvie. In the pulsing of his veins and the pounding of his heart and head and his sweat dripping to the concrete floor, the song hits its stride. Heavy bars, thrumming with reverb, match the rhythms of his shaking body. He has a vision. He pictures himself from above, driving a highway, driving his father's old truck, headed west, and west, and west, until he's somewhere that reminds him of those old Westerns on TBS late at night, a place where hard-asses go to rob banks and live free. It's so real it seems like a memory, different from how his mind used to work on meth, or coke. His mind churned then, too, but this isn't so flitting, so falsely sheen. He can barely make out his own eyes through the grime on the windshield. He sees the lines on his own young face, something no drug has shown him before. The song ends. Judah drops to the floor, his body a heaving mess of flustered youth on the concrete.

· · ·

FALL 2008

Once Ben mounted the cypress log onto the stanchions he'd built to support it, the remaining tasks fell into place. He allowed himself to imagine how much longer it would take. Months, most probably. His manic high was wearing off. Visions came, unsummoned, of various methods of self-mutilation. At night he wallowed in them. In his worst moments, he imagined his exit a retribution. To whom, for what, he couldn't say. On-site, he put aside these visions, but as work drudged on, he felt a slackening of energy, a slowing of the mind. Despite his outright dismissals of the problem, the mirror at night showed him the effects of his mood plainly.

Anne noticed. After he went two weeks straight without saying nearly anything, she set him up with a psychiatrist, a family friend who promised to charge half her usual rate. Despite his resistance, not wanting to seem ungrateful, he acquiesced.

For Ben, the psychiatrist's office was as foreign as Iraq had been to his eldest. Laminated certificates and diplomas lined her prefab walls. A fake potted plant in the corner reached out to him like a leper from Numbers. An electric fountain cycled water over plastic rocks. With hair permed like the eighties and giant glasses hiding her eyes, the psychiatrist sat behind her desk. It was lacquered but cheaply made, which shaped his impression of her as a person who cared more about appearances than quality. Still, he'd been taught better than to judge on first impressions, and so he sat down opposite the desk with an open mind.

"Welcome," she said.

Ben nodded.

"Anne told me what's going on, but it'd be better if I heard it from you. Okay?"

"Yes, ma'am."

To his surprise, Ben unloaded the most intimate of his troubled thoughts, ones he'd never shared. He talked about his problems with

Anne, the pain of rebuilding over and over. With that grind soon to be finished, he wondered aloud: What would be his use after that? Days when he had no strength and the pains in his knees kept him laid up, his mind would wander. He envisioned the shapes of tools hanging from the garage walls, the dark forms of chainsaws and miter saws, the machete resting against the workbench and the nail gun hanging from its knob. Figuring a certain kind of talk might force this woman's hand, he didn't add how these images gave rise to a variety of grim possibilities. How, ultimately, his rifle would work just fine. When she asked about suicide, he didn't say anything.

She changed the subject. "What about Judah? Don't you have use in his life?"

"He might could use somebody," Ben allowed. "I'm gonna let him stay in the garage when he gets out of prison this time. I could get him to cut the grass, do odd jobs. Having him around *might* help me, but I damn sure know it'll help *him*. He needs all the help he can get."

Anyhow, Ben allowed, that was some ways off. His boy's latest sentence wouldn't be up for two months. He looked at the psychiatrist's desk, couldn't help but wince at the sight of its unevenly leveled top.

. . .

LATE WINTER 2009

The day Judah got out of prison, Ben was waiting for him with two rifles in the back of his truck, ready to take him hunting. They drove to the woods west of the lake. These were Ben's father's lands, up near Blood River's origins, where Ben had hunted since before he could remember. As a teen, Ben built a deer blind near here that still stood, and he made for it now. In a half hour they pulled onto a grassy clearing beside a dirt road. Ben parked in front of a concrete slab overgrown with weeds, where his father's childhood house had once stood. They walked a half mile into the woods following a trail until they came upon the blind. Judah climbed up into it. Ben had brought a camouflage jacket, and he threw it up to Judah, who put it on. Ben climbed up, wearing his own camo and an LSU hat. He set the rifles down and they slumped in the blind and leaned against its wooden wall, ankles dangling over the railing's edge. From his pocket, Ben offered his son a peanut butter sandwich in a Ziploc. "Just half," Judah said. Ben ripped it. Together, they ate. It was midafternoon, and the sky was gray and the air was damp and cold.

The easiest entry into conversation, Ben figured, would be LSU football. He complained about Les Miles's propensity for taking risks. He had a talented enough team. How on earth did he think fake field goals and going for it on fourth downs would continue to work? The irony was that none of his gambles had failed yet. This frustrated Ben. It went against his notions of hard work. Faking a field goal against a better team felt like cheating. It would be more dignified to get beat.

"He's an outlaw, Daddy. It's just his nature. You used to be that way. Don't you know you can't do nothing about that?"

"One day, it's gonna come back to bite him," Ben offered.

"Maybe. But until it does, let's just enjoy the ride, huh?"

So much for *that* as a starter. Maybe Ben could try something else. "I'm just about finished with the house," he said. "We've been sleeping in it for a week now."

"Yeah?"

Ben offered the canteen. Judah drank. "Not much else has changed, though."

Judah nodded. Ben had the urge to put his hand out to the boy, bring Judah's head into his arms, but he didn't.

"Your momma's got me seeing a psychiatrist," he offered.

Judah laughed. "Yeah? What's that about? You been working yourself too hard again?"

"I suppose."

Judah took his father's squint-smile as a sign of his father's enduring will. He offered the old man a playful pat on the shoulder. "Same old Daddy," he said.

Ben guffawed. "I reckon," he replied, though he knew it wasn't true. "What about you? You the same old Judah?"

They talked, but Judah had long since mastered the art of telling his daddy what he wanted to hear. Ben had no way to tell if Judah would stick to any plan of recovery.

"I know I can't ask for nothing," Judah said. "I'm day to day. I know the kind of people I need to stay away from."

Ben had no new advice. "I guess time'll tell, won't it?"

Like Connie had predicted, Ben proposed an arrangement: the Home Depot job, free rent in the garage, the rest of it. "But I swear," he added. "I catch you red-eyed, I'll beat your ass."

Judah smiled. "Yes, sir."

They sat in silence in the blind, watching and waiting. The air cooled as twilight approached. Ben's bones stiffened. His back tightened. Near dusk, a crunching of twigs: a doe, by itself. With silent glances, they debated whether to take a shot. Such a tiny thing, no great prize. But Ben wanted to take something away from this trip, a head on the wall to commemorate his boy's return. Not for himself—he'd already planned when and how he'd do it (this very shotgun, that very weekend)—but for the boy: a reminder, always, of the way they were at their best. Ben lined up the animal in his sights. "Say the word," he whispered. For a single beat, the doe raised its head and chewed, unaware. A moment later, Judah said, "Now."

. . .

THAT TUESDAY IN LATE SUMMER
OF 2009, 10:30 PM

The garage's heat swells. Judah's exhausted but he can't sleep: Sylvie. Should he text her back? Was she serious this morning about a job? Had she known he'd be at Home Depot this morning?

He rises from his mat, walks blind through his parents' yard to the main house. Since the murder-suicide, since that morning he found his parents' bodies, the house has remained empty. He could sleep there and no one would say anything. Technically, it belongs to him as much as it does to any of his siblings, but that wasn't part of the plan. His father's plan was black and white: *Live in that garage, boy. Mow that grass. Take those classes. Work that job. Build you some character, maybe stop being such a dipshit, maybe get yourself a goddamn education, and maybe, just maybe, one of these days, this house could be yours.* He's not there yet.

With a spare key beneath the mat, he enters to silence. Walks through the dark living room, avoids furniture by memory. Heads to the kitchen, grabs a case of beer. Brings it to his father's study—first time in here since that night. Closes the door, cracks open a can, notes the room's odors—the sappy pine of the unpainted door; the dingy smell of grease, like the mechanic's shop where his father got Judah's truck fixed before his release. Sits down at the desk, another Daddy original, made from a salvaged door found on the curb of a rich man's house. Looks about: tacked to the bulletin board, invoices from Home Depot for rebuilding materials; beneath the keyboard, a calendar scribbled with reminders— notes, for this very month, for appointments with a Doctor Salinski. Dosages, too, for drugs he can't pronounce—Clonazepam, Zyprexa, Trazodone—scribbled in the daily squares.

On the monitor, the digital stars of a screensaver fly at Judah a million miles an hour. No doubt they've been scrolling by since the gunshots two weeks earlier. A simple move of the mouse will show what's behind that curtain. Does he want to see? Sitting here still feels like snooping on a crime scene. He taps the spacebar. First, an amateur builder's blog, lined with pictures of houses constructed in various styles. Behind that, a supplier's website with insets of brackets and hinges for purchase. Behind that, a weather site tracking storm threats. The page reloads to reveal a hurricane gathering right now over the Virgin Islands.

It's too much. Judah clicks away, lands on a spreadsheet with financials related to the rebuild. He follows the columns, reads the numbers: government loans from FEMA, tax credits—oh, how his father liked to brag to anyone who'd listen about how Obama was paying for all this work!—amounts from Home Depot, purchase orders for items bought on credit, invoices for friends and family who'd helped. Finally, a large red number at the bottom of the screen. Reaches for another beer.

Five beers later, Judah's still at the computer. Having circled back to the weather, his mind's lost in a sea of numbers and images of the new storm gathering in the Gulf. Latitudes and longitudes, wind speeds, expected storm surges. Too much. He wades into a desktop folder labeled Kids. It's filled with photos his mother had collected of Judah and his siblings through the years. A pick-me-up for Daddy in his depression. There are more of Judah than the rest, mostly from early high school before he'd begun using. He can hardly believe he ever looked that innocent. No tattoos, no stubble. The clearness in his eyes is nearly enough to make him cry. Too much. He clicks over to the animated GIF of the approaching hurricane.

Again, too much. He leaves the room, returns to the garage. Feels in the dark along the wall until the small teeth of the chainsaw bite into his skin. Moves his rough hands downward to its handle, pulls it off the wall. Its weight surprises him, sends him stumbling backward in a drunken stupor. He takes it to the yard, sets it down beside the one water oak still standing. Goes to the shed for a gas can and a funnel. Fills up the tank and returns for a ladder, which he carries out to the oak and lays against its trunk. Chainsaw in hand, he climbs up to the first branch. Stars shine in the new moon night. He places the chainsaw in a crevice between trunk and branch to secure it while he pulls the starter.

Before the motor catches, he hears car wheels on the gravel road. No headlights. A Pontiac Sunfire turns the bend. Its dark form inches forward. Sylvie. Did she get his address from Brennan? Had she always known where he lived? She kills her engine. She gets out and leaves the door ajar, the car's inside light shining. That constant beep. Blind to Judah in the tree, she heads for the garage. Judah calls out to her in a shrieked whisper.

"Sylvie! You're gonna wake the neighbors."

She freezes in the middle of the lawn. "Damn, Judah. What the fuck?" She walks beneath the oak and looks up at him. "I got something for you." She takes an Altoids box out of her back pocket and opens it. Shards of meth shine in the starlight like geodes. "Is that a chainsaw?" she asks.

Judah looks back toward the house. A yellow square of light appears. A silhouette rises in its frame, walks toward the window and raises it. Daddy's face appears in the square. He looks out on the yard.

"Judah!" he yells. "That you?"

"Yes, sir."

"What you doin' in that tree, boy?"

"Saw the weather report. Storm in the Gulf. Couldn't sleep. Thought I'd cut down some branches. Keep this oak from falling on the house."

"Boy, you crazy as all get-out. Go to bed 'fore I come out and whip you. I don't hardly know what else to do with you, son."

"Yes, sir." Ben lingers at the window a moment, then shuts it. His silhouette disappears as the yellow light goes black.

Sylvie looks toward the house and back up at Judah. "Who the fuck are you talking to?"

"Hush up, 'fore he hears you."

"Before *who* hears me? Jesus Christ, Judah."

"What?"

"All I'm saying is, it looks to me like you could use a pick-me-up."

"I'll be fine."

"I'll just leave this here," she says. "Give yourself a break. You're gonna work yourself crazy. Shit—maybe you already have." She places the Altoids box on a root at the base of the tree, walks back to her car. "Call me when you figure yourself the fuck out," she says.

Judah hears her ignition turn, the roll of her wheels down the gravel. Silence. From his perch, he looks back at that perfectly square window. Just a spot of black surrounded by gray. No sound. No movement. He hangs his head, wanting to cry, but his eyes light upon the Altoids box resting on the tree's roots. Its crystal offering shines like diamonds. He closes his eyes to escape the sight. In the blackness of those passing moments, visions come of the pixelated white stars of Daddy's screen-saver. Behind them, a dozen pitiless windows await perusal. If he'd have looked closer at them, what would he have found? Crouching in the still embrace of the stolid oak, eyes clenched shut out of fear, he watches the infinite constellation fly past him at a million miles an hour, a mirage soon to be dissipated by the faintest hint of a hurricane gust, the slightest movement of his eyes, the least twitch of his body in any direction.

After the Incident, Mary Vásquez Teaches Burlesque

WELCOME, TREASURES, AND thank you for signing up! I'm
Marina Valentina, your Head Mistress for the next four scorching-hot
weeks of the summer. I assure you that, despite this laughably Catholic
gathering space in which we have convened here in the heart of Deep
Ellum, you're in good hands. I've been classically trained in ballet. In
fact, I once danced in a Russian company, which, during my tenure, put
on such timeless wonders as *Paquita*, *Swan Lake*, and *Giselle*. Those,
ladies, were glorious days. That garbage bag in the corner? It's filled
with my old, bloody pointe shoes. I keep them here to remind me of the
hours of sweat I poured into that craft, and to preserve the memory of
strong Ukrainian hands gripped upon my once-tiny waist. Granted, I
never rose above the rank of apprentice. Honesty with oneself, kittens,

is the first step to becoming a burlesque performer. One cannot tease and chide effectively without self-awareness. But my failure to advance was due in part to a torn ACL, and also to, as many of you might guess, a man.

Where was I? Ah, yes. Experience. Not only did I once dance classically, you Dallas divas. I've also appeared on the covers of local magazines, including *Burly Queen*. I know what it's like to be in the spotlight. I know what it means to pose. Yet look at these thunder thighs! Look at this muffin top! I'm not lithe anymore! I'm no longer perfect, but does that stop me, future divas? A quick glance in your welcome packets at the pictures of me teasing onstage will give you your answer. In fact, despite my recent gathering of additional loveliness at the hips and bust, I have even occasionally caught a sidelong glance from my uncle, who is bishop of this archdiocese, former pastor here at St. Thomas Parish, and whose sudden presence we must guard against. For, you see, just a few days ago, after my trial, he threatened to—wait! Listen, and hold still! Is that the sound of footsteps in the hall? Shhh! Wait here, my darlings, while I check . . .

It seems only to have been Tony, our late-night custodian, a dear old black man we shan't shy away from, for I can already tell that he appreciates the guile of our meetings. He nightly roams the halls of this half rectory, half rec center, this palimpsest of the profane and the sacred. Over time I have come to feel his presence as a kind of salve to what I've experienced that has rent my heart so mercilessly. Rest assured, we can depend on his kindness as blessedly as Miss DuBois ought to have been able to count on that brute of a brother-in-law, down on Elysian Fields.

Now again, I must ask. Where was I? Ah, yes. My qualifications. What else, aspiring foxes? What beyond my confidence, my experience, what beyond my *beauty*—and I don't say this with pride. It's merely a fact, one you must come to believe wholeheartedly about yourself. Beyond these, what qualifies me to teach you in the ways of a stage seductress? Perhaps it is my knowledge of the *history* of our oft-denigrated pursuit. As surely as you anticipate learning to shimmy

in three-inch heels while nonchalantly pulling off opera gloves in time
to a sultry swing beat, I will tell you of that venerated deportee, Charlie
Chaplin, and his words regarding the classically American beginnings
of our humble endeavors as chorus line members, backdrops to offbeat
comedy troupes at the turn of the century. In Week One, I'll trace
for you the evolutions in showgirl personas from pre-cinematic days
to the latest Vegas incarnations of *Cirque du Soleil.* The best dancers
understand the historical context of the pasty twirl. They get why our
certain brand of irreverence has come to be so revered. In the time
after this one incident, when I'd fallen from grace with The Bishop My
Dear Uncle and relinquished ballet to follow a terribly handsome and
reckless boy to New Orleans, I found it such a comfort to learn about
these things. What a wonder to read about these fancy-free women of
the past! Those, sultry vixens, were the first moments I conceived of
my own reincarnation.

Perhaps, too, I'm qualified because of my knowledge of costumes and
their relation to our art of illusion. Believe me, fallen angels, there are
multiple pleasures latent in how you layer yourself in mystery! Look,
for example, at my gorgeous and enigmatic outfit. If you peer beneath
this tattered, handwoven dress that was worn at the time that my (wink
wink) great-great-great-great-great-great-great-great-grandmother was
(wink wink) offered as a prize to Cortez on arrival to Veracruz, you
will notice the ridiculously formal overtones in these close-knit thigh-
highs I'm wearing underneath. And look how these white opera gloves,
camouflaged by the Nahuatl jewelry of my (wink wink) ancestor's time,
echo the Jazz Age and distract from the more usual stimulants to the
careless masculine gaze. Or how the makeup I've applied is a nod to
the early Spanish colonial period as much as it is a tribute to the early
pinup days and the silent film years. Or how, underneath the bodice
of my costume, this flaming red-and-black basque not only constricts
and pushes up my bodacious ta-tas front and center but also projects a
sense of dominance and control. Perhaps, if you're astute as you look at
my luscious legs, you will notice the ornate silver buckles on my garter,

their spit-shine polish that glints in the light sometimes, depending on my gait and location in a spotlit room.

Yes, costumes elevate us above spectacle—this is, indeed, an art form, dulces—and in the tradition of folk craftswomen everywhere, we will, in Week Two, learn the joys of redecorating ourselves by fashioning two ashtrays into a bra, gluing an ironic excess of rhinestone to any material, making fake angel wings from supplies available at Big Lots and Hancock Fabrics. These can be the first steps to creating a character for yourself, for in no other pursuit is the cliché quite as true as in this one, that the clothes make the woman. Whenever it rains and my knee swells with humid ache and I begin to feel the nostalgic pull of the old ballet days, or whenever it's sunny and the harsh light conjures the smell of the dumpster beside which I wa—well, at least, in those anxious days just after The Bishop My Dear Uncle officially looked the other way, I'd merely slip into one of my Marina Valentina outfits, stand before the mirror, and the past would be nowhere to be seen in that gilded frame.

And have you yet noted my ability to talk either like a high-society courtesan or a vaudeville tramp? Here, then, is another of my credentials. This acquired skill comes from being raised by a priest and erudite man of the world, and also from extended exposure to the bars and venues where I perform. The point: we must always, deliciosas, keep audience in mind. On the one hand, they are drinkers and rabble-rousers, artists and performers, ne'er-do-wells and the most generous of the service industry. On the other hand, they are the educated and elite: high-minded professors and CPAs, self-proclaimed young professionals, dealership managers, even clergy and government officials, the two-faced of this town who would never admit to having seen us, but who also never miss a show. When I'm not onstage at House of Gypsy, the nearby dive where our class will end with your recital, you can find me behind the bar trying to save money to pay for my recent litigation, serving drinks and listening to the stories that audience members tell each other about our performances. The asides of those tactless crowds are priceless. In sharing them with you, I hope to provide not only a snippet of tasty town gossip, but also a window onto who these gazers are. Such knowledge, such intimacies, these are the bones of our fine art that will keep you standing proud and naked on stage, even as your thighs quiver in front of a most hostile crowd.

Perhaps it will not surprise you to learn that, while cast out of this urban prairie and living in that delightfully trivial city of New Orleans, I wrote a burlesque column for a local rag. The more you shine your own light on these odd corners of the world, the more you will understand how to move. How to perform. I don't claim, fair ladies of the twilight, to know your interests outside this class. I only suggest that, if they do not already include a curiosity and passion for all things burlesque, then I will take it upon myself to show you why they should. For, even accounting for the fleeting escape our pursuit affords in moments on stage, how can you consistently enjoy yourself without knowing such things? If you have done the history homework that should accompany regular practice of your burgeoning routines, then your body will speak your intelligence, and that will be what is remembered. When I am dead and gone, I'd like to be known as—well, a beautiful woman. Okay. Preciosas, if this aligns with your sensibilities, know that you have come to the right place.

My grandmother, she is a classic picadora. To this day, she admonishes me for my terrible tortillas. "Mija," she says, "why can't you *do* these? Eet's *seemple.* You just do like *these.*" The ability to tightrope between infuriating and endearing, that is a skill I cannot ascribe to the many fine instructors I've studied under, nor to the many prodigious dancers I've seen grace stages hither and yon. I can only ascribe it to my grandmother. And so it must be with you, you Magdalenian madams of the metroplex. You must strive in these weeks to find the thing you possess that you did not work to achieve, the thing that defines you beyond your ambition, the thing you were born with. First, you must find it—fret not, frisky ones, I will help you in that endeavor—and once you do, you must work your patooties off to accentuate that quality.

Ah, but do not let them know you have worked! This is the death knell of any great performance. The dancer cannot allow the audience to see her panting. Do you think I am not nervous now, introducing myself to you, who have each paid $350 for my expertise when I am new to this, and when it has no doubt become evident that we are stealth burlesquers for whom the soulless, two-tone tolling of the front door's electric bell might at any moment herald the unexpected arrival of The Bishop My Dear Uncle? Imagine it: I am somewhat young (this heartbreaker will not tell in years), while a few of you—and forgive me, mis amores, for presuming—but some of you might have occasion to contemplate how much more *experience* in life you possess than me. I know this, yet look how I smile! See my confident posture! How I look you in the eye! I do not let you know, my darlings, how unsure I might be, which of course I am not. Complete honesty with oneself, absolute mastery of one's audience!

Let me show you around. You may wonder why we are meeting here, in the workout room of this parish's rectory. First of all, we will be happy to have use of the multiple facilities available to us here. While members of the diocese access this space during the day, we will always meet after hours, lest we provide more than the improbable chance of confronting The Bishop My Dear Uncle. We will therefore be free to explore the body and spirit in our own way. Of course, he holds the key to this establishment, and so we must stay on guard. Though his emergence this late is unlikely, I pray that the anxiety produced by this possibility might encourage you to aspire to the most devilishly provocative of mindsets. In most rooms of this sacred space, there is a Bible. Everywhere, crucifixes. Relics from Rome blessed by the Pope himself, whom my uncle knows personally. Remember these facts, for in this way, you might most authentically discover that nugget of rebelliousness that lies within you, and that will become the bedrock of your stage routine.

As you have no doubt surmised, our use of this space originates in my dubious connections to this establishment. And so, even now, we must watch for him. If, while we're separated, he happens to enter, you will know him by his Clooney-gray hair, his puppy dog eyes, his perfect brown skin, his poker face. Do not approach! His looks and unassuming grace are his greatest assets. He will lure you with disarming stories meant to accentuate the light of his oh-so-holy refinement. If he corners you in my absence and asks what you are doing here, advise him you are taking tap lessons. If he asks why tap lessons require the audacious clothing you will no doubt be wearing, I leave it to you to invent a perfectly coquettish and manipulative response that will distract and delight him. Consider this a part of your training and be assured that, upon my return, I will handle that lightly tanned sophisticate in the ways I always have.

How? you might ask. *How do I know this will be okay?* Truth be told, I have a certain familiarity with this place and its leader that, when combined with my own seductive powers of charm and guile, affords me certain privileges. And so, at my heartfelt pleading, which he has never had the folly or fortitude to deny, we have been graciously allowed to use this space at night—so far as he knows, for the purposes of teaching "dance." He feels a certain remorse, shall we say, and he still remembers my ballet days. And so, with proper cajoling, he has come to fancy the idea that I might maintain some connection to things that give me pleasure.

Aside from these matters of convenience, I've chosen this modern space downtown with an eye for its lack of history. As you parked and entered, you likely ignored the aluminum siding and square windows, the linoleum floors. But the ability to put ordinary things to use should not be overlooked. Here, you will learn the value of finding possibility for tease and humor in what seems most ubiquitous. Case in point, vírgenes de la night stage: the walls of this workout room were once plain and mirrorless. Not at all workable for our purposes. Look how I have improved things by providing the dance mirrors against the wall, even encasing them in a frame of crushed red velvet curtains bursting with cartoon hearts embroidered with rhinestones, fitting them with sequin-encrusted wheels so we may roll away our vanities when the day's work is done. In honor of these lush features, I've referred to it, as you will note in your welcome packet, as the Velvet Room.

What is that, you say? That the cheapness of my handiwork is visible? Well, you did not *say* so, but judging by posture and gesture, I see that some of you must *feel* this way. Perhaps some context will provide you reason to believe in the superiority of the sale-priced. Perhaps you will be pleased to discover that in upgrading this room this way, I have not consulted anyone. I made these changes weeks ago and have yet to hear complaint. In fact, The Bishop My Dear Uncle recently relayed how one of his parishioners complimented the décor. "You're lucky to have someone with a woman's touch, Father," the crazy viejito was reported to have said. Unlike my uncle, I do not aspire to explain how the mind of the lamb works. I only know what I have seen, and that is this: the most egregious of audacities will be tolerated, even smiled upon, should you enact them with utmost taste and confidence. Such is the charm of the burlesque performer. We do not accentuate existing authenticities that please the majority. No, we laugh beautifully in the face of mundane profanity.

And now walk with me out of the Velvet Room, past that glorious image of ourselves in the mirror as we sashay into this hall of darkness. I'll now close the curtains on the mirrors, for our attentions are turned briefly away from our own movements. Allow me quickly to check for him . . .

. . . and now as I join you in the hall, note the harsh light of these fluorescent bulbs we shall otherwise learn to avoid. Follow me, and we arrive at the changing room. Note the ordinary lockers, the unstained benches made of four-by-fours fit for the firm asses of young athletes. Note the smell of stale bodies and attune yourself to your own sweetness in its midst. We are soft things, and this space helps us know it. This room, with its concrete floors and unpainted walls, has been designed with rapidity and transition in mind. Though instinct might urge us to shun it, we must learn to embrace not its aesthetic, but what it signifies of a fleeting moment. There should be no dressing room that feels like home, no temporary sitting place that comforts. This, I know well. As performers, as refugees from reality, we should embrace eternal return to these places. Your time spent here, your preparations in these rooms, will become the most sacred of rituals, for they remind us of the need to go on, to leave things behind, the necessity of pursuing something else, something greater, more tempting, more beautiful.

In your welcome packets you will see I have assigned you each a numbered locker. Open yours now and make sure there are no stale remnants of churchgoing workout fiends in your new personal space. The locker is yours for the duration of our class. Decorate it with chiffon, or lace, or taffeta cutouts, or whatever might become part of your routine. I once did this in this same space, newly returned from New Orleans, and even more recently, newly besmeared by the untoward attentions of a mo—never you mind that. The point is that, in just this way, your decorating should be undertaken not with the goal of improving the locker's desirability, but rather to remind you of what you hope to become. In this spirit, we will refer to this room, with all due irony and affection, as the Chamber of Immaculate Reconception.

Follow me this way, and pardon the echo as we walk through the shower and now on to the pool. You might not have thought, Arlington harlots, that such an artless tub would be useful to your training. But in Weeks Three and Four, as we learn basic burlesque steps, you will find that the siren call of the water, its baptismal quality, allows us to deliberate our movements, to consider our bodies, to force us into a slowness akin to grace. If you have never seen the bottom end of a pair of synchronized swimmers rising out of the pool, ragtime beat echoing in the natatorium's rafters as their thighs move like sharks in heat, then you have yet to understand the kind of mind-warping beauty to which we aspire. Though it is true that The Bishop My Dear Uncle uses these lanes every morning as a refuge of solitude from which to gather some deluded perspective on his officious workdays, I hope our presence might counter whatever lingering negative energy might remain at this late hour. And so, let us hereafter refer to this as the Pool of a Thousand Graces.

Through this door we exit and return to the hallway. With the light now on and the length of it to walk, you will note the pictures of saints lining the wall. Theresa, of ecstasies and visions. Stephen, the stoned seer. Paul, who stoned Stephen. Agnes, martyr and patron saint of chastity and rape victims. Holy Mary, Mother of God. And, of course, St. Thomas, this church's namesake, the one absolved of the stain of his famous faux pas (it was *doubt*, temptresses—*doubt*). We, of course, add names to those venerated here. You'll notice the framed prints I've brought to the Velvet Room, of Gypsy Lee, Lydia Thompson, Dita Von Teese. We adore them as well, though as my uncle does with these other haloed ones, we must be careful not to worship them. With them, with me, you must only ask for guidance in answering the call to the odd and ignoble action that our stories and bodies can impart.

But wait! What is that sound? Do you hear that two-tone chime? Do not be harried, my hussies. We knew this moment would come. Gather yourselves in the hallways, beneath the vacuous glares of those long-dead saints, and await my return . . .

· · ·

As you've no doubt ascertained, I've just returned from a most passionate argument with the Bishop My Dear Uncle. Perhaps you did not hear the intimacies we whispered between those unfortunate shouts. There are times, my sweets, when a spat unfolds in ways you cannot return from. Suffice it to say, our pursuit was questioned. Rather, *my* pursuit. And here, fellow floozies, I drew a line in the sacred marble of this lobby with my stiletto-spiked heel. For, as I will teach you, ours is a physical art, and you must always prepare yourself for the inevitable time when your success on stage depends on your ability to strike your heel down on a stool, expose your stocking-encased calf, and hold the stare of a man, never once wondering where your hands should go.

And to that man of the cloth, I pointed out the hypocrisy of a priest these days making claims on sexual appropriateness. He responded with a poker face of indignation, and then quietly uttered a threat that both of us have known could strike me down at any moment—a threat related to my identity, to my actual ties to this space (forgive me, my Texan trollops, for having kept this secret). This, my Jezebels, shook me to my core. I praise all that is precious and trivial in this world that my grandmother was not there to hear these awful words. I stood a moment, unsure how to respond. And then, it came to me: a true thing to say, a way to send him reeling, to assure our space in this building forevermore. For, you see, my bellas, I happen to know of a certain crime that happened near the back entrance of this place, a crime I know for a fact The Bishop the Dear Father had occasion to wit—ah, but what does it matter, my Lone Star strumpets?

Upon hearing my retort, he paused for a moment and then moved backward without turning, without looking away—like a vampire who, after conniving for an invitation into a home, stoically refuses to acknowledge defeat and retreats into the night. Look even now, dear treasures, at his portrait, commissioned by the diocese, which hangs on the wall beside these venerated saints. See how his blank face reveals nothing of his intentions, how the red and black of his sleek and official robes keep his hands well hidden beneath their folds. Father Benicio, he is called. He is no father to me. Though his glasses intimate a man from that austere and despicable era of Cleaver and Sullivan, Lucy and Lassie, I assure you that, even just now, he was wearing them as if no time had passed since then. I have traded on my wiles before, my Pussycat Dolls of this Corporate Prairie, but after tonight, I have no other devices upon which to rely. I have only, as it yet has always been but will not ever be, my youth, my beauty.

Follow me now, back into the Velvet Room, where we shall put aside that awful row. Notice how different it feels in here with the mirrors curtained. Sometimes, after practicing alone at night, I forget to close them off and when I return, I hear the sounds of 80s radio gems blaring while the parishioners follow the lead of an aerobics instructor. I spy on septuagenarians missing steps as they look at themselves and I smile, wondering what sorts of students they would make. Who can say what mysterious power the looking glass holds over even the humblest of us? It is our greatest challenge, in fact our duty, to learn to harness its power, to make its effects into something we can share with those who come to watch.

And so, my new family, we have reached the end of the tour. We have ended where we began, though a change is nevertheless upon us. I've remained in character for the duration of this welcome. Soon, though, so that you might see the true art of the façade, I will relinquish my title, divulge my true identity, and we will together explore the origins of a character as mysterious and beguiling, as seductive and sultry as Marina Valentina, titillating traitor and translator that she was and i—

I HEAR YOU, FATHER! YOUR CLAMOUR DROWNS OUT MY WISDOM, AND I MUST NOT YET YIELD TO YOUR DEMANDS. GRANT ME ONLY THIRTY SECONDS MORE, I IMPLORE, AND KNOW THIS: YOU ARE WRONG TO IMAGINE THERE IS NO ONE ELSE HERE! LOOK AROUND: DO YOU NOT SEE US? THE OPPRESSED, THE NAKED, THE HUNGRY, THE FORGOTTEN, THE CLEANERS OF YOUR BATHROOMS, THE SERVERS OF YOUR FOOD, THE WHISKERS-AWAY OF YOUR GARBAGE? THE HOMELESS? THE LEAST OF YOUR BROTHERS AND SISTERS? HAVE YOU NOT PLEDGED YOURSELF TO THE BETTERMENT OF BOTH SHEEP AND GOAT? GRANT ME, O ANOINTED CLERIC, ONLY THIS, THE GRACE OF A DIGNIFIED EXIT, AND I PLEDGE THAT, DESPITE YOUR WILLFUL TURNING OF A BLIND EYE TO MY PLIGHT, I WILL BOTHER YOU NO MORE!

Once more, I must apologize, my only friends, for this outburst. I can promise in all good faith that it is the last we will suffer. For now, keep your eyes on me. For now, let the lights stay dim, and let the mirrors sleep in the void behind their curtains. They are tired of showing us ourselves, much as the parishioners who daily stand before it must ultimately tire of their own façade after too much gazing. In this case and at the end of every class night, you will see this, how vanity closes in on itself, even if you should still feel its weight and ubiquity. Such is the nature of the burlesque performer at the quiet end of a solitary night's work on a dive stage in Deep Ellum, only the echo of her stilettos upon the alleyway pavement to keep her company as she walks to her van. Take one last look at the curtains, their red opacity, and note how they reveal nothing about you. With this lonely thought, turn away from the wall of mirrors, toward your humble mistress, and let us begin.

The Laurel Wreath

WHEN VITO REY DIED, the owner of St. Amelie's Bar sent his widow a wreath of laurel. Vito had been fifty-seven, but still the heart attack was sudden, and Darby felt compelled to make a gesture. Of what, he couldn't say. He was sure she despised him, and with good reason. St. Amelie's had kept Vito, a thin-faced Tom Waits of a drinker, away from his family for much of the last ten years. And yet at the bar, he'd often told affectionate stories about his wife's sharp tongue, her strict and even-handed ways with the kids, her impatient reactions to his passivity. In the telling, he'd seemed a tender absentee, and she a reasonably irrational wife.

Just days before he died, she came to St. Amelie's to hunt Vito down. Her name was Darlene, and Darby never forgot the sight of her. Tall

and awkward as a giraffe, she walked with a rangy gait and kept her
lips pursed tight. Wearing a pair of cutoff jean shorts and a wifebeater
stained with spaghetti sauce, she made right for Vito, her face lineless
despite twenty-five years of motherhood, her deep-set blue eyes glaring
with fury. She could've passed for her early forties, Darby's age. She
switched her anger on and off as she alternated between addressing
Vito, then him. "You goddamn waste of a man!" she shouted at Vito.
"Seth's been crying for hours: *Where's daddy? Where's daddy?* You know
what I told him? That you'd be home soon. Now pay for your drink and
come the fuck home." Then, more softly, to Darby: "I'm sorry, mister,
but you must have a family. You understand, right? I'll be out your way
real soon." And then back to Vito: "If your drunk ass ain't back in ten
minutes, I'm gonna shoot the tube outta your TV. You know I love
you, you shit. Don't make me do that."

In combination with Vito's affectionate accounts, that memory
made her seem like the kind of reckless, semicompetent woman Darby
could've imagined marrying, if such a life had ever come to pass. But it
wasn't affection he intended to communicate by sending the wreath.
Had he given it more thought, he likely would've figured her reaction
to the gift as a way of measuring the distance between bartending and
parenthood. Also, he prided himself on his instinct for interacting with
people on the edge, and though she wouldn't expect the gift, he felt sure
she'd receive it in a spirit of goodwill. He'd learned to trust his instinct
in awkward situations. Good bartenders had that skill, but they didn't
normally make a first gesture. That made all the difference. For once,
he couldn't mend things by reacting. He simply had to wait.

. . .

For patrons who asked, Darby liked to trace his bartending career back
to a single moment in childhood. When his parents were still together
raising him in the Marigny, they'd put him to bed and have friends over
to the house late. Once, a group of them were drinking cheap beer in
the living room and arguing about Dutch Morial's bid for mayor. "The

thing is," Darby's dad said, "Dutch ain't even black. Look at that stringy hair. Shit, just look at his skin. *I'm* darker than he is." No one knew how long Darby had been watching from the doorway, but he made his presence known with a single, simple retort: "*You* have stringy hair, Daddy. Could you run for mayor?"

No more than eight, he stood there with his Cookie Monster pajamas draped off his slight frame. While everyone laughed, he smiled just enough so that it looked like he'd intended sarcasm. His mother joked that he'd make a fine bartender one day. "Get me a Turkey on the rocks, son," his dad said with a straight face, then burst into a laugh meant only for adults.

Amelie hadn't really been that kind of mother. Darby's father's influence had led to those scenes. Once he ran off, she changed. She stopped smoking and started going to church and volunteering at St. Vincent de Paul down the street. With her husband's income gone, she took an office position during the day. Since there was no one to watch over Darby in the summer, she started bringing him to the office. Within a week, everyone in the building loved him. Even the humorless executives tolerated, sometimes enjoyed his presence. Without calculation he understood when to shut up, how to be cute at the right moments, when it was okay to strike up a conversation with the secretaries, what to talk about with the bosses in the break room. He told the men stories about his sports teams and their successes, and he asked the women polite questions about their families, then sat with his head cocked and listened. When he sensed they needed to work, he retreated to his mother's cubicle, sat down at the word processor, and typed out *Thanksgiving* and *Christmas* and the precise number of days left until they arrived. When the workday ended and his mother's colleagues left, he'd tell them goodbye, sending them off with a polished line: *See you tomorrow, Ms. Angie; Say hi to Max for me, Mr. Baldwin; Thanks for the math help, Ms. Cathy; Nice talking, Mr. Lowry.* He never got a name wrong.

Amelie went full Catholic as Darby grew up. When he moved out after high school and she'd paid off the mortgage, she retired and started spending time at St. Vincent, tending its azalea garden with care each morning, decorating the altar with its flowers as the church's liturgical seasons came and went. She became a Eucharistic Minister. She led RCIA classes. She prayed constantly.

His mother's religious conversion deepened as Darby slip-slid through a lonely sequence of odd jobs in his late teens and twenties. For a time, he was a gum buster for the city park service, scraping old wads off of the undersides of picnic benches and swing set seats. Then, a gravedigger. Then, a golf ball diver for the course at English Turn. Then, a counter clerk at a fast-food restaurant, until he finally settled on a job with IMAX once they came to town, cleaning their screens to keep the images fresh. Throughout it all, his bosses and coworkers, had they ever been asked, would've reported that he was a pleasant man, easy to talk to about most anything, the kind of agreeable guy one thought about only long after he was out of your life. With hardly any money, he didn't socialize much, and he began to understand that, for him, a wife and family would not materialize simply by force of time and circumstance.

In December of 1999, Amelie died suddenly of a heart attack. It wasn't pretty. He didn't hear from her for a few days, so he decided to drop by the old house. When no one answered, he let himself in, and she was three days gone on the floor, already decomposing in the living room's humidity that refused to be brushed away by the ceiling fan spinning on low. It was Advent, and her wreath still lay neatly on the dining room table. The first two purple candles were burned down, but the pink one, which she would've lit that Sunday, hadn't been. The wreath was made of laurel, and to distract himself from the horror of her body, he focused on the oddity of that choice: most wreaths at the church he remembered from his youth were made of pine.

In her will she left him a small sum of money and the house, which he didn't want to return to. Still, it didn't seem right to sell it. One day not long after the funeral, as he went through her things, a woman in a pink suit with permed hair stopped by, one of his mom's church friends. Amelie had left behind a number of belongings at St. Vincent's office, and the woman was delivering them. In a box that could hardly fit through the door, Darby discovered silver sconces, half-used votive candles smelling of vanilla, paintings of Mary and Jesus and the crucifixion, strings of white lights used to decorate the altar, and a huge collection of laurel advent wreaths she'd made over the years as gifts for the shut-ins of the parish. The woman told the story: Amelie had taken on that task with quiet resolve and confidence that her visits with those shut-ins, along with the wreaths she made them, would help give those sad, cooped-up spirits the resolve to send their Christmas prayers to heaven the proper way, even if they couldn't make it to Mass. The woman in pink didn't say why laurel, and it pleased Darby that there was something unexplained, however small, about his mother's religious devotion.

Taken by the depth of her commitment, not wanting to sell the place or live in it, he decided to convert the house to a bar, name it after her, and decorate it with her things. It was the best way he could think to honor and acknowledge her religious turn at the same time that he could fulfill her prediction for his livelihood. There would be no kitsch in this place. He'd sincerely loved her, and he believed that, deep down, she always knew he was meant to do this.

Over months, he used the small inheritance to transform the house. Inside the crumbling shotgun, he knocked out the walls between the living room and the master bedroom. He installed an air conditioning unit in the window next to where her bed had been. He built a bar against the side wall, then started decorating. He hung her advent wreaths around the place and lit the door and the area behind the bar with the white lights. He set her votives in red candleholders, then placed them on her sconces and put them up on the wall. He hung her paintings of Mary and Jesus over his childhood bathroom to indicate it was unisex and put the crucifix on the exterior door. He laid the smaller wreaths on the tables and at the corners of the U-shaped bar with the pink and purple candles still in them. Finally, he hung a framed, airbrushed black-and-white of his mother at eighteen over the cash register. In this way, St. Amelie's was born.

. . .

It didn't take long for him to get a reaction from Darlene. The day after he sent her the wreath, she came into the bar. She didn't say anything, just sat down and ordered a whisky sour with Johnnie Walker Red, the same whisky Vito always drank neat. Darby made it and set it in front of her. He considered giving it to her on the house, then thought better of it. She let it sit, stirring it with her straw and looking up at the TV.

"You need anything else?" Darby asked.

"My youngest is set to start high school this year," she said. "I'm still not sure how I'm going to pay for it."

"He's going to private school, then?" Darby asked.

"Jesuit."

"Good school. City's run by Jesuit boys, seems like."

"I don't want Seth to have anything to do with this city, certainly don't want him running it. That'd be the day."

"This place has its flaws."

"Mainly, it's just the drinking," she said.

Normally, when strangers talked that way, Darby would say something at his own expense. But now, that would've seemed like an admission of murder, or at least of accessory. The silence hung for a bit, and then she spoke again.

"You know, there's a band at the Polo Lounge tonight."

He didn't know how to read this statement. He was suspicious, of course. This trade had evoked that in him.

"Polo Lounge?" he asked.

"The bar at the Windsor Court. I hear they have a three-piece tonight."

Her eyes gave nothing away. She kept stirring the whisky sour, looking down at it. Darby waited for her to look up. He wanted her to see his eyes. When she did, he smiled. "I haven't been there in ages," he said. "What time's the show?"

That night, Darby drove downtown to the Windsor Court Hotel. He wore a suit, as the dress code required. It was his only one, an old seersucker number that used to be his father's, and he kept hunching over to feel its fit as he waited for Darlene at the bar, nursing a soda water with lime. Two decades before, in the one semester he'd attended college, he'd known a few classmates in the music school. They'd get the chance sometimes to play with their professors here, and Darby came once to see them. He remembered being surrounded by well-dressed men and perfectly postured women in late middle age having conversations about the jazz legends they felt the band resembled. Darby liked hearing his friends compared to Duke Ellington and John Coltrane, even if he knew it was bogus. Telling them about it afterward, he relished how each took it—some satisfied, others baffled, others exasperated by the cocksure calm of their audience. These were among the first moments he'd ever found joy in surveying the goings-on of a drinking crowd.

Darlene walked in wearing a white silk dress with an empire waist, cinched there with a wide black sash. The fabric fell in folds to well above her knee, and she wore black heels that exaggerated her height and awkwardness. She held her purse at her waist with one arm and scanned the room for Darby's face. He raised his glass and smiled, then offered her his seat as she walked over.

"I see they haven't started yet," she said.

"Have you been here before?"

"Used to come when I was in college."

"So did I. That would've been in '87, I guess."

"I've got you by a few years. I finished in '78."

Darby did the math, came up with somewhere between fifty and fifty-two. About nine years' difference between them.

"Is it like you remembered?" he asked.

"Exactly."

"Would you like a drink?"

"Whisky sour, with Johnnie Walker Red."

He looked at her playfully. "Is that an old favorite?"

"A new favorite, I guess."

Darby ordered it for her, and a gin and tonic for himself. They toasted to nothing, then settled in to watching the crowd. The place filled slowly as the musicians set up in the corner by the curtained window. By the time they'd drained a couple drinks, the room had the consistent chatter of a respectable party, and the band soon started. The mild instrumentals didn't demand dancing, and they stayed at the bar, pretending to follow the rhythms of the music.

After a few numbers, the band took a break. The dapper pianist adjusted his bow tie and spoke to the crowd evenly. "Welcome, everyone. I'm Johnny Menera, and this is the John Menera Trio." He indicated the drummer, who thumped three sure snare beats in recognition of his name. "And Karl Davic on bass." The bassist nodded without smiling, played an ascending scale ending on a high note in time with the drummer's cymbal crash. From the bar, an elderly woman in an ankle-length sequined gown sashayed over to them.

"Darlene, dear! I haven't seen you in ages! You look absolutely div*ine* in that dress." Her jewelry flashed as her hands moved with her speech. She looked at Darby coyly, waited.

"Hello," he relented, "I'm Darby Clark. Do you know Darlene from school?"

"From *school*? Well isn't *that* a compliment! No, honey. I know Darlene from her days at the PT*A*. We had our kids at the same school, at De La Salle, back before they gave in and went coed. My youngest was a few grades ahead of her oldest. They played together in the band one year. How *is* William?" the woman asked.

"Down on his luck, now," Darlene said. "Just got laid off, but someone'll pick him up."

"Well, of course, dear. He was always such a *prince*, you know. He must be missing his daddy," she added, and looked right at Darby. Darby held the woman's gaze until she went on talking about herself. When she finished, she said goodbye to Darlene and walked away.

"Quite the charmer, your friend," he said.

Darlene didn't laugh.

"At the bar, Vito always talked about you, you know," Darby added.

"Well, the children talked about him at home, too."

"What would they say?"

"They talked about his art. That was the one thing they admired about him—that he used to paint, many moons ago. And it was true. He was talented, you know."

"He never talked about that."

"Well, he never did anything about it either, but he could have been decent. Or at least, he could've made a living at it, I suppose."

"What kinds of things did he paint?"

"Oil on canvases mostly. Landscapes from the lakefront, scenes from the Quarter, local musicians, that sort of thing. The kind of art that tourists buy. I still have some of them, but what am I going to do with them? They're not worth anything, and all they do is remind me what a waste he was. All he ever did was—well, *you* know."

"He never told me about his painting."

Darlene smiled. "Way back when, he'd always be at it. There was this one time I'm sure William remembers. A trip we took once to the Smoky Mountains, when William wasn't yet in school, before Vito sold his eas—"

She stopped midsentence, mouth agape. She grabbed Darby and dug her fingernails into his shoulders. Her face turned white and she ducked her head. "Oh my God," she said. Her hands started shaking. Darby didn't know what to do but hold her there, at a distance. He heard a voice near the back of his head, and for a brief moment its familiarity soothed him until he realized it was Vito's. That gravel and lilt. That softness to how he vocalized assent. The way his sentences faded away. Unmistakable. Darby couldn't turn around. He was too scared.

"I heard Cabo was quite relaxing," the man was saying. "I wish I could've made the ceremony." He was talking to someone else, but Darby couldn't hear what the other man said. The longer the conversation went on, the more paralytic Darlene's posture became. The voices hushed, and out of the corner of his eye, Darby saw the man pass him by and turn to face the bar. Darby could view him then in profile. He wore a suit, which he'd never seen Vito in, and his posture seemed poised, sober. He had the same drawn face Darby remembered from all those years at St. Amelie's, but he seemed less morose, more controlled. Darby couldn't stop staring, and then the man stared back. Darlene was still clutching his shoulder, her back to the man now.

"I'm sorry, do I know you?" the man asked.

"Well . . ." Darby managed.

"Name's Kent. Kent Spillman," he said, and he extended his hand. At that, Darlene turned around.

"Hello, Madame," Kent said to her. He reached for her hand and kissed the back of it. She couldn't manage a word. Kent seemed unfazed by the loss of color to her face. It happened too fast for them to ask any questions, but as they watched Kent Spillman nod politely and walk back toward the crowd of sophisticates from which he had emerged, they each came to realize with certainty that he was not Vito. Though he couldn't say what prompted Darlene's acknowledgment of this fact, Darby read her face closely enough to see she'd reached that conclusion. For Darby, it had been the drink the man ordered and the way he ordered it: hand up in the air with resolve and a slight arrogance to how he searched for the bartender's eyes, then locked onto them when he made contact. It became even clearer to watch him now among his circle. In that setting, he looked more surely like a businessman meeting up with colleagues after a day of attending panels at a conference somewhere in the CBD. This was a scenario Vito had never known. Darby turned back to Darlene, who tried to smile. The band, which was set to begin again, saved them from the awkwardness of talking more about it.

"Thanks again, everyone, for coming," Johnny Menera said, and then they were off with a brass standard arranged for piano. Darby and Darlene clapped politely in recognition when he came to the hook. Johnny smiled and played on, riffing on the melody to make it suit the trio's instrumentation, even though there was no graceful way to do so.

Darby and Darlene each glanced occasionally at Kent Spillman and his crowd of seven or so, who'd taken seats at a trio of hand-carved couches across from the bar. Some of them faced the musicians, and others of them, women with cat-eye glasses and drinks held out beneath slender, braceleted wrists, kept their attentions on each other. Darby felt compelled to watch the man's drinking behavior, to imagine the stories he was telling. Darby watched Darlene zero in on the man's simple, silver wedding band, and so he did, too: it spoke of a reasonable marriage, one with a definite sense of contentment held close to the chest, a private happiness never articulated to strangers. He wondered then whether Darlene had ever shared such sentiments about Vito—or if, in fact, she'd merely sacrificed herself for the sake of her children. Sometime in the second set, without either of them noticing, Kent left his party and walked off, presumably to some elegant hotel room that neither of them would ever see the inside of.

Before the trio finished, Darlene placed an empty glass on the bar beside Darby, leaned to whisper into his ear. He could smell the bland scent of her generic shampoo. He focused on it as she said, "I'm sorry, but please excuse me, Darby," and got up. Darby understood then that no moment of anticipation, no moment of dread awaited him; no kiss, nor any sign of affection. They hadn't shared glances since Kent's departure, and the small but certain distance between their barstools had locked her body away from any sign of intent or exchange. She left for the restroom and never came back. When he realized she'd gone for good, he ordered another gin and tonic at the bar, and when it came, he swirled his drink with a toothpick. It occurred to him to run after her, but what would he say? What would be the point? With a wave of his hand to the bartender to sign for the bill, he acknowledged that he would probably never see her again.

· · ·

On the way home, a cop pulled Darby over on Canal Boulevard, near Carrollton.

"Been out on the town tonight?" the policeman asked.

"Down to Windsor for a show. Headed home now, sir."

"Where's home?"

"Down off Bienville, on Scott."

"That's right by the—what was the name of the theater used to be there?"

"Movie Pitchers."

"Movie Pitchers," the cop echoed.

"That's right. Movie Pitchers. Get yourself a movie ticket and a pitcher of beer."

"Okay, yeah. From before the storm. Look, you realize your taillights aren't working?"

"No, sir. I didn—"

Just then, across the boulevard, something like a firecracker pop sounded, and both he and the cop turned to see. Two black kids ran off into the darkness, and immediately, the patrolman set out on a dead sprint after them, holster slapping his thigh as he raced away. There was nothing for Darby to do except watch. The cop ran across the parking lot of an abandoned grocery store, then turned the same corner the two boys had.

Darby considered his options. Should he wait? The cruiser behind him still had its blue lights flashing. With its door ajar, he could hear the police radio calling out garbled messages in code. Subconsciously, his brain conjured images of Darlene: tending to Seth and William, pining for the Kent version of Vito, brushing her teeth, looking in the mirror. He heard two more shots in the distance, out of sight. He searched out his window for any hint of where they'd come from, but saw nothing. If *I'm gonna leave,* he told himself, *it's gotta be now.* He pulled out onto the road and started to drive away, but curiosity stopped him. Half a block down, he pulled into a driveway, turned off his lights, and put the car in park. It was late enough, he drunkenly decided, that whoever lived here wouldn't notice him, and that he'd still be close enough to watch what happened when the cop came back.

With its green indicator lights illuminating the dashboard and the AC running, the interior of the car felt cool and safe. Though he'd lowered the volume, the stereo whispered Irma Thomas's "Ruler of My Heart" beneath his attention. It'd been a good five minutes since the cop ran off. He appeared then at the corner of the abandoned grocery store, walking slowly, alone, wiping his hands on his stomach. He walked back to his car with his gun holstered and his face fixed straight ahead. When he got to the cruiser's front fender, he turned in Darby's direction. Inside the car, a DJ ended the song by naming it and then read off a schedule of upcoming concerts across the city. Midway through, his voice came to a baffled halt. The cop kept watching. Darby tried to focus on his eyes, but he couldn't help imagining the old volunteer at the radio station, stooped over the desk, struggling to pronounce the bands' names.

Just then, the door to the house opened. An old black woman in pajamas looked down at Darby from the porch steps, half scared, half poised to strike. A light shone in the open doorway behind her. It must have caught the cop's attention, because Darby saw him looking closer now. Darby didn't know which one of them to face or what to do. The old woman approached the car cautiously, and the cop watched the scene unfold. Darby wanted to leave before she made it to his window, but he was afraid she would yell and the cop would come after him, so he stayed put. In a panic he grabbed a pen and notepad from the center console and wrote: "Wife died. Mechanical problems. Off soon. Sorry." He put it up to the window and watched the woman read it. She looked at Darby's face, and the anxiousness in his expression caused her to back away, never once flinching until she reached her front door and closed it. Darby turned back to look at the cop in the distance, who was still watching. For a moment, it was a toss-up, what would happen. Then the cop smirked and shook his head, opened up a notepad, and began writing. Darby sat stone-still until the cop got in his cruiser and drove away. Only then, with the face of the old woman peering out from behind the curtains of her living room, did Darby put the car in gear and drive home.

· · ·

In the next few days, Darby waited, but he didn't hear from Darlene. He half hoped to see her the next day at St. Amelie's, but only the regulars showed, and he had plenty of time to think. He thought about her. He thought about the absent stool beside him once she'd left the Windsor Court, and about the note he'd written in the stranger's driveway. *Wife died.* He thought about Darlene's children. The older one, William the unemployed, he'd probably have to spend more time at home now. And Seth, who knew? In time, he could become another regular at St. Amelie's.

While his customers fixed the world with debate, Darby read the *Times-Picayune*, looking for mention of what had happened that night on Canal, but he found nothing. There was plenty else to gape at: the trial of the representative who'd been caught with ninety thousand dollars in his freezer, new details on the cop who'd stolen a car from a dying man in the aftermath of the storm, the latest on the trial of the officers who shot evacuees on the Danziger Bridge. Still, his proximity to the episode on Canal gave it import, and he put the paper down with frustration, with the misguided sense that this was the only transgression that had gone unreported.

It occurred to him to do the smallest bit of his own research. Call the morgue to see if two young black men had been found, call the station to see who'd been on patrol in Mid-City. Then call the paper with the facts. He imagined the fallout. His tip would lead to an investigation, which would lead to an exposé on the NOPD, which would be the spark to turning around racial relations in the dying city. Of course, he would be tested. In the beginning, the cops would vilify him, but that would just give him a chance to show his true character. He'd accept whatever slander and unfair treatment he'd receive from them. (He imagined they'd no longer respond to calls from the bar to break up fights.) His persistence and competence would cause the paper to look closer. Justice would prevail as a result. Ultimately, he didn't even need the fear of being found out by cops to keep him from starting his research. It only took a lazy raise of an empty glass from a man at the end of the bar.

A week later, a stranger walked in carrying a laurel wreath. Darby had never seen the man before. Around twenty-five, he had a few days' worth of stubble on his face, and he wore a T-shirt and jeans that dragged the floor as he shuffled across the bar in a daze. Paying no attention to the newness of his surroundings, he took a stool and sat by himself, clearly not expecting anyone. He looked up at the TV news, and when Darby prompted him, he ordered a High Life.

"Are you Darby Clark?" the man said as he put the bottle to his lips.

"That's me."

The man nodded. "I'm William Rey," he said. "Vito's oldest."

Darby extended his hand, and William took it. "Vito was a regular here. I was sad to hear he'd died," he said.

"He was kind of a bastard, to be honest."

"His wife, your mother, she came in here once cursing his name."

"About her," the son said. Clear-eyed, he looked up from his beer at Darby, waiting for a response. Darby didn't say anything, and then William spoke.

"She's gone missing," he said. He explained that, that afternoon, his younger brother had come home to a simple note she'd left on the kitchen counter: "I've gone away."

"I've gone away," Darby repeated. His aptitude for social graces escaped him.

"Just like that. We tried her phone, but she'd left it behind. Her car was in the garage. We checked her accounts, and it looks like she's cleaned them out. Cash withdrawal."

"I don't know what to—"

"Seth called me about it just now. He's still just a kid, you know. I don't know what to make of it. That's why I'm here. He said there was a wreath on the counter next to the note." William then placed it on the bar. "Seth told me she'd talked the last couple days about a man named Darby Clark, guy who owned a bar around here."

Darby regarded William with compassion and unease. He thought about Darlene and he thought about what she could be thinking. He should say something, but what? Would he try to explain the feeling that had compelled him to send her the wreath? Would he discuss their date? Would there be use in describing the appearance of Kent Spillman? Perhaps, at some point, the story of the incident with the cop would be a welcome distraction, minus mention of his note. Whatever he said, it couldn't just be banter. The conversation would need to last awhile.

William looked up at the TV. The national news was focused on Senator Obama's bid for election. No music played on the jukebox, and Darby let the talking heads fill the room. The window unit in his mother's old bedroom sputtered and choked out lukewarm air. William put his elbows on the bar and rested his chin on his folded hands. Without looking at his new customer, and in a manner that suggested nightly routine, Darby pulled two purple candles and a pink one from beneath the bar, put them in the wreath, and lit them. The evening was early, and there was plenty of time for the telling.

Oh, But to Be a Hearse!

"BIG BAD NURSE & THE HEARSES! MON NIGHT! MERMAID LOUNGE, 1100 Constance St!" The ad, printed in washed-out stencil on an 8 × 11 sheet and tacked to a telephone pole on Frenchman Street, caught Hans-Georg's eye amid a palimpsest of other band flyers and notices of lost pets. Beneath the headline, a dot-matrixed, black-lipped punk girl was shredding a star-shaped guitar, snarling. Behind her, two gray smudges of other guitarists—the Hearses, presumably—held a beat. *This city,* he thought. He would have to tell Milena about it later, on the phone.

But there were so many things he'd wanted to share that he simply forgot in the wash of other, crazier things. Case in point: in his two weeks since moving to New Orleans after being hired on at an engineering firm, he'd already forgotten the incident on Decatur with the goth girls who'd warned him he was vampire fodder because of his light-colored clothes and then hissed at him, baring their filed canines. Memorable as that was, he forgot about it after witnessing a stranger dressed in a purple wifebeater and black parachute pants walk straight to him in a café and say, "You never did pay me, but if you still want it, I got that boot in the back of my van." And he forgot to tell her about *that* in the wake of the midafternoon traffic jam on Common Street for a mass of women and men in red dresses traipsing across the road, cocktails in hand. And he forgot to tell her about *that* in the wake of having seen, out his office window at ten in the morning, five elephants trumpeting as they moped down Julia Street like drunks walking off a night's debauchery. This, ultimately, was the only nugget he'd offered her.

For Hans-Georg, trying to talk to his Milena on the phone, he thought at first those stories weren't really stories worth sharing: they were unconnected anecdotes that each wanted to outdo the others as better proof of the importance of frivolity in this town. And what good was frivolity in this time of their serious commitment? He was young. Committed. Driven. Myopic in his ambition, as the part in his blond hair and the straight line of his thin lips announced. But curious, too. And when it came to having a tolerance for these wondrous oddities, he was starting to realize that Milena was, as people in this country might say, a regular homecoming queen: when he mentioned the elephants, he could hear her polite smile through the phone's bad connection. Only when he offered a justification—the Ringling Brothers, it turned out, had docked at the Julia Street Wharf on the river—did she seem satisfied. This troubled him, for he had begun to discover a secret joy in the unexplained. It was a kind of spiritual mystery he had difficulty explaining, even to himself. He'd spent his time at this, his first job out of engineering school in Munich, designing ways to connect steel beams to glass windows. He hadn't taken much time to look around. Now that he was, he noted Milena's practical mind with less affection. And so, he held these oddities to himself, like shaken bottles of beer he knew not to pop open.

Likely, he supposed, this was a phase. He'd come out of it, finish up his contract, and return to Munich to marry as they'd planned. Anyway, there wasn't much chance to discuss it. She worked graveyard shifts as a nurse back home, and he slow-motioned his way through long hours here. On the phone, they stuck to conversations about whether she'd found a flat for them, which of their Austrian cousins they should invite to the wedding in Innsbruck.

Monday afternoon in Hans-Georg's office building, the vending machine fell on a man and crushed him. As medics wheeled the body away, a group of onlookers gawked, Hans-Georg among them. A bra strap dangled from the dead man's shoulder, his fingernails painted a vibrant red. "Devil's due," someone said. Hans-Georg hadn't met the guy. What had been his story? He looked at his watch: quitting time. Would he tell Milena? Or maybe instead, he thought, he'd go see what was what at the Mermaid Lounge.

Godfather

TO GRANT MERCEDES'S wish, we had to find this old priest in a cheap resort town called Tecolutla; if I was okay with it, the *we* should include me. Or anyway, that's what Manuel told me over the phone that morning. "She wants you to be there," he added. He told me how things had gone the night before when they all got back to his apartment from our final planning session at the Hotel California. The argument started innocently enough. He and Tommy had needled Mercedes about this baptism business. Why expose Tita to anyone official in Mexico, they argued. The fewer to know about her before she crosses, the better. Wouldn't there be a document certifying the rite? Couldn't the certificate of baptism later be used against them? Or, might it not work the other way? Wouldn't a priest require a birth certificate to perform the ceremony? And in that case, how would it be possible to find a priest willing to baptize the child on such short notice?

This had all sounded like bullshit to Mercedes. She felt ganged up on. She told them flatly that she didn't care what the rules were, and she didn't care about anything so petty as the bureaucracy behind a birth certificate. What was that in the face of a child's soul? What was that in the face of performing a rite that that been performed on every single member of every single child in her family, going back as far as the time of the mixed-race great-grandchildren of Cortés? "Híjole," she had said, "my mother and father would have wanted this!"

This, the trump card.

Tommy and Manuel let it drop. Tommy explained to his father: the only reason she'd ever gone to America—Louisiana, at that—in the first place was that her mother had been murdered when she was a girl. "At the Acteal massacre," he said. "The one at the church in the jungle. The day her husband disappeared. Her parents, they were churchgoing people. Very devout." And so, on Mercedes's behalf, at Tommy's begrudging behest, Manuel was calling to see if I would come.

"Where is Tecolutla?" I asked. "And why there? Why not here, in Poza Rica?"

"An hour away. My mother had me baptized at the church there. The same old priest still runs that diocese," he said. It was the only religious place in the world, he reasoned, where his name might have any pull, where he could ask a priest to do something like this. He'd made a few calls and arranged for the old man to perform the ceremony.

We took off late that morning, scrunched together in Manuel's truck, four of us in a row with the baby on Mercedes's lap. The truck's cabin jostled us about as we rolled over uneven roads with holes from where the rain had washed them out. The road cut through tiny towns carved out of the jungle that surrounded us. Every few miles, a street-side vendor sold something preposterous—pickled chicken necks, Batman action figures, always Coca-Cola—at the spots where the traffic had to slow to pass over earthen speed humps. Tommy asked Manuel about Tecolutla. As Manuel responded, Mercedes asked Tommy to take the baby, but he paid such close attention to his father that he didn't notice her. She turned to me then. Gladly, I accepted the child.

We came out of the jungle on a road that ran along the Gulf. Suddenly we were in a dreamworld version of Mexico where the sea sparkled as the sun rose high in the sky. Where the paper flags hung over the streets promised cheap fun. Where even the fun didn't need to be taken seriously. Souvenir vendors populated street corners, holding up PVC piping from which hung luchador masks and huaraches, plastic skeleton dolls and crucifixes with the puncture wound in Jesus's side bleeding down his ribs. Manuel fended them off with waves of his index finger. We turned on a road that went up a hill away from the sea. As we climbed it, banana leaves brushed against the chassis. At the top, an adobe church looked down on the hill from its perch, its coral window treatments and white bell tower pristine in the sun. To the side of the church stood a small office painted the same colors. The town looked nothing like the wasteland of Poza Rica, where I'd arrived the week before from Cameron, Louisiana, to consult with Manuel on his waste oil treatment business. He pulled his truck into a parking spot and we got out.

"This is some place," Tommy said. "You sure you don't want to just stay and live here, sweetie?"

Mercedes looked at him like a petulant child.

"My mother used to take me here from Veracruz once a year, on my saint's day," Manuel said.

As Manuel reminisced, Tommy listened like the son he was. Mercedes glanced around, pleased with the look of the church. We walked in a motley caravan through the portico and into the rectory's lobby. There, a woman in a blue blouse and jeans welcomed us and spoke to Manuel. I looked around at the pictures of Juan Diego and la Virgen de Guadalupe on the walls. Eventually, an old priest donned in black emerged from the hallway and waved us to the back with a kind smile. As he led us down a hall, he put his arm around Manuel and spoke to him fondly. I couldn't understand their words, but it seemed like the old man was asking about Manuel's mother and father. The priest put his arm gently on Manuel's shoulder as they reminisced. We came to a conference room, not unlike the one at the Hotel California, except for its bookshelves, which housed endless volumes of hymnals, stacks of musty missals, framed photos of priests posing with important-looking people. The priest asked us to take a seat. At that point, he recognized me for the gringo I was: "I see we have an American, yes?"

I nodded.

"Welcome," he offered. "My name is Father Antonio."

"Keith," I said, and extended my hand.

"Where are you from, Keith?" Despite his brown skin, he had no trace of an accent.

"Denver."

"Ah, Denver. I was there once, in 1993. Do you know the Cathedral Basilica of the Immaculate Conception? The one on Colfax Avenue?"

What could I say? "Yes. My parents were parishioners there."

"Ah!" he said. "And so, did they baptize you there?"

"I don't know," I said.

"Well, you might remember that in 1993, Pope John Paul came to Denver. Our bishop granted me a dispensation for the travel. Lovely city, Denver."

"Yes, it is," I said.

"And we have a little one here, yes?" He turned to Mercedes to decipher whether she was following his English. Seeing she wasn't, he returned to Spanish. Because I couldn't understand his words, I focused on his continental air. With his shock of white hair and gnarled hands, he looked feeble, but judging by his smooth face, it seemed impossible that he was old enough to have baptized Manuel. Tommy and Manuel and Mercedes took turns speaking to him, and he acknowledged them with soft nods. Despite my lack of Spanish, he made eye contact with me as much as the others as he spoke. He rose when he finished, and we all took his cue. He led us back out into the portico, and as he made for the door, he spoke to me again: "We'll see you in just a minute," he said, and then he was gone.

As we entered the church, its size and quiet signified its holiness. Up in front, an old woman knelt before a votive she'd lit to the side of the nave. When she heard us close the massive wooden door with a creak, she didn't move. We walked down the center aisle, my hard-sole shoes clicking and echoing in the vast, high-ceilinged space. The midday sun shone brilliantly through the stained glass mural behind the altar. Shafts of dust swirled in the sunbeams and made the shadowed portions of the church seem darker than they were, the votives' red holders more reverent.

As we reached the front pews, Manuel genuflected and made the sign of the cross, a begrudging nod to old childhood traditions. Tommy did the same, with all the tactlessness of youth. Mercedes made the gesture in the manner of a believer, even as she held the child in her arms. I awkwardly imitated her and took my seat. We sat in silence, waiting. The old woman kneeling in front of the candles arose and crossed herself. As she turned, I saw that she held a rosary. She walked past us on her way out, and as she did, she smiled at me and patted me on the shoulder.

Mercedes knelt beside me and mouthed the words to a prayer in Spanish. Tommy and Manuel both held the same seated posture—slumped, hands in their laps, heads tilted up, both staring straight ahead at the engravings etched into the stone pulpit before them. I marveled then at the art's detail: human figures gestured to each other and upward at heaven, signs and symbols aplenty in the smooth stone firmament above. The stained glass windows featured on every wall revealed that same level of embellishment. Each one had a mural with a story on it: Jesus at the well with the Samaritan woman, a flock of sheep and their shepherd, John the Baptist visiting Mary and Joseph for the first time since the Savior's birth—each of them, I imagined, the work of an artist or a believer, a penitent or a craftsman, or anyway someone who wouldn't have considered the role that oil might have played in its construction.

The massive wooden door squeaked open behind us and I turned to see. Father Antonio stood at the precipice, donning a green vestment that covered his collar and his black shirt. He held the same expression as before, but the garments transformed him. His walk exuded authority. When he extended his arm high to wave at us, the cloth came with it and created the illusion of a wing running from his wrists to his hip. He no longer appeared as a man Manuel had called for a favor. Master of this space, he acknowledged me. I bowed in his presence.

As he approached us in the first pew, Mercedes stood up with her child. The rest of us followed suit. Father exchanged whispered words with Mercedes, and she nodded her head at his explanations. After draping a folded white cloth over his forearm, Father Antonio turned to me.

"So, you will be the godfather?"

I'd been dense enough not to fathom my official role in the ceremony. What else could I say? "Yes, Father," I replied.

"All right then. Are you ready?"

We walked up to the baptismal font on the right of the altar, a marble monolith filled with holy water. As Father Antonio crossed in front of the tabernacle, he bowed deeply. Not wanting to mess anything up, I followed suit. We gathered round the font. Father Antonio lit the paschal candle beside it and started to recite a prayer from a book held in his hands. Occasionally, he looked up to prompt Mercedes and Tommy for a response, and they gave it. Entranced by the rhythm of his speech and my own remove from the Spanish he spoke, I didn't recognize when he was talking to me. At least not until he paused, and the silence held long enough for me to look up and see that he was smiling at me patiently.

"I'm sorry, Keith. The question was, 'Are you ready to help the parents of this child in their duty as Christian parents?'"

"Uh, yeah. Sí," I said.

He went back to Spanish, continuing the rite. When he paused for a response, Tommy and Mercedes echoed my words: sí. And later again: sí. Soon enough, because I kept thinking of the word I was embodying—godfather—I thought of the scene in the church where

Michael Corleone's niece is baptized, and only because of that could I decipher the words that Father Antonio must have been asking us all: Did I reject Satan and all of his works? Sí. I thought of a movie thug pulling the trigger on courthouse steps. Did I reject all of his empty promises? Sí. I thought of migrants crossing the border even in that moment. Did I believe in God, the father almighty, creator of heaven and earth? Sí. I thought of my uncle, who raised me. Did I believe in Jesus Christ, his only Son, our Lord, who was born of the Virgin Mary, was crucified, died, and was buried, rose from the dead, and is now seated at the right hand of the Father? Sí. I thought of my own dead father, the picture of his kind face in Uncle Stock's house. Did I believe in the Holy Spirit, the holy Catholic Church, the forgiveness of sins, the resurrection of the body, and life everlasting? Sí. And I thought, finally, of Tita, the child cradled in the priests' arms, the American *ita* of Poza Rica, the fragile soul whose body I would ferry across the Rio Grande and on to New Orleans in the coming days like some kind of fucked-up saint.

PART II
Manuel and Tommy

Mysteries of the 19th Olympiad

MANUEL STOOD SHOULDER to shoulder in the Plaza de las Tres Culturas with law school classmates who were chanting "¡México, libertad!" But while his friends thrusted posters upward in earnest outrage, Manuel kept his arms low. He was holding a painting he'd recently finished. *Bird Infected by the Sky within Her,* he'd titled it. He'd naively imagined he might sell it at this protest. He'd told himself that if he could, it would be all the motivation he'd need to drop out and apply for admission to INBA: Instituto Nacional de Bellas Artes. Art school.

"What's with the canvas?" a law classmate asked.

"Yeah. What's with the bird?"

Manuel didn't respond, just shook his head like they wouldn't get it.

With wry pleasure, they played the part. This was easy for them since they didn't know of his plans to drop out. He tended to secrecy that way.

"You're a fucking weirdo, dude."

His friend Diego, also a disaffected 2L like Manuel, smiled and patted him on the shoulder. "When is Garín going to get up there and speak?" Diego said. "Or even Perelló. They're the goddamn reason we all came."

"The leaders of the student movement?" another classmate responded. "*That's* why you're here? Speak for yourself."

"What are you talking about?" Diego asked. "Why are *you* here?"

"Betancourt," the boy replied.

"The con law prof?" Diego prompted.

"El mero chingón, güey. The very one. He's supposed to be here tonight."

"And so?"

"He supports the movement openly. Everyone loves him, especially the higher-ups in the administration. He's like a god to them. Anyway, it would be good for him to see us here."

Diego caught Manuel's gaze. Manuel rolled his eyes, and they took a moment to judge their peers. They were dressed in tan suits and skinny ties, their clean-shaven faces the essence of conformity. Such effete fussiness put Manuel off, especially here, amid the vivid chaos swirling in the pre-Olympic air like *Starry Night*. Seeing these straightlaced white-collars protest was like watching cattle ice-skate—both the animals and their action foreign, the two together appearing like a scene from Márquez's new novel more than anything else Manuel could imagine.

"Dude. Your sign is in my way," one of them complained to another. "I can't see anything. How will we know when Betancourt is coming?"

Manuel looked at the sign. It read: Estudiantes Contra La Represión.

"No, dude. *Your* fucking sign is in *my* fucking way." The other boy's sign read: Estudiantes Para La Justicia. "Anyway, what are *you* really here for, Diego? Do you actually believe that being here is going to make any difference?"

"Well, yes. But that's not the only reason."

"Out with it, then."

Diego held quiet. He seemed hesitant. "My brother," he finally said. "I need to speak with him about something."

Manuel had no idea Diego had a brother. In their year together at law school, he'd never mentioned it.

"Listen to Mr. Mysterious. *I need to speak to my brother about something.* Okay. You want to be like that? Be like that. What's it to us?"

With that, they raised their fists and chanted in a bored monotone for Mexican universities' right to operate free of military intervention. As they panned the crowd for Betancourt, Diego tapped Manuel on the shoulder. "Let's find somewhere else to talk," he whispered. They eased away from the white-collars and maneuvered through a dense mass of protestors. The plaza held an unromantic slab of historic stone construction that echoed Mexico's past. The ruins of an Aztec temple stood next to a Spanish cathedral founded after Cortés's conquest. That stood next to a hulking, Soviet-bloc tower called the Chihuahua Building. The three structures formed a U, inside which ten thousand protesters had gathered. From a balcony of the Chihuahua Building, organizers spoke with import and bombast through the mouthpiece of a megaphone. The night was young, and the angry speakers were, too.

As Manuel and Diego sifted through the crowd, the kaleidoscope of humanity churned and revealed its patterns. Priests in black stood next to blue-clad janitors. Drab teamsters chanted with brightly colored students from the art school. There were even a few elderly gray souls a part of the scene, viejos who'd probably witnessed the Revolution. And then, of course, plaid-coated professors and white-collar students from UNAM, the national university, where Diego and Manuel attended law school. And though neither of them said anything aloud about it, both noted the green of military presence on the edges of the square—men in riot gear with machine guns, the granaderos hired by Chief of Police Cueto, under orders from el Presidente Ordaz himself. They stood sentinel like eagles zapped into stone statues, forced to restrain their natural urges to hunt prey. After ten minutes of walking and excusing themselves, the two friends arrived at a small clearing on the edge of the massive crowd.

"This is crazy," Manuel said. "This has to be at least twice as big as last week."

"Seems that way."

"What were you talking about back there? What's this about a brother?"

"His name is Ancho. I never told you about him?"

"No," Manuel replied.

Diego seemed shifty. "He's a—well, he's a granadero, Manuel. But it's not what you think."

"He's here? Working tonight?"

"Yes."

"Um, no. You never told me about your thug brother."

"We're not close. He left a note under my apartment door today. Said he wanted to meet me. I don't know what he wants."

"Any ideas?"

"He's hard to figure sometimes. Anyway, what's with the painting?"

Manuel held it up. A stoic white sparrow flew in profile. She was cut crudely out of construction paper that had been dyed and textured. Manuel had cut a hole where the bird's heart would be. In it you could see the austere blues and whites of a sun-drenched, puffy-cloud sky. *Sky Bird*, he called her.

"I see what you're going for," Diego said, nodding as he examined the painting.

"Lay it on me," said Manuel.

Even here, they reverted to their typical mode. Diego: short, shaven-headed politico, pontificator of the evils of the PRI, and the only law student who'd ever bothered to carry a conversation with Manuel about anything besides who the shittiest teachers were and the various under-handed ways to get chosen as editor of the law review. In this very plaza, an ancient square that had witnessed Aztec caciques cut out the beating hearts of seventy terrified men and the Spaniard mutilation of a Nahuatl king with sixteen arrows pierced into his torso before he was burned alive, Manuel and Diego met often to speak of the hollowness of Rivera's murals, the need for a more focused political statement from today's Mexican artists. They spoke to fix the world with debate—arreglar el mundo. They spoke like mezzanine-level philosophers, like luminaries without obligations to torts homework. They spoke of artists like Xavier Esqueda and José Cuevas—the genius of their choices in composition, the role of the frame in interpreting their art. The upcoming Olympics, they argued, would be a time not only for Mexico to shine but also for the country's political realities to be exposed to the world. "The time is coming, my friend, when an artist could get shown in a gallery by asserting the right kind of political fuck-all," Diego had said. "You know, like Warhol in the States. Like Lichtenstein." They were a bumbling, unstoppable force for airy discussion, a dynamic duo of *fuck it*, of *ay*, *cabrón*, of *ay*, *chingón*, of *a la chingada*. In a bloody, violent country like this, they sometimes asked no one, what good were laws? What good could men endowed with the responsibility to interpret them possibly think they could achieve?

"Your painting reminds me of Cuevas. It has a multitextured quality, you know? A deceptive simplicity. And there's something staid about it. As if it doesn't care if you like it. Which I like."

Manuel stroked his chin at this musing. He appreciated Diego's remarks. His friend harbored no artistic ambitions of his own, but Diego took seriously the role of critic. Manuel liked to imagine them in fifteen years, himself a respected artist in the Distrito Federal and Diego the undisputed voice of antireason in the critical world, a voice to push the country's artistic aesthetic in specific and radical directions. Manuel had discovered an intimacy with Diego, founded on art but reaching beyond that toward the bottomless fathoms of his ambition. He didn't take it for granted. He couldn't and didn't want to imagine his burgeoning life in art without his friend.

On the balcony, Raul Garín, president of the national strike coalition, started gesticulating and ranting. As he spoke, his megaphone morphed his voice into warbled echoes of anger. In response more to the passion of the man's gestures than the content of his words, the crowd responded with canned chants, raised fists clenched. Manuel and Diego watched.

"Why did you bring that bird tonight?" Diego asked.

Manuel told him.

"Who do you think is going to buy it? This isn't a market, Manuel."

This obvious truth, articulated, sobered Manuel enough to keep him from retorting right away. After some thinking, though, as he listened to Garín rail against the government's occupation of the Instituto Politécnico Nacional #5, he thought of something: "And I guess your motives for being here are nothing but pure. You and your granadero brother's motives, I mean."

Manuel said this as a blind lashing out, but in Diego's wince, Manuel saw he'd landed on a truth. He didn't know exactly what it was, and he didn't know if he wanted to find out. "I'm sorry," Manuel offered. "I know it's foolish, to think I'll sell something. That's not even the point, anyway."

"Well, you've come a long way from those early paintings. Anyone can see that."

"They were pretty bad, right?"

In those first naïve attempts, Manuel had represented the futility of existence abstractly. He'd painted a series of blue rectangles entitled *The Bitter Ovens of My Melancholy Dreams, #IV, 117, and E.* He painted a brown blob in the shape of a beaker and splattered it yellow with the whimsical and untrained drip of a Jackson Pollock wannabe ("I like your painting of that disaffected goat," a girl he'd shown it to had told him). He even took a dead mouse, dipped it in a murky green synthetic, and smeared a junkyard piece of chrome with its carcass: *A Second Use for the Dead*, he called that one.

All this heady creativity led to no showings, but an allowance for law school still came from his clueless father in Veracruz. He feared what his ex-military old man would do if he discovered Manuel was considering art school. After all, the man had worked in counterintelligence for the Americans in World War II. Still, Manuel persisted in his belief that a life of artistic pursuit was plausible.

"Listen," Diego said. "I'm going to see Ancho. Let's meet here in an hour, okay?"

"An hour?" Manuel said. "Seriously, what are you doing?"

"Don't worry about it," Diego said. With that, he took off, and the morass of bodies subsumed his form.

Despite knowing the long odds, Manuel began to search for anyone who might be interested in his painting. He caught a woman's gaze, and to his surprise, she made straight for him. She was short, with gray eyes and gray streaks in her jet-black hair. In the assertiveness of her posture, Manuel imagined her a fellow lover of art. She was not.

"Excuse me, sir," she said. "I am a reporter for *Bild-Zeitung*, out of Hamburg. We have witnessed protests there, too. Some of them violent. Can you tell me please why you are here, and what you hope to accomplish tonight? Will you interfere with the Olympics next week? If so, what do you hope *that* will achieve?"

Manuel had never articulated any connection between the movement and what he painted. Mostly, he'd milled about at demonstrations and meetings, culling conversations for artistic inspiration.

"This is not our fathers' Mexico," Manuel found himself saying.

"Okay," said the scribbling reporter, disappointed. "And what, exactly, was your father's Mexico?"

Manuel scanned the crowd for Diego. He would have the right words. Others were being interviewed. What were they saying? And what would the saying accomplish? When all the articles were published, when they'd all been read and assembled in some collection of astute readers' minds, what sense might be made of all these cacophonous utterings, this constellation of so many fundamental urges played out and quashed over the grim succession of Mexican months? Especially when so many were probably, like him, just here to see what was going on. He imagined then a flock of words—Presidente Ordaz's, Chief of Police Cueto's, Diego's, Betancourt's, his law buddies', his own—he imagined them in the sky like geese, first in a V, each word bird a black phrase in a blue expanse of the heavens heading toward some common and safe and distant land, each suddenly flustered into its own chaotic trajectory by a clip of staccato questions like gunshots from reporters, each message then made to fly of its own accord, with no sense of unity with the others now floating in a vast and darkening sky.

"What do you mean?" she repeated. "What was it like, your father's Mexico?"

When he hesitated again, she sighed. Tried another tack. "Well, then tell me about this painting you're holding. Does it mean something in terms of the movement?"

"There's a sky of sun and clouds in every bird," he said. "It represents—" but he couldn't think this way. He just painted. He was no critic. Where the fuck was Diego?

"I don't know why I'm still here," she said.

"Many of us paint this way," he replied. "We don't paint directly about the movement. We paint with the emotion it stirs in us." This felt like a true thing. It felt good to say it aloud to this woman. She wasn't impressed, but she gave him one more chance.

"So, you're part of a school of artists, then? With some specific, aesthetic notions of how to represent all of this anger and frustration? Is that it?"

Her condescension beat him. He sighed. "No, actually. I'm just a law student. I just paint on the side."

She raised an eyebrow. "A law student? Are there many of you here?"

"Yes, there—"

"That's so interesting! And what have your professors been saying about these government interventions?"

"Actually, a couple of them are here tonight. They—"

"Here tonight? Are you serious? Where?"

Once again, he sighed. "I'm sure that if you can find the group of well-dressed boys in skinny ties and tan suits, you'll be able to track them down no problem."

With that, he walked back into the fray, closer to the balcony of the Chihuahua Building, where Perelló was speaking on the question of what would be done if the protestors' demands weren't met. All around, people seemed to listen. To agree. To be emboldened. Manuel put his painting by his side and tried to become a part of the fuss.

Up ahead, he spotted Diego. He was speaking to a stout, stern-faced man wearing a white glove on his left hand. Ancho, presumably. The two of them exchanged nods. Over the reverberating voice of Perelló on the balcony, Ancho brought his mouth to Diego's ear and spoke. Diego nodded in collusion. He handed Ancho a piece of paper, and Ancho pocketed it. They looked at each other with grave import, with a baffling kind of hunger. Manuel realized three things: (1) everyone with white gloves was military police, even those not in riot gear, all of them likely hiding, as he could now see Ancho was, some form of automatic weapon; (2) the angular shape of Ancho's jaw resembled a particular laborer depicted in Rivera's *Dream of a Sunday Afternoon in Alameda Park*; and (3) whoever Ancho was, he wasn't Diego's brother. Though Manuel was close enough to walk up on their scene, he didn't speak out in greeting. Just stood apart and watched.

Surveying the crowd, Ancho folded his arms and spoke with annoyance. Diego shrugged his shoulders in response. Ancho nodded. They were commiserating over something. Something, it seemed, unrelated to the protests. On the balcony, Perelló yielded the megaphone to a short, mustachioed twenty-something in a striped shirt with energy to burn. Manuel didn't recognize the new speaker, but the crowd surged forward at the sight of him and carried Manuel a few paces in the wash of their excitement. In the process, he moved closer to the colluding pair. From this new vantage, in the rhombus of space in which he could view their bodies, he saw that Ancho had lowered his arms to his side. Diego had, too. They were holding hands, their thumbs rubbing just beside the tip of Ancho's rifle. It only lasted a second, and then Diego withdrew and clapped in faux support of the mustachioed man's rant. Ancho scanned the crowd, looking for agitators.

Awash in that sight, Manuel kept watching. Just then, Diego spotted him. His face lit with recognition—no hint of anxiety at being caught—and he raised a hand in earnest offering. Manuel smiled back. Diego walked toward him, but a group of soldiers pushed a crowd of students into a heap of faltering limbs. Manuel backed away. He scanned for Diego, but the mob had tumbled into the spot where his friend had stood. Somewhere in the miasma of bodies and voices, a familiar-sounding voice called Manuel's name. He couldn't place it. "Manuel," he heard again. No faces registered. He turned toward a girl he thought might've been the caller. She wasn't, but his look of expectancy registered with her, and she spoke to him.

"You are looking for someone," she said, "but there is only all of us."

She wore a protest sign around her neck. It read: Presidente Ordaz—Come out on the balcony, loudmouth! She scanned his left hand. Seeing it bare, she sized up his tattered pants, the painting he held, his plaid shirt lined with garish white buttons. "What are you?" she asked. "Some kind of violence watcher? Why are you here?"

"Why are any of us at any of these things?" he responded. How could he explain?

"These gatherings, they are shapes in the dust," she said. "Fast-approaching squalls that come and pass before you know it."

"What are you talking about?" Manuel asked.

"But that does not mean they have no significance. They are, in fact, a bold proclamation of the end of days. They foretell of a death-laden future. Blood emptying into the gutters. And will all the violence be worth it?" she asked the sky.

He imagined she thought so. He shrugged. She smirked back at him. "Are you trying to impress someone by being here?" she asked.

"What about you?" Manuel replied. "Are you with labor? Are you a student?"

She laughed. "What do you think?" she said. "Of course I'm a student. My friends help organize, you know. You look lost."

Manuel, in fact, was gazing aimlessly over her shoulder for Diego. "I'm looking for my friend."

"Who's your friend, little boy? You look like we need to find your parents and take you to bed."

He appeared young for his twenty-one years, but he didn't react to the slight. "I have to go," he said. He pushed through the thickening crowd to escape the woman's eeriness. And then, at a distance, he saw Diego again, this time as if he were a stranger. He was pounding his fist into the air, alone. He held no sign, though he donned the usual drab garb of the protestor. He was just standing like nothing strange had just happened. As Manuel approached, anxiety constricted his throat. Had Diego bribed Ancho for something? Were they lovers soon to abscond? And had Diego provided his lover with the names of dissenters? What, in the name of all things Mexican, might Manuel possibly say to him now?

Maybe Manuel could return to his painting. The white sparrow— you see, Diego, his stoic expression, it's in profile because we're really only seeing things two-dimensionally these days. There's more to the movement than we can see. You know how we talk. We have no idea what we're saying. It *is* a blast, though, right? But now, I see what we were missing. What *I* was missing, anyway. And I wanted to represent that in the bird, you see. And the sparrow's stoic expression? Think of it, that monotone face some of us have, even now, even right fucking now as we're standing in this plaza and shit is happening all around us that is real. We're platicando, asking strangers why they're here. Talking blindly about our fathers' Mexico. Wondering where the right person is. And all this time, the thing that's real, the thing that makes us who we are, it's *inside* us. We really *do* care about our futures. We really *do* think that the movimiento matters. How could we not? We're young, and the gift of youth, I'm starting to think, is not knowing, just being. And how can any of us not feel the power and the glory of this moment? It's a part of us, to react this way to soldiers in our university's halls. Just like the sky is a part of the bird. Which is why I've cut out the belly, to expose the truth of the clouds and the sky within her. And yet this doesn't faze her! She doesn't change her expression on the outside. She doesn't let on that she's got this burning desire of flight at her core. But you're meant to ask: What does it mean, that she's so unfeeling on the outside while all of this truth is there inside her belly? This is how we are, Diego. This is how I am, anyway. This is how I've been this whole time. Who the fuck have *you* been?

A green flare streaked across the darkening sky. Like a toxic comet, he thought. Or a child's smear of crayon across the gray construction paper of the night. Everyone, de repente, quieted. In the still thereafter, like a distant thundering of hooves upon the dust, there appeared above the Spanish cathedral and the Aztec temple a pair of military helicopters in the sky, hovering. Faces tilted upward. The buzzing of blades echoed against ancient walls. On the balcony, the mustachioed leader dropped the megaphone to his side. The helicopters' floating made it seem like the moment would stay suspended forever—each side staunch in its unspoken assumptions, the choppers' blades keeping unstable peace with their fierce sense of the present.

Shots rang out. The crowd screamed and churned. Bodies around him were clubbed by the batons of granaderos. Diego—was it Diego?—ran into one who beat him over the head with the butt of a rifle until he bled from the mouth. A herd of frightened sign carriers knocked Manuel down. A steel-toed granadero boot thudded into his side like a swung mallet. A rib cracked. He rolled into a fetal ball and screamed out into the night. Others trampled him, too. He grabbed an ankle just above a dress shoe and pulled the body down to pull himself up. Once on his feet, side throbbing, he glimpsed down onto the terrified sophisticate he'd used as a lever, the man's perfect glasses framing his professorial face, and then Manuel lost the visage in a wash of pants and arms, shoes and torsos. He doubled over, trying to protect his side. Next to where he had just lain, a spike of wood from a falling picketer impaled another student who'd been trampled. Manuel forced himself through a thicket of boys into a small space of breathing room. He heard the staccato fire of machine guns. People ducked and screamed.

The helicopters swooped low, firing into the crowd. Wind blew his shirt open at the waist and he held his side. Megaphoned voices of authority boomed over the chaos from the choppers, but he couldn't hear the words.

The blunt pain of being trampled ignited his bones. Breathing shallowly to avoid the worst pain, he walked toward the plaza's center, against the grain of the rushing crowd. He imagined it like a hurricane. In the center there'd be an eye where he could rest while the turmoil swirled about. If he just kept walking against the flow, he'd end up there. He walked for what seemed like hours, only moved a few meters. He kept seeing the same stained glass window of the church, blue and looming over him at the same distance. Bloodied bodies limped across his line of vision like zombies. Students shrieked and granaderos bellowed incomprehensible orders. He forgot his own pain in the presence of others who'd been shot, others trampled so badly they couldn't rise.

In a flash, then, he saw a ghostly figure. It stood at the edge of the square in standard-issue military fatigues. Square shoulders rigid. Legs spread just enough to be menacing and disciplinary. Disappointed and staunch. Eyes glowing red. No movement. Stolid. The man caught his gaze and shook his head, as if warning Manuel not to do whatever he was thinking of doing. Manuel looked away. When he looked back, the man was gone.

. . .

The next morning, back in his one-room flat, Manuel called Diego's apartment. No answer. He looked for his friend's name in the newspaper accounts, but the articles were vague, no names listed. Feeling the tender flesh of his trampled side, he pictured Diego with Ancho's hand in his. Thumbs rubbing. That paper being passed.

The sirens having faded, rib still throbbing, Manuel ignored the burning city outside his window. Turned to his canvases. Started on a cycle of paintings. Each canvas, a different witnessing of that red-eyed ghost. In the first one, he painted the scene by memory: staunch figure of discipline and terror, dressed in green, arms at his side. In the next painting, he painted the figure to the exact specifications of his father: first adding epaulets and the insignia of the army, then pasting on an ink-black mustache and arching a severe angle of eyebrow. In the third, he depicted the figure as Ancho, with a white wristband and head shaved down to stubble, fashioning then a shield beside a rippling bicep, and then adding Diego next to him, marked bloody with the red badge of his collusion. As nightmares of the protest invaded his sleep, he added others, too, in the periphery, always with other voices from other times in his life—Garín, Perelló, law classmates, his mother— voices he imagined booming off the canvas from the angry confusion of his subconscious. Always with Diego painted in, too. Always Diego, staring. Always Diego, openmouthed. Always Diego, not saying.

By the time he'd finished four of the planned seven paintings (one for each of his nightmares), the Olympics had ended with a reverent extinguishing of the torch. As churchgoers leave a vigil when the candle has been snuffed, the world took its cue to beg off. Newspapers never named the dead. Diego did not resurface. That, it appeared, was that.

But Manuel continued painting. As he did, he recalled a story his father had told him about his own childhood—how, long ago, the old man had prayed the rosary nightly in hopes of escaping the rural Veracruz of his youth. And now, bead by bead, canvas by canvas, the glorious mysteries of this lifelike life were revealing themselves to Manuel as gradually as an earth tilt. Completing the series, he did not wonder what Diego would think, for his friend was no longer there. Diego existed only in Manuel's frames now, if he was anywhere. And even *that* Diego, who could say who he was?

Weeks later, having heard rumors of the former law student's artwork about the movement, Professor Betancourt called Manuel to ask if he could see them. Showing the pieces to his former con law prof, Manuel waited for him to ask about the recurring figure, but Betancourt refrained. Just stroked his chin. Likely, Manuel thought, he was already formulating stories he'd tell his colleagues about them. At the end of the cursory examination, he offered Manuel fifteen thousand pesos for the entire series.

How many times had Manuel dreamed of a moment like this? He thought to smirk but didn't. Only shook the man's hand. Betancourt shook back, nodded like a Medici. "You're quite talented," he said. "These paintings, what do you call them?"

Diego would've gone for a direct title. Unassuming. Let the art speak for itself. Let critics effuse with bullshit meaning. But this was Manuel's moment. The beginning of something. Inventing a name for the series, Manuel understood that he would never paint about the movement again. "Mysteries of the 19th Olympiad," he said.

Betancourt nodded in approval. Stroked his chin again. "You've got something here," he said.

"If you say so," Manuel replied. With that, he slid his canvases into a box lined with cardboard sleeves and shoved them into the hall. When Betancourt followed, perplexed, wondering about method of payment, Manuel shut the door on his buyer and his art, and then turned back toward his living room and sighed, wondering what madness he would paint next.

The Baller Ganked the Rock

"IT'S HIGH TIME you started showing yourself good around here, Tommy," said Mom smiling, and she gave me a dollar and a pen. "Buy your sick Grammy a card from the drugstore and write her a note. Don't talk to strangers and look both ways when you cross the street."

I put on my socks and tennis shoes and went out mumbling to myself. There were many cards at the K&B around the corner but I finally picked one that said, "I love you." The line was long and I waited between a fat lady and a man in a tie until it was my turn.

"Just this card, sir," I said meekly.

"Just a card? You don't want a envelope? Or a ribbon?"

I didn't answer and he saw me hesitate and he grew impatient:

"C'mon, boy, what you want?"

"I don't know," I stammered.

He saw it in my eyes and laughed, saying, "Come back when you figured it out."

I fell out of line embarrassed and returned home defeated.

"Where's the card? What did you do, silly, lose the dollar?" Mom asked.

"I'm sorry. I didn't know if you wanted an envelope. Or a ribbon. I'm sorry."

"Silly goose. Haven't you seen me at Christmastime writing cards? There is no ribbon, except on the presents."

"I guess not."

"Boy o boy, I tell you. Ask him for an envelope to go with it."

I went back to the K&B man and said, "I want it with an envelope."

With a smirk on his face he asked, "What color envelope? Baby blue, romantic red, olive green?"

I wasn't ready for that.

"I got a line here, kid," he sighed. He was laughing.

I returned quickly to Mom, who laughed too.

"Again? No card or envelope?"

"A green one? A blue one? A red one?"

"What color is the card?"

"White and red."

"Then get a red envelope." She sighed heavily.

"How was I supposed to know? Sorry."

"Silly goose. Tell that old man you want a red envelope and to quit pulling your chain."

I went off quickly and yelled at the man as I walked in the K&B, "The card, with a red envelope."

"Eighty-nine cent."

I reached for the dollar, but it wasn't in my pocket. I looked in the other pocket and down my shorts. The man's face lit up with laughter.

"You lost your money. Your poor ma!"

"I'll be back," I mumbled.

I returned to Mom empty-handed.

"Baby, what now?" she asked.

"I forgot the dollar."

"Or did you lose it?"

"I don't know."

"Boy o boy o boy. Here's another dollar. Think you can do it all right, or you want me to come with you?"

I shook my head no and took the dollar in my hand and went off to the K&B, mumbling to myself and not thinking of anything. There was an older boy on the sidewalk where I had to pass who was dribbling a basketball. He was putting it through his legs and spinning it on his finger. I tried to avoid him but I wanted to watch too.

"At's right. I'm a baller. Check me out, fool. Bet you can't ball like this."

I said nothing but he could tell I wanted to play.

"Watch the rock, boy."

He put the ball in his hand and presented it like a magician showing his cards. Then he spun it around his right hand and caught it with his left and spun it around that hand too. His hands were moving everywhere but the ball stayed stationary and rotated like the earth.

"You wanna ball?"

I only looked at him.

"You gotta pay to play."

I didn't understand what he meant.

He faked the ball at my head and I flinched. "You gotta pay to play."

I still didn't get it. Some of his friends called to him and he went away dribbling, so I went on to the K&B.

"The card with the red envelope. Here is the dollar."

"You some kinda white boy."

"The card with the red envelope, please."

"Eighty-nine cent."

I gave him the dollar and he gave me the envelope and the card in a bag. Walking on to Grammy's house I reached into my pocket for my pen to write the note on the card but it wasn't there. I didn't want to go back to Mom again. I walked up and down the block looking for my pen. The boy with the basketball was gone.

I made my way to streets farther and farther away from Mom and Grammy's block to look in garbage cans for a discarded pen but I had no luck. Soon I was far from home but I heard basketballs bouncing in the distance at a school and I went to see. There were other boys. The boy from my street was there and he was bouncing his ball. We were the youngest ones.

"Y'all better watch me. I'm a baller," the boy said.

"Yeah, you a baller." They were teasing him. They were all dribbling and shooting and laughing and talking easily.

"Peep this move out, baller," one of them said and then dribbled through his legs and round his back and then faked at the baller's head. He flinched.

I ran home fast as I could even though it was far and sneaked into the backyard to get my old rubber ball and came back and dribbled by the side waiting for a game to start. They all watched me and I liked that.

"C'mon, let's go. Ball up," one of them said.

They needed another player so they picked me up. I put down the bag with the card and the envelope and put my ball on top of it.

"Take it, white boy," one called to me and passed me the ball. "Can't nobody stop you, white boy." They were laughing and joking and standing around waiting for me to do something.

I didn't know it till then but I am fast and good and so I scored a lot of points and made them look silly.

"Damn, boy, what you is, ten?"

I didn't respond.

"I be got-damned. I ain't been getting crossed-over by no little white boy." He was a man.

By the end of the game there was a crowd gathered watching but I didn't see the boy from my block anymore. My team lost and so I had to get off but I stayed and watched the other games. For a long while I thought about winning and about doing the trick the boy had done with the ball in his hands like the earth moving. Making the hand motions without the ball, I mumbled, "You gotta pay to play, bitch."

"Who you callin' bitch, white boy?" came back a clear and pretty voice.

I turned and saw a girl who had been watching the game. She was wearing Adidas shorts, a tank top, and a backward Saints hat and was sucking on a lollipop. She smiled at me and I lost my heart to her.

I couldn't speak so I could only motion for her to follow me and I was lucky that she did. I led her to the jungle gym and we climbed up into it and watched the pickup games through the bars. I still couldn't speak but I smiled at her and she smiled at me. Putting my hand against hers I felt the natural smoothness of her skin and thought how different it was from my other hand that was holding on to the bars. I squeezed her hand and swallowed. She knew I was nervous then but she was still looking at me and smiling. She put her sucker back in her mouth and I could tell it would end. She got up to leave and I reached out to her.

"I gotta go," she said.

"Where?"

"To the store for Mama. She axed me to get some pork and beans for supper and it's gettin' on."

"Will you come back?"

She said yeah, but when she mentioned her mother I remembered my mom and I took in a quick breath of panic. Untangling myself from the jungle gym I wandered back to the basketball court to pick up my card and envelope and ball, but they were all gone. I stood still and bewildered.

"White boy, you looking for yo shit?" one of them said.

"The baller, it was him," another replied.

"The baller ganked yo rock, dog," a third said with no feeling except for almost laughing.

"And the card and envelope, too," I said to myself. But I didn't blame him. When I was walking down the street and people asked me what I was crying about I said, "I lost my grammy's card." It was better to have it that way than for them to know it was stolen.

I went home to admit failure and ask for more money, but Mom wasn't there. I grabbed the key from under the mat and went inside and took a pen and some quarters and quickly left before she might return. I walked down the block back to K&B. It was late and the old man was at the end of his shift.

"Aw hell no," he said. "What you want now?"

"This card with a red envelope," I said seriously.

"Boy, you *fool* crazy."

"I have the money."

"Ain't this a son-of-a-bitch. I gotta right mind to go down to your mama and tell that woman what you been up to, boy." He went on talking and talking and I didn't listen. Instead I got angry. I threw my pen at him and ran out the store. I thought about going back home but then I started to think about the basketball game and how good I'd been. I started to dribble an imaginary basketball and act like I was dribbling past people and jumping high and dunking on them.

"You got to pay to play," I said aloud.

I wanted to find the boy with my card and my envelope and my basketball. I walked all around the neighborhood but he was nowhere. I went back to the school with the jungle gym to see if the girl would come back. I climbed up into the bars and waited in the twilight, wondering what I would say if she came. I admitted to myself that the girl had given me feelings I never had before. As I waited and dreamed I heard whispers in the coming darkness. I looked in the direction of the sound and saw two bodies standing next to the court. I could tell by their voices that one was a man and one was a woman. They spoke softly but their voices carried in the breeze, and I thought of how it was like me and the girl earlier. It was not what they said because we didn't say anything, but how they weren't sure of how to be. Their voices filled me with curiosity and I smiled because I knew they couldn't see me.

But they went on and what they said sounded funny and made me feel like I shouldn't be there.

"I don't have the money," she said, annoyed.

"Dime bags ain't on layaway. You gonna pay one way or another."

"I don't know what you talkin'."

"Girl you fuckin' crazy. Ain't nobody here. Come on."

He put his hand on her arm and squeezed and she said ouch and slapped him, and the man hit the woman across the face. Then he was on top of her and there was screaming. I forgot my grip as I watched. I slipped enough to make a sound with my foot against the bars that they could hear. I didn't look to see if they stopped cause I heard the man yelling hey and then the quiet after. I crawled out of the jungle gym quickly and took off running as fast as I could. It was dark now and I didn't know where I was running, but I didn't look back and I didn't stop until I couldn't run anymore.

When it was over I found myself in a part of town I'd never been in. It was a big highway intersection and there were green and white signs everywhere: I-10 East New Orleans, I-110 North Scotlandville, I-10 West Lafayette Mississippi River Bridge, US 61 North Saint Francisville, US 61 South New Orleans. There was no sign for Mexico, where Mom had said that my dad was from, and I was very lost and there was no telling how I would find my way. There was a convenience store by the exit ramp. Should I ask the clerk there? But then I remembered the man at the K&B and thought better of it. There were lots of lights on everywhere and people were out and about. I saw a pay phone outside the store and made my way to it. I had the money from the card I didn't buy. I opened the phone book and there were all kinds of names I never saw before, but then I remembered that the girl hadn't told me her name. And the older people at the playground didn't use names either. I stood there for a second and wished I could at least have my basketball back, and then I knew there was only one way I could get another one. I put coins in the phone and dialed Mom beneath the store's streetlight.

In the City of Murals

IN THE FIRST DAYS of the couple's unlikely marriage, it became the airbrush artist's habit to follow his American wife about the tiny kitchen of their rented house, daydreaming aloud to her in Spanish as she prepared dinner. Most often, he shared his plans to open a screen-printing and art shop in the small town where they lived, near Bayou Teche.

"Hoy hice el letrero, Pearl. Mañana lo montaré." *I made the sign today, Pearl. I'm putting it up tomorrow.*

She understood only her name and mañana. Spiced chicken cubes sizzled when she spilled them into the pan. His hands held her sides to feel when she needed to move past him, for there were many places for her to be when she cooked. He continued in Spanish:

"It's big and blue with black letters: M A N N Y ' S. Each letter is in a different font. I made the *M* and the *S* big, and they connect, like an underline. The apostrophe is a little shirt. You can come soon and tell me what you think."

As he paced behind her in the small room, he had to watch for cabinets ajar and the sharp edges of counter corners, and so he could not look at her as they moved like a two-car train from the counter to the stove to the sink.

"I'm going to make the first shirts for the festival tomorrow. Would you like me to screen one for you?"

She stood over the faucet washing her hands of raw chicken and chili powder, the room thick with the smell of cumin and cilantro.

"Mmm, bueno," he whispered into her ear.

She understood that word, too, and smiled. During their brief courtship, she'd prepared him Cajun dishes from recipes handed down to her by her mother. Since the wedding, though, she'd cooked with tortillas and onions, tomatoes and cheese. He liked the shift, but the new dishes didn't resemble the food of his childhood. This was his fault. He could've shared more about his life in Mexico, but he wanted to think of himself only as American now. For this reason, Pearl's imagined version of his youth in Veracruz became a false oasis shimmering at the edges of their interactions. But because he saw how it made her feel about him to imagine it, he didn't want to dissolve her vision. And anyway, he liked her attempts at Mexican food, even if they weren't authentic.

They returned to the stove so she could prepare a sauce. He let go of her and walked to the living room, where he felt her gaze as he looked at one of his pieces tacked to the wall above the old couch. It was a sparrow in profile cut out of cream construction paper. In the middle of its breast he'd burned a hole through which showed light blues and whites the color of the sky and the clouds.

"Would you like me to make you a shirt from this print?" he asked her in English.

She smiled at him. "Yes," she said.

She chopped garlic and chilies for a sauce and put them into a cast-iron pot with onion. She took store-brand cheddar from the fridge and cut a big cube into a pan to melt it over the stove. Though this was a special dinner, the fresh vegetables had left no money for good cheese. She placed a stack of tortillas in a cradle of foil and put them in the toaster oven to warm. She joined him in the living room then to wait for dinner. They sat down on the couch, a hand-me-down from Pearl's mother, and sank into its broken springs. He draped his arm around her, and she laid her head on his chest. He could feel the weight of her wrist against his abdomen.

"Are you sure the loan will go through?" she asked. The sauce bubbled beneath their words.

"Of course," he said.

"It's been a while."

"That's why I went ahead and started. I didn't want to wait on the bank forever."

"Even if you didn't know about the loan? But what did you have for collateral?"

"This is a small town. They understand the problems of starting a small business. Yesterday, Harry—"

"Harry. From the bank?"

"He said that he would visit the store tomorrow to give me the final yes."

"He's said that twice already."

"Which is why he won't cancel again."

She asked if Harry had questioned his citizenship. He deflected the question, but she persisted. "I know you're a dual citizen," she said, "but that doesn't matter to them."

He reminded her patiently, for the umpteenth time, that his mother's family had lived here respectably for years. He was, in fact, only half Mexican. His grandmother, a quiet and humble member of the Prejean family known in these parts for generations, was a friend of Harry's aunt. When, as usual, this didn't assuage Pearl, he resorted to defending the promise of his business based on how their small town had recently begun to support the arts with the inception of a new local festival. Yes, he was new here; no, he wasn't a gamble.

She admired his confidence though she didn't share it, and to distract herself from her worry she focused on his looks. Her Manuel had jet-black hair, and he was much taller than most Mexicans. He was light-skinned and you could see traces of his ethnicity in his facial structure, both the Cajun and the Mexican, though when he spoke Spanish, most people around here usually saw only the latter. As he'd told her, he was capable of speaking English without an accent. As a child in Veracruz, he'd learned English well enough from his mother that he knew from an early age what it should sound like. When he concentrated, he could make himself sound American, but mostly he found the effort distracting. To think about his own words too much made him forget what he was trying to say. And so, more often than not, he spoke with a slight accent, just enough for people in Rayne to question whether he was foreign.

"What if it doesn't go through? What will we do then?"

He didn't want to think of it. With savings, he'd bought airbrushes and screen presses and inks, and he'd even succeeded at getting a $500 line of credit, but only the bank could front the money to rent the store space. He'd secured this first month's rent with the old, senile landlord by borrowing from Pearl's father to pay upfront, promising additional months' payment with the eventual loan approval.

The loan application had asked questions that had indeed made him nervous, and so he'd fudged. Where it asked for income projections for the first year, he ballparked and bullshitted the best he knew how, exaggerating his work with an art education venture in the Distrito Federal to show proof of past financial success. Where it asked for a personal financial statement, he mentioned how he'd saved two thousand dollars before applying (it had really only been five hundred), and he drew on his fleeting law school days to give them jargon about a studio he'd managed in the months just after the Olympic massacre in Mexico City—a time when financial sustainability, he wrote, was difficult to achieve. Where it asked for tax returns from the prior three years, he confidently included the Mexican documents, reassured by the absence on the form of any question that referred to nationality. He hoped these answers made him look worldly and not simply Mexican. The waiting period was stressful, but the ability to become whoever you needed to be at any given time—wasn't this what made for a good businessman?

Pearl's concern carried their silence. He ran his fingers through her hair absentmindedly, and she sighed to remind him she was there. "Well, dinner smells bueno, doesn't it?" she said.

She got up from his embrace and returned to the kitchen. As she left, his arms fell from her body and into his lap. He watched her from the couch through the open doorway between the two rooms. The cheese had melted, the sauce had thickened, and now the toaster oven, filled with tortillas, dinged. Pearl collected silverware and napkins and brought them to the living room. She placed them on the old black trunk in front of the sofa. She took two tortillas from the toaster oven and laid them on a plate. She dumped the chicken into the sauce and spooned the mixture into the tortillas. She dabbed the melted cheese on top and brought the meals to the sofa. As a gesture of thanks, he smiled at the offering, and Pearl took it as her due. They dined to the clanging of railroad bells at the end of the street, where soon a freighter came thundering by. Their glasses rattled on the trunk as they ate. When the roar and rush faded, the glasses stopped jittering and they were left with the familiar sound of a train in the distance blowing its horn.

"To my Manwell," she said, trying to pronounce it like he'd taught her. "On the eve of his new business."

. . .

He dressed the next morning in one of his self-made T-shirts and a pair of jeans. He combed back his hair and plucked the stray hairs from his nose and eyebrows. When he finished, Pearl was waiting for him in the kitchen. She'd made him a bag lunch, like her mother always did for her father, and now she gave it to him with a smile.

"Good luck," she offered.

He smiled and kissed her on his way out. Walking along the railroad tracks into town, his huaraches exposed diamond-patterned bits of his feet and left his ankles bare. The sun shone bright in front of him, hovering just above the pines and live oaks on the side of the road. Along the way he passed Saint Joseph Cemetery. In the small plot, tombs stood aboveground to survive floods. Grass and weeds grew in rows between the stones and led back to the church's sacristy. As he'd heard twice already in his short time in Rayne, it was the only Christian cemetery in the world that faced north-south. Looking out at the graves, he gave a soft laugh at the thought of how Harry had explained it to him:

You see, cemeteries are built east-west so that the headstones face east, the setting of the sun and all. Here in Rayne, when we built the railroad depot, folks wanted the church to be moved closer to it. Well, they weren't going to have a new church without a new cemetery, so they built Saint Joe's. But for whatever reason, they put the headstones facing north. By the time the city realized what it'd done, a heap of us'd already been buried. You can't just dig up your own kin for the sake of some symbol. Dead people don't know which way the sun sets.

It reminded him of the old junkyard near his family's house in Veracruz. As a kid, he'd sneak out of the house at night to get away from so many people. He made his way there by the moonlight and then lost himself in sorting through rusted bumpers, broken headlights and mountains of flattened chassis, plastic cupholder rings and hubcaps. Imagining what else they could be, something beautiful they could become: those had been the first times he'd considered being an artist.

The railroad ties showed themselves in front of his feet, trailing back to Texas and Mexico behind him, stretching east in front of him to New Orleans. He passed the church and walked into the tiny business district, where his rented store space awaited. Approaching it, thinking of his own murals project, he thought of the murals on the concrete slabs beneath the single interstate exit for Rayne. The concrete there had been painted with big frogs in bright greens and pastels. They donned big mouths and smiles. On first arriving, he hadn't known whether to take them as a sign of welcome or drunken revelry. A sign by the concrete slabs announced Rayne to visitors as Louisiana's City of Murals, and also the Frog Capital of the World.

Murals of frogs adorned storefronts on Main Street, too. Walking the main drag, he studied them closely. They were painted over the outer brick walls of the hardware store, the side of the convenience store, and even the city court building. Some depicted frogs in top hats at a town meeting, their necks swollen as they ribbited or spoke. Some were realistic depictions, like the one on the side of a warehouse of two tree frogs, painted a light lime green with red eyes and thin, black, vertical pupils that stared out at all who passed. Others were like fairy tales that depicted frogs in conversation with snakes and birds. Everywhere, frogs.

Summer would end in two weeks with Labor Day weekend, when Rayne would celebrate its first annual Frog Festival. The mayor had promoted it across south Louisiana, and he boasted that visitors would be coming from as far away as Opelousas and Baton Rouge to see the murals and hear the Cajun music. They'd even booked Clifton Chenier. Manuel had already begun to make templates for T-shirts. He'd brainstormed phrases for airbrushing and screen-printing: Rayne's Ribbiting Experience, Frogging on the Bayou, Rayne Frog Fest '72: A Hopping Good Time. He'd talked to authorities in town about setting up a booth at the festival that would advertise Manny's, but a formal process of obtaining appropriate permits stood in the way, and time was slipping by in the settling in and the getting used to his wife.

He came upon his rented shop, sandwiched between a Baskin-Robbins and a jewelry store. The plateglass windows on either side of the wooden door were tall and narrow. Manuel had printed Grand Opening leaflets at the local copy shop, taped them to the glass, and distributed them to neighboring shops, and they fluttered now with the passing of cars down the street. He looked through the window but couldn't see very far back in the weak light of morning. His new hand-painted wooden sign leaned against the glass from the inside and announced him to the community.

The door squeaked as he opened it. Turning on the lights, the fluorescent bulbs buzzed and filled the empty spaces between the things he'd taken such care to arrange: a circular rack of plain T-shirts to the right, bought wholesale from a distributor in Lafayette; behind it, a collection of his canvassed art stacked upright for leafing; to the left, the sales counter with a register, a calculator, a fan, a phone, the loan papers, and an air compressor from Pearl's father; behind it, the large square workbench for making shirts that held a scattering of felt letters, a few wooden screens with fabric stretched tight across them, and an iron standing upright; above that, on the wall, a shelf of aerosol and liquid paint cans, purchased from a dime store; next to that, the ticking clock, which read five to nine.

He examined the space like a priest alone at his altar before mass. He rested Pearl's bag lunch on the workbench, walked to the circular rack of T-shirts, and passed a hand through their shoulders. They rifled through his fingers like fresh playing cards. He walked behind the desk and picked up the phone to check for a dial tone. He ran his hands over the sanded wood of the desk, a present from Pearl's father, a woodworker in his spare time. He breathed in, and the store smelled of aerosol paints and new T-shirts. A cutout piece of cardboard stared back at him from the window. *Open*, it said. He smiled, until he realized that it was facing the wrong way.

No one gave patronage to Manny's in those first few hours of business. People stopped at the post office across the street and looked through his window. A few even pointed and spoke, though he couldn't hear anything but the buzz of lights and the quiet hum of the fan. He spent his time preparing shirts for the festival. He made many in kids' sizes with cartoon designs. The phone rang once, but it was just Pearl checking to see how things were going. She had called a number of local businesses to ask directions to Manny's, a kind of free advertising. He chided her for it, but she was immune to his complaints, deflected them by telling him he should eat the lunch she'd fixed.

Near eleven, the door squeaked open: his first customer. The woman was striking. She wore a tight T-shirt tucked into her jeans and carried a pink purse that hugged her side. She had high cheekbones, her brown hair was pulled back into a ponytail, and she had a tight, compact face. Her nose was mousy, and the independent way she moved about the store made him think it best not to welcome her. Some people liked to be left alone. She browsed with intent, rifling through his art prints. The door whined open again, and he turned to see a man in a business suit burst through.

"Hey there," he said.

"Hello," Manuel responded.

"Hotter'n hell." The man took off his sunglasses and clipped them to his collar.

"Yes, it is. May I help you, sir?"

The businessman stroked his pockmarked face. "Y'all have any-thing—I don't know, some of those flower-type shirts? Not for me, mind you. My daughter, she wants one with this leaf on it, like a seven-fingered one. You got any of those?"

Manuel smirked. "We don't have any, but I can make one for you if you like."

"You mean, special order it?"

He could hear the woman leafing through his art in the back, but he focused on the man.

"Yes. It will cost five dollars. I can have it ready for you in fifteen minutes."

"Fifteen minutes, you say. Five dollars? Hmm." He stroked his face again and thought. "Why not? Gotta act on impulse every now and again, you know? Keep yourself honest, right?"

"Yes, sir. Would you like it on a plain white?"

"What's that? Oh, the shirt. Yeah, whatever you got'll be fine."

Manuel drew a quick sketch on paper with a green bit of charcoal, a marijuana leaf. It was textured and shaded so that it appeared to be three-dimensional.

"Is this what she wants?"

"That's it! How'd you know? Must be you kids. Y'all all think alike, huh?"

"You can come back later to get it or you can wait and watch." He was speaking more for the benefit of the woman.

"I've got a lunch meeting with the boss. Can I come back in an hour?"

"As you wish."

"Hey, thanks, buddy." He smiled and looked around the store. "I like this place. You new to town?"

"This is my first day."

"Hey, great. Well, good luck. See you after lunch."

"Goodbye, sir."

After the door closed shut, he was left in the woman's presence. He didn't eye her, though he wondered if she might feel ignored since she could now compare his warm welcome of the businessman to his silence at her arrival. Or maybe she'd fondly noted his attention to how to treat different types of customers. Too late, he realized he was verbalizing his worries out loud, in Spanish.

"What?" she asked, turning to face him.

He dismissed his mutters with a wave of his hand and smiled. Her face gave nothing away. He stretched a plain white tee across the bare wooden screen and smoothed over the taut fabric with his hands. Hunching over the workbench behind the sales counter with a black marker, he outlined the silhouette of the leaf on the torso in quick and certain movements.

"How much is this one?" she called from the art rack. She held up a print of his sky bird, the one that hung in his living room. "I like it."

"Thank you. I made that one only last week."

"You made all these?"

He nodded.

"Wow."

He smiled and let a bit of air out of his nose, something like a gesture of thanks.

"So, how much for this one?"

"Fifteen."

"Not bad."

He returned to the marijuana shirt. He sprayed it with green aerosol, blurring the sharp contrast of the thick black line against the white of the fabric.

"I think I'll take it," she said.

He stopped his work to address her. "I'm glad you like it."

"The sky showing through the bird, that's what I like." She put it on the counter. He kept his eyes on the register, focused on the procedure of making a sale. He took a twenty from her, punched the numbers and the sale button, and watched as the register rang and the money drawer opened. It was empty.

"Well," he said. The woman laughed, and they smiled at each other. Manuel reached into his pockets and took out his wallet. He offered her the correct change and apologized.

"Of course. Don't worry about it. It must be hard starting a new business."

"There are many things one never thinks of." He put the bird in a bag, handed it to her.

"Thanks," she said.

"My pleasure. You are my first customer. May I frame your bill and put it on the wall?"

"Isn't that sweet! But don't you think you could use the money?" she said and winked.

They held the stare, and then she said goodbye and left. He was alone again, though this time with something to do. Turning his attention to the businessman's shirt, he grabbed the aerosol can and sprayed the paint onto the white of the cotton tee. When he'd filled inside the black outline with green, he put down the can and turned on the air compressor. As he waited for it to warm up, he grabbed his airbrush and a few plastic bottles of liquid paint from the shelf behind him. He connected the airbrush to the gasket atop the bottle and also to the end of the compressor's rubber tube. The airbrush had a button at the top that released the air, and a trigger at the bottom that sent the paint into the tube, but it lacked the usual control at the tip that mixed the air with the paint and sent it smoothly down onto the fabric. He could thus control the mixture of air pressure and paint, and hence the thickness of the line, only by placing his thumb over the opening, like a garden hose. Once the business stabilized he'd be able to afford a better airbrush and another two small compressors for each of the primary colors, which would allow him to work quicker. For now he could only rely on his father-in-law's.

Manuel took the airbrush in his hand and placed the tip almost against the fabric. He opened the valve and moved it along the middle of each part of the leaf evenly, following the outline of the permanent marker. A smooth green line appeared on the shirt. It would only take a twitch of the thumb to ruin it, yet he moved swiftly and without any thought of a mistake. He drew the stem. Its dense color stood out against the soft, earthy shade of the rest of the leaf. He finished the piece and turned off the compressor. His thumb was moist and green. A metallic taste hung in the air and mixed with the paint fumes. He stepped back from the shirt and looked at the leaf. It was a simple design, but well executed. He turned the fan on high and placed the shirt in front of it to dry. The loan papers fluttered at the corners.

He wiped his hands on a rag and looked out the window. It was nearing the lunch hour and people were milling about on the street. He walked outside and the brightness hit his eyes and forced them into a squint. He stretched his arms above his head and felt the warm air against his skin, pleased at the feel of the sun against his ankles. Cars inched down the road. No one was in much of a hurry. He could distinguish each separate motor. A waltz sung in French drifted out of the music store a couple blocks down. A steady stream of kids and mothers and fathers made their way in and out of Baskin-Robbins. Men in suits dropped letters in the mailbox outside the post office. The faint smell of Cajun cooking wafted to him from Lola's Restaurant. A mailman walked the block and put envelopes in the slots of businesses' doors.

Harry approached, and Manuel called out to him.

"Hello, Manual. How's your first day?"

"Henry, my friend! I just sold my first print and made my first shirt. Come in." Manuel ushered him through the door like a king into the shop.

"Great! The festival ought to help you get started."

"Yes. I'm making frog prints for the children." He pointed to the shirts he'd airbrushed that morning.

"Good," Harry laughed. "Looks like the frogs around town."

The men looked at each other through the heat.

"So, do you have good news for me?" asked Manuel.

"Listen, Manual, I don't want you to get the wrong idea here."

"Is something the matter? The papers are sitting right here, ready for your signature."

"Well, there's a thing I need to ask you about. About your past."

"What past?" He thought of his time in the Distrito Federal, the student protests he hadn't attended prior to the Olympics, the massacre on the grounds in front of the church. But these thoughts passed quickly: this was a place where things like La Noche de Tlatelolco weren't mentioned, weren't even known.

"Your past business experience. Looking over your loan application, you mention your experience at a—at what sounds to me like a *charity* in Mexico. I'm just not sure—"

"It was artistic work, like this store will entail."

Harry sighed. "I'm sure it was hard work, but things are different here. I don't see much experience in *America* listed on the application."

"Are you saying that the loan is rejected?"

"Well, Manual, there are lots of questions I don't have answers to, like why you went ahead with renting the store before knowing about the loan."

Because he was driven. Because of urgent premonitions. What other answers could make sense?

"And well, and so, what's your experience with business in *America*?"

He had none; he hadn't even thought to make up any on the loan application.

Harry sighed audibly, satisfied at having made a point on solid ground. "I don't mean to be judgmental, but I'm sure you see why I can't approve you. I'm sorry, Manual, it's just not good business. Knowing you and your grandmother, my gut tells me to give it to you, but you have to see it's an investment for us. I'm sorry."

Manuel kept his thoughts from escaping his lips, either in Spanish or English. Harry tipped his hat and left. A hot draft of air touched Manuel as he watched Harry open the door and walk out of sight. He didn't move, just stared through his store's window to the street. He breathed a heavy sigh and ran his hands through his hair, gripping at his scalp and pulling the skin of his face tight up against his bones. He put his green thumb to his lip and winced.

Looking down at the brown bag, he realized he hadn't eaten since the previous night. Reaching into it, he found a note, "Please put this in the mail. Best of luck! Love, Pearl." There was a letter addressed to her father, and he knew what it must be about. To put it out of mind, he stuffed the envelope in his pocket. Reaching farther down, he found an egg sandwich with vegetables, and he took it out. The eggs had been scrambled lightly, mixed with just a bit of milk so they were fluffy, with diced bits of green pepper and onion. The toast was browned just right. As he put it to his mouth, the door opened again. It was the businessman.

"Hey there, buddy! Great news!"

Manuel could hardly muster a smile, but he put down his sandwich nonetheless to listen.

"Guess what, friend? Boss man just told me he's moving me up to the New Orleans branch! Said I been doing a crack-up job, and it was about time I saw something for it. Giving me a day off next week to go on up and look for houses. The wife and kids and I wouldn't move for a while, I suppose, but he got me so excited, I got to thinking maybe I should ask him to let me go for the day, and so I did, and he said okay!

You believe that? Twenty-five years of service, and they finally throw you a bone." He rubbed his pockmarked face. "I tell you."

"Congratulations. Your shirt is ready."

"Would you look at that? Ain't that something? Georgia—that's my daughter—she'll just flip when she sees it." He was all smiles. "I'm sorry, friend, how much I owe you?"

"Five dollars."

"Here you go—and don't worry about the change, hear?" He put a twenty on the counter, took the shirt, and looked it over. Manuel watched him feel the texture of the painted marijuana leaf with his hand and put it up against his chest, guessing at the snugness of the fit.

"Hey, buddy, you do some damn fine work. Best of luck to you with the shop. Take my card. You should call me. I got some people at the office looking for some stuff for the festival. I see by the frogs you're gearing up for the show. City of Murals, I tell you. That's something, ain't it?" He handed Manuel the card and left, smiling.

The clock showed it was only midafternoon. He put the card in his pocket, picked up the papers from the bank, and threw them away. All about were paints and shirts and airbrushes and screens for printing and the compressor and other things borrowed or bought on credit. The luck of this space being available, the chances of it being owned by an old Cajun whose wits were far gone enough to forgo checking Manuel's earnings before agreeing to rent it—these things seemed now in retrospect a cruel string of useless luck.

The egg sandwich lay uneaten on the counter in front of him. He picked it up and bit into it, watching people walk by his store as he chewed. The egg was soft and cold against his palate and he kept it in his mouth a long while, feeling the vegetables give beneath his teeth and wishing that he could just eat the rest of the day, never getting full and never getting hungry. Sooner than seemed fair, the sandwich was gone, and there still remained the balance of the afternoon till closing. Opening the register to put the businessman's twenty away, he saw the other bill from his first sale. It reminded him of the sky bird print and the woman who'd bought it. Only then did he remember that he'd promised his wife that he'd screen it onto a T-shirt for her. It was gone now, sold, and though it probably didn't matter, he thought that maybe it was a good time to paint her a new sky bird. He worked on it the rest of the afternoon, but he was distracted by customers who came in and browsed without buying. He never got around to finishing it. He only got as far as the clouds and the sky.

At closing time he took the two twenties from the day's sales out of the register. He straightened them against the counter and pocketed them and then closed the shop and went to the bank to make change. Waiting in line between belted walkways, he looked through an interior window and saw Harry talking to the businessman. They were laughing and joking together, and he couldn't hear their words through the pane of glass. At the teller's station, he asked for forty ones out of the two twenties so that the stack would be more substantial in his wallet.

As he walked toward the house where his wife was waiting, he looked at a tree frog mural on a warehouse wall. The red eyes stared back, in search of small prey. He passed more frog murals, the fairy tale one and the city council one and the others. Turning west onto the country road that would take him by the railroad tracks, he stuck his hands into his pockets and felt his customer's business card and Pearl's envelope. She would likely be on the porch with a cup of diluted lemonade for him and a handful of questions he couldn't answer.

He thought of the businessman and his trip. The man's daughter was probably his age. "Veinticinco años de servicio," he muttered. A car approached, a navy blue, mud-flecked Chevy Nova, and trying to make light of his situation, he stuck his thumb out in jest. But it stopped and the boy inside rolled down his window.

"You need a ride? I'm headed for New Orleans," the boy said.

"Is that a Nova?" Manuel asked. He gave a soft laugh when the boy shrugged. He kept his hands in his pockets. "Do you know what 'No va' means in Spanish?" he asked.

"Can't say I do," the boy said.

"No va," Manuel said out loud. The cemetery lay in the distance. The boy's car faced him. The Nova's engine idling was the only sound. It was a humid evening in the City of Murals, far from his home and yet very near the new place he rested his head at night. Manuel faced west, the glare of the setting sun angling straight into his eyes, and yet he was aware of it only as a backdrop, as if it were no more or less than a mural.

The Language of Heroes

NEAR ONE IN THE morning with New Orleans still three hours away, the Wolfpackmobile blew out a tire. We were coming back from a tournament in Memphis, and Coach Lynch had turned onto a remote state road because he thought he knew a shortcut. What a hypocrite. "Shortcuts never get you anywhere!" he always shouted when we cut the end off of a slide drill in practice.

The Wolfpackmobile was this half-van, half-bus, secondhand death trap painted in our university's maroon and gold. In black scripted letters, it read *Wolfpack* along the chassis, and near the gas tank, a graphic-design student had created the image of a lonely wolf staring blankly at nothing. There was no pack to speak of, unless you counted the wolf on each fender. Even then, you could barely tell they weren't just shaggy dogs. To boot, the thing had less legroom than a school bus. Our big men bunched themselves up like accordions or draped their tree-trunk legs across armrests and into the aisle. With their mouths open and their eyes closed, their big, limp bodies looked like corpses out of a war scene from *The Iliad*, which I was reading in the bitch seat in the back, where a hump in the floorboard covered the back tires. I had to sit there because I was a freshman. It was some stupid rite of initiation. Lynch, an ex-marine, encouraged it.

When the tire burst, the Wolfpackmobile jolted, then vibrated down the highway as rubber flapped against the pavement. Lynch guided us to a stop on the shoulder. No one moved. We'd played two games that day, and a lot of guys were wiped. I put Homer down and looked out the window. I couldn't see anything except for a shadowy ditch filled with wet weeds in the moonlight and a black mass of opaque pines beyond that. For a literature class, I'd recently read "Night, Death, Mississippi" by this poet named Robert Hayden, and for the past two hours in *The Iliad*, Achaeans and Trojans had been dying left and right, darkness veiling eyes on every page. Looking at that wine-dark ditch, I couldn't help but feel like a little lost soldier in a Trojan wolf-horse headed for carnage.

As Lynch turned off the ignition, Remy looked at me from across the aisle and shook his head. We were two of the freshmen that year, new recruits who shared a few classes and were beginning to see the shape of our dismal future with the Wolfpack. Before the season, there'd been a "press conference" set up for us in the campus athletic building. A reporter and a photographer from the school paper stood off to the side smoking cigarettes, waiting while Lynch directed us into a pose, as if he were a photographer, too. No one else was there except Remy's parents and my mom, who beamed. In the picture, which came out the next week, Lynch is standing behind us with a goofy grin on his face and his hands on our shoulders as we each sign a blank piece of paper. Afterward, Remy and I commiserated over the spectacle, and we asked each other if this was a sign of things to come. It was.

Lynch and Coach Bellows got out and inspected the damage. Sitting over the bad tire, I could see their faces below me. They bent down to look at it and then stood up and looked at each other. "Fuckin Wolf-packmobile," Lynch said. They stepped away, closer to the ditch. Bellows made a few short phone calls, then relayed some news to Lynch. I couldn't hear them, but I hoped that whatever they came up with would be better than their game plan. We'd played Middle Mississippi College that night, a team like us with marginal quickness on the perimeter and undersized post men, with a single, major difference: they won regularly. Still, watching them warm up, I thought we'd have a shot. Coach's plan was to make it a half-court game and run set plays he thought no one else knew. So much for that. We lost by twenty-five. Nine games into the season, and after a state championship as a high school senior, I was still waiting for my first W as a college athlete.

After a couple minutes of strategizing, the coaches came back onto the Wolfpackmobile and woke everyone up. Lynch stood at the front and addressed us. "All right, troops. Here's the situation: we got a blow-out." A whispering chorus of deep, sleepy *fuuuuucks* echoed around me. "We don't know exactly what happened, but it must have been a stick or a twig or something, or maybe it was a raccoon. Could've been anything out here, you know?"

Lynch's explanations were always infuriating, even when you weren't stuck in a cramped bus with a bum tire. My first college practice, just two months before, he'd started by telling us about the practice jerseys we'd been waiting on for a week. "All right, troops. Here's the situation. The jerseys are coming in here real soon. They're gonna look pretty sharp, men. Pretty sharp. They're reversible, and at the top, in big letters, it says PACK, and then beneath that, in smaller letters, it says BASKETBALL. PACK. Then BASKETBALL. PACK. BASKETBALL. Just like that. There's shorts, too, and over the thigh, it says it again. In big yellow letters, it says PACK, and then below it, BASKETBALL."

If the Great Krzyzewski of D-III athletics repeated those two words once, he did it a dozen times. But it'd been laughable then because it didn't matter. In fact, it was good because it shortened practice time. Now, we were on the side of a state road in backwoods Mississippi. I didn't think he'd ever stop listing the names of the places Bellows had called about our breakdown. Eventually, he explained that a tire was on its way from a Walmart in Jackson, and we'd have to wait about two hours.

"Now, I'm pretty sure I saw a café open back there. I don't have any more meal money—we used it all up back at the Burger King in Oxford—but if you have any cash yourself, you might want to get some food. Let's move it out, troops. There's a bend in the road, and then you'll see the place I'm talking about."

Our maroon and black warm-ups swished out into the humidity. My uniform was sweaty and moist underneath my outer layer; there had been no showers at the gym in Memphis. It sucked to be walking, and having sat in the back, I was one of the last off the Wolfpackmobile. Remy, with his long, slow gait, fell back to where I was. He was a solid six-eight, and they listed him in the program at 260. His shoulders were slumped and he walked like a powerlifter defeated by a hard workout. I figured he hadn't gotten very far into *The Iliad.*

"What page are you on?" he asked me.

"Just got Book XXIV left."

"I think I'm gonna ask for an extension. Ridenour's gotta understand." I didn't say anything.

"Come on. Don't do this to me. He knows we're both on the team. He'll wonder why you finished and I didn't."

"Why would he know we're on the team? Coach told us Dr. Ridenour was antisports. I know *you* didn't tell him."

But I could tell by his eyes that he had. God knows why. Probably thought in his good-natured way that honesty was the best policy. "You really think we're gonna get home in time for you to write five pages?" he asked.

"Now that we're going to a place where I can write without throwing up from the bumps in the road, I might be able to jot some ideas down."

"It's like two thirty in the morning. We probably won't even make it back to New Orleans in time for class."

The diner appeared on a stretch of the highway that passed for the Main Street of some town. Storefronts looked like façades, buildings were connected at their sides, and the café had a covered patio with rocking chairs and tables with checkerboards set up in front—like Cracker Barrel, except this was the real thing. Inside, square tables were covered with tablecloths that had chickens and geese for designs. Old bumper stickers were stuck to the wall. "Heritage, not hate," read one with a replica of the rebel flag. Right next to that, a stuffed turkey was mounted on a plaque. A sign above the door read: Fat Shirley's.

"Aw, *hell* no," J-Rock said.

"This ain't no joke," said Shareef.

"Yeee-haw!" said Caramel, then lowered his voice: "Seriously, Coach, you got to get that tire. We got to roll out 'fore something *happen* up in here."

Nobody was in the place. I couldn't believe it was open. As we found out later from the waitress, they stayed open for the late-night bar crowd to feed the drunks before they went home. It wasn't near enough to closing time, so it hadn't yet picked up.

Players arranged themselves in groups—Dizzy and Tack, the other two freshmen, sat in a booth by the door. Remy and I took one in the corner. Three big men took seats at a table with B, our point guard. Shareef, Caramel, and J-Rock (who was white only by the color of his skin) sat at a booth with their headphones on, clowning each other. The Dallas boys, Doop and Scoop, sat at a two-seater and started playing paper football. The coaches sat by the window and made calls on their cell phones. A waitress numb with fatigue made the rounds, starting with the big men.

"I don't want to fuck you over, man," I told Remy. "It's just that I've never turned in something late before."

"Me neither."

"So you think he would give you an extension?" I asked.

"I think so. I mean, these are extreme circumstances. Epic, even." The waitress asked us for our drink orders. From across the way, J-Rock yelled at me: "Babyface! When you gonna have that paper ready, dog? My teacher been sweatin' me."

Remy looked at me, not judging, just wondering how I would handle it.

"Talk to me tomorrow, Jarren. After practice," I said.

"That's my *boy* over there. Been hooking me *up*. Ain't no *joke*."

"Tommy handle his *business*," added Caramel. "Dude reads through the *night*. Motherfucker don't *play*." All of this being said, of course, for my benefit, to keep me going on with it. I hadn't wanted to do it, but they all knew my ACT scores before they even met me. That's how Lynch would brag about his recruits. Since our school didn't give out athletic scholarships, Coach had to either pull strings to get good athletes in or else get guys with mediocre game who could get an academic scholarship. Either way, it was a losing proposition, but he tried to make it look good, and if he didn't have something like court vision or a killer cross to brag about, then he'd use grades. The first thing Caramel and J-Rock ever told me was the story of how Coach had boasted to them about me in the spring.

"Ah, Jarren, lemme tell you, this kid's got a great jump shot. He's six-two, 180, got a 31 on his ACT. Real quick, too. Not a great leaper, but he got a 1390 on his SAT, and lemme tell you, he averaged 14 points a game at the 5-A level. He's got a quirky motion when he drives, but he's real smart. 4.2 GPA. Real sharp kid. Not a great leaper, though. Not a great leaper."

And so, J-Rock picked me out right away. After our first practice, he came up to me and gave me a textbook, told me to copy the first two chapters and put a title and his name on the front page, then walked away before I could say anything. He was our best player, and we couldn't afford to have him ineligible. I didn't want to do it, but I felt a certain unspoken pressure from a few of our seniors, and my naive desire for acceptance from fellow athletes won out. They never paid me,

but they got me back in other ways. On a weeknight after I gave the first
of many papers to J-Rock, he came by my dorm room late.

"You ready to roll?" he said.

"What? Where?"

"Get dressed, Babyface. We goin' out."

He and Caramel took me riding down Saint Charles in his old,
beat-up Cutlass. We stopped at a liquor store and they bought me two
32s of Woodchuck, the same for themselves. Mystikal was blaring from
the stereo. In the front seats, they bobbed their heads back and forth,
taking swigs every now and then from their brown bags. As we cruised
down the avenue past all the mansions, I wondered where they were
taking me. You should understand, I was coming from a Catholic high
school where I had been a good little Catholic boy. I'd never gone to
a bar, never cheated, never had sex. A true baller I was—nothing but
the gym and homework. My mom imposed a ten o'clock curfew all
the way through graduation (not that I ever went out), and she was
petrified that, somewhere along the way, I'd turn. And I guess that,
now, I was turning.

They took me to the Quarter, where they illegally parked in an
abandoned construction site. When we got out, I saw that they'd each
finished both their 32s. I'd only finished three-fourths of one. I took
a quick gulp of the rest of it and tossed the bottle through the open
window into the back seat. I took the other one for the walk.

"You better drink up, Babyface. We gonna be at the club soon."

They weren't the slightest bit tipsy, and they walked fast. Pussy was
calling them forward, keeping me behind. I worried and hoped that a
girl might want to dance with me.

At House of Blues, it was Service Industry Night, and as J-Rock said,
the hoes were *bouncin'*. The first thing they did was to get these five
girls—and I mean each one of them phenomenal—to dance with us.
"These three are for you, dog," said J-Rock, and he raised his bottle up,
gave me one with his other hand, and forced a clink. The girls got up
on me, made snarling slut faces and rubbed against me. I'd never been

touched like that before. I tried to bend my knees and not focus too hard on their proximity. My eyes were planted firmly on their waists, my peripheral vision picking up their curves, until I looked up. J-Rock and Caramel were laughing. Apparently, I'm a horrible dancer. Drunk as I was, I hammed it up, shaking my ass out of rhythm, and the girls pretended to be amused. The night went on like that. Every so often, J-Rock disappeared. Word was, that's where he got his nickname: he liked to do lines sometimes when he went out.

Around five that morning they dropped me off (alone) in front of the dorm. "Get some Zs, Babyface. I'm gonna light you up today," J-Rock said. Practice time, seven o'clock, was coming soon, and it was a known fact, and a legend to us freshmen, that Jarren practiced his best after going out hard. And lucky me, I'd been recruited to take his spot at the 2 when he graduated, so I had to guard him every practice. He was true to his word. At practice that morning, he kicked my ass. We were both reeking of alcohol and a little dizzy at first, but he shook it off within a few trips down the court. It never wore off of me. He hit every kind of shot with me draped all over him: he crossed me over, hit jumpers, teardrops, circus shots in the lane with his off hand. He even went backdoor on me and caught an alley, his nuts in my face as he hung on the rim. On the way back down the court, he whispered into my ear: "31 ACT? 31 PPG, bitch!" At a certain point, you had to laugh. I mean, it was brutal. Coach even felt the need to pull me aside. "Tommy, man. It's okay. You know, he's pretty good! Now be a soldier and get back out there!" Seeing how even that emotional Einstein could tell I needed the consolation, that was the true insult.

Fat Shirley came with our drinks. "I'll have the Trucker's Special," Remy said.

"Just water for me," I said.

"Come on, dude, what do you want? I'll spot you."

"All right, a plate of scrambled eggs. You have anything caffeinated besides coffee?"

"Mountain Dew," she said.

"Bring me two of those, please. Thanks, Remy."

"Hey, whatever it takes, dude. That's what I'm here for, to pay for the caffeine you need to finish what I can't even start. Fuck me," he said. "What are you gonna write about?"

"I don't know. What do you think of it so far?"

"Not my cup of tea," he said.

"Not your cup of tea? But you watch professional wrestling."

"I think I'm gonna like *The Odyssey* more."

"Yeah, me too."

We wanted to be wanderers. And well, there we were, wandering through Mississippi. If Lynch was our Odysseus, we were going to be in trouble. Or maybe Remy or I was the hero, but neither one of us had a Penelope then, neither of us had fought any damn wars.

"Ridenour's a clown, right?" he said.

"All the profs are clowns, but why do they save the real nutjobs for the honors college?"

"Because you learn more from a nutjob. They're usually geniuses. What do you think about Weinhauser?"

"Nutjob."

"A smart one though, right?"

"Yeah, sure. What's that noise he makes after he calls on you?"

On we went. It was good to feel like we were getting a handle on things, even if we were really falling way behind. The later it got, the more people came into the diner, most of them really drunk. With our size and matching warm-ups, some gave us stares when they walked in, and some looked a bit longer at Caramel and Shareef and Doop and a couple of the big men, and you had to wonder if anything would happen. We were a mixed bunch, half white and half black, maybe a little less white if you counted J-Rock black or me half Mexican, which no one did. You could even pronounce my last name, León, just like regular old Leon if you wanted. There was no way anyone was going to look at me and see anything but white. The dirty blond hair always guaranteed that.

A pair of men came in and sat at the table behind Remy, in my line of sight. One looked like where he was from—he wore a red and black plaid shirt and a pair of jeans—but the other caught my eye. He looked vaguely French; he was super thin and he had a handlebar mustache, and he wore tight white pants with a silver buckle and pointy shoes with a sheen of fresh polish on them. He looked like he was in his late twenties, and his friend looked a good ten years older. Though I tried, I couldn't peg their friendship.

"No John Boy tonight? No Daryl, neither?" the one in plaid said. "Looks like the blacks took another night off."

The other shrugged his shoulders. "Slow night, I guess," he said.

I looked to see if anyone on the team had heard, but I was the only one. I looked over at Caramel and Shareef. I didn't know Caramel well, but Shareef, he was an honest-to-goodness good person. He was 19, with a baby. He went from practice to school to work, and then home. I never saw him out. He didn't complain about his lot, never seemed to think himself anything special for all that trouble. He was quiet, subdued, even after a phenomenal play. He struggled in school, but he was trying. Once, he asked me to help him with a paper—not to write it, just to sit down with him and help him understand what he needed to do to make it better. I did the best I could, but who knows how it turned out. "Thank you, Tommy Leon," he said when we finished with it.

"I got something," Remy said.

"What do you mean?"

"To write about. I've been thinking here."

"Shoot."

"Isn't it weird how Achilles, who's this great warrior, is pretty much a bitch? I mean, especially that part where he sends Patroclus out disguised as himself. What a pussy. So you didn't get your trophy whore. So what, you know? Your boys are dying out there."

"Yeah, that was pretty lame. He comes through in the clutch, though. You'll see."

"I don't care what he does. I'll still think he's an asshole. Beyond redemption, Tommy. Beyond redemption."

"You don't say."

"And don't get me started on Agamemnon. There's a real weasel for you."

The local men kept talking behind Remy. I couldn't hear the words because Remy was yakking it up about *The Iliad*, but I watched their lips move, their body language and their eyes.

"Say, Tommy, who do you think would win head to head, Maravich or the Stilt?"

"Don't try to goad me into that garbage again."

"Come on, dude. Humor me. Look where we are."

"It'll just end up like the Milli Vanilli argument."

"You gotta go with Wilt, right? He could just back down the Pistol every time."

"Okay, fine. Let's do this. When would Maravich miss, Remy? Answer: he wouldn't."

"Outside shooters always miss eventually. And I stand by Rob and Fab. They could dance, and so what if they lip-synched? They were flopping around all over the stage. Just talking would've been hard. What do you want? And 'Girl You Know It's True'—it's a great song. I don't care who wrote it."

"Say it's a game to ten: Maravich wouldn't miss in the first ten shots. I guarantee it."

"Wilt would block one, and that'd be it. And 'Blame It on the Rain'? Come on. Oh, all right, fine. I'll give you Maravich 10–9 if you'll give me that song."

The food came and we ate it like hyenas. The five bucks apiece we'd spent earlier at Burger King hadn't gotten us very far. Our mouths full, the talking stopped completely. Through the quiet, we both could hear the boy with the mustache at the table behind Remy: "Seriously, what's with all the Democrats tonight? Where you suppose they're coming from?" He said it in a matter-of-fact tone, as if the term were simply factual.

"Dude, did you hear that?" Remy said, looking at me. I had the view of their table, not him. Looking at the man with the mustache over Remy's shoulder, I thought how he hadn't seemed like someone who'd say that. I glanced down at my plate, recalling moments at holidays when my uncles would talk this way. I wondered if Caramel or Shareef or Doop or any of the big men heard it.

"Was that line straight out of some bullshit Matthew McConaughey movie about the South?" said Remy.

"Pretty crazy, huh?" was all I could manage.

Remy shook his head for a moment, as if deciding something. Then he stood up, all six-eight of him, and turned around. As he did, the team looked up to see what was going on. "Excuse me, sir," Remy said to the man with the mustache, "I couldn't help but overhear what you just said about all these Democrats showing up. You have a problem with my teammates?"

I saw Caramel and Shareef look up and watch. The man with the mustache looked around, saw the eyes upon him, saw the size and number of us in maroon and gold. "Listen, you seem like a nice young man. I'm not trying to cause trouble in Shirley's place, so why don't we let this go."

"So then you said it," said Remy.

"I'm not sure you—"

"If you said it, sir, I'd appreciate it if you would apologize." He was as polite as you could be.

"You want me to *apologize*? You don't know much about me, do you?" The place was charging up.

"And you don't know much about us, sir."

"I suppose I'll never have the pleasure."

The man stared up at Remy. Remy turned it passive-aggressive, raised his hands in the air in defense, and said, "Look, whatever. I was just offended, and I think it'd be best if you didn't say that again while we're here, that's all."

It hadn't occurred to me to be offended—only embarrassed—and I disappointed myself by realizing it. Voices crept back into the room.

Already, Caramel and J-Rock were snickering across the way under their breaths.

"Christ, what a day," the man in the mustache said to his friend.

"Just keep it to yourself," said Remy.

"I suppose we'd all be better off that way," the man said, and that was it. Remy sat back down, and everybody went back to eating. The two men didn't say anything else, and after we were done, we stuck around, still waiting for the tire man from Jackson. The two men finished, and when they left, they had to walk right by Remy, then by Caramel and J-Rock and Shareef. Nobody looked at anybody. When the door shut behind them, a couple of the big men and Caramel busted out laughing. Shareef slumped down into his seat and put his hands to his face. Doop watched them through a window until they were gone from sight. I caught Lynch's eye while he pretended to listen to someone on the phone. I saw that he'd followed the exchange. He was smirking at it, but when he saw me looking at him, he turned somberly back to the conversation on the phone and acted like he didn't notice that I'd seen him.

After the tire got fixed, Lynch rounded us up from the café's porch and we walked back to the Wolfpackmobile in clusters. Remy and I walked next to a group of our teammates.

"What was that about?" asked B.

"That dude called some of us bitches," Remy started, "and somebody needed to let him know that—"

"Damn. Remy said, '*You gotta let em KNOW!*'" said B.

"Remy was ready to *blow*!" said J-Rock. "You ain't no *joke*, boy!"

"I wish that cracker woulda said something to *me*," Caramel said, and then acted out a series of punches. There was general laughter at the production. It reminded me of clips I'd seen of Muhammad Ali in his glory days.

"Caramel, bruh, you stupid," said Shareef, his posture a bit too perfect for Caramel's taste.

Caramel laughed. "Shareef, dog, you trippin'." He looked at Shareef and started to say something, but then we passed by one of the big men, a dorky white guy with this tiny white headband stretched out over his crew cut, and Caramel couldn't resist saying something.

"Duane, dog, somebody need to be *straight* with you, bruh. You need to take that headband off 'fore it make you retarded."

Everybody busted out laughing at this, even Shareef, who didn't want to. "Aw, that's cold, bruh," he said. "Why don't you let that man be? He just like to wear his headband like that. What he doing you?"

We got on the bus, and J-Rock told everyone who didn't already know what Caramel had said about Duane's headband. Remy and I took our places in the back, me on top of the tire hump again and Remy across the aisle, sprawled out and too tired for conversation. If I were him, I'd have been churning over the confrontation, but Remy was just solid like that. He rested his head against the window and closed his eyes.

The Wolfpackmobile groaned as Lynch accelerated back onto the road. By that point, the Mountain Dew was flowing through my bloodstream, and I got back to *The Iliad*. I had forty pages left, and New Orleans was still far away. In the front, the excitement over Caramel's headband joke dulled into fatigue, and within thirty minutes, mine was the only light on. The only sounds were the engine and the tires on the highway. The farther we got from Fat Shirley's, the more easily I could focus on King Priam's big trip to Achilles to beg for mercy.

We got back to campus around five in the morning. For us freshmen, we just had the walk across campus to our dorm. Lynch gave us a long-winded explanation of how we'd move back practice today to the afternoon. "And troops," he added, looking right at J-Rock, "don't forget to take care of the books." J-Rock raised his eyebrows and looked right at me.

Remy and I headed home on foot. Campus was dark and deserted except for our residential quad, which was lit up. On the porch outside our dorm, a couple of late-night smokers sat on benches, burning off a night out.

"What are you gonna do?" I asked Remy.

"I can't do it, dude. I wish I could. I'm just gonna get a couple hours sleep, then go to Ridenour's office. He ought to understand. What about you?"

I didn't say anything. We entered the dorm and pushed the elevator button. We rode up together, and as usual it took a while. He stood there, exhausted, with his duffel bag on his shoulder like it was nothing. I had to put mine down.

"That was really something," I said.

"What's that?"

"Back at the diner. What you said."

"Yeah, that's Mississippi for you."

The elevator opened and he stepped out. "See you in class," he said, and then the doors closed.

When I got back to my room, Charlie, my roommate, was sleeping. I took off my sweaty jersey and put it over the computer speaker to mute the startup sound as I turned it on. When Windows loaded, I looked at the clock: 5:49. Class started in just over three hours. Sentences and thoughts would have to come fast. In Word, the black line of the cursor blinked at me, disappearing then reappearing every few moments on the blank white of the screen. It was waiting for me, but I wasn't ready. Remy had waited for me, too, I imagined. At the diner. To say something. I hadn't been ready then, either. Still, I knew I could do this.

I started to type, and what came out at first was how much of a bitch Achilles was, the irony of the King having to beg *him* for mercy, instead of the other way around. What was the point of all that divine talent on the battlefield if something so pathetically human could keep you from joining your countrymen in the fight? Of course, in the context of a war fought for the sake of a woman, such behavior couldn't be surprising.

For a while, I dabbled in those kinds of banal insights, until I finally stumbled onto something real: it wasn't just that Achilles and Paris and so many of the rest of them were bitches. It was their words, the language these deluded characters used to couch their petty positions into some kind of great stance they were taking on principle. With that revelation, the argument deepened, and I quickened my pace, skimming the book for examples of that kind of speech.

I could hear Charlie breathing as I typed on, one eye on the clock. Dog-earing and underlining from the text, I made my way deep into the body of the paper. Dawn crept through the edges of the curtains until they were outlined by a rectangle of faint light. When I got within a paragraph of finishing, I read over what I'd written. It was sort of half-baked, but I knew it would get an A. Already, in two months as a college writer, I'd figured out that if you had talent, content rarely mattered.

The alarm buzzed. Charlie rustled under the sheets, and the sense of being alone vanished. *Achilles, what a pussy,* I thought. No wonder Remy hated him. Boy was my mind racing. I turned off the alarm, and Charlie flipped back over on his bed. In the new, sentient quiet, I looked beside the computer at the wall, where our team's picture and schedule was tacked to a bulletin board. I'd marked the prior eight losses with an L, and now I marked the ninth. Above the schedule, I saw the team photo. I stood in uniform, looking out with the vacant stare of seriousness we'd been ordered to hold. I remembered how, just behind the photographer, in the rec center weight room, some students had been working out for themselves, paying us no mind. If we'd have been D-I athletes, they'd have stopped and watched, but we weren't. I sat in the front row with the guards. Remy stood behind me, smiling wide despite the order of sternness, the only happy face in the whole bunch. He didn't deserve any of this losing. At least now he wouldn't have to worry about Ridenour, if he didn't want to.

In a final read-through, I picked out overwrought sentences and phrases like *juxtaposition of Achaean deaths with passages of Achilles's articulate sulking,* and *shocking complicity in the nefarious deception,* and *couching his desires in the call of duty.* I cleaned up the language, tightened the argument. When I thought it was done, I read it again, thinking with nostalgia of how I used to run through Maravich's ball-handling drills after practice in high school, making myself do them perfectly twice in a row before stopping for the day. This writing, I thought, this should be just as considered, even if I had a good guess that Remy wouldn't accept it. That was just the kind of guy he was. And this, I started to fathom, was just the way that I was. I looked at the clock: fifteen minutes to class. It was time for me to give up this fight. I put Remy's name in the corner at the top of the first page and, thinking of words I hoped he'd approve of and that I guessed old Ridenour might find intriguing if he ever saw them, I gave the lame-duck piece its title.

Frog Festival

PEARL HAD WAITED until then—after all the expletives had been shouted at the walls that held his paintings, after throwing a bottle of tequila at his sky bird and cleaning it up (she had missed, and was thankful for it), after carving away with a knife the outer surface of the soap bar in the bath that might have touched his dirty skin, after painted whispers of guilt over her anger given some unforeseen tragedy had been airbrushed away, after some of the resentment had been replaced by solitude and sadness, after most of the recurring thoughts and images of Jesse had been pushed back into the recesses of her mind—to call her mother.

As bath water ran into the tub, she brought the phone to the toilet where she sat. She played with the cord as she dialed and became intensely aware of all the waiting: for the water to warm, for her mother to pick up the phone, for the door to open to the sound of his voice, for the sudden worry about a pregnancy to pass. Her mother answered, said hello, and then it was silent for a long while.

It wasn't something to admit, that your husband had left you, and she could hardly bring herself to accept it. All week she had cooked dinners for two, setting the trunk with plastic forks and napkins and waiting, but then the food had run out and there was no more money. Rent would be due soon. She feared the mailbox and the jostling sound of parcels placed inside, for even in the few days since Manuel's disappearance, a credit card statement and the electricity bill had arrived.

"Oh, Mary May," her mother said. She could picture her mother and how she was probably thinking more about the shame of his actions than anything. And she was probably taking sips from a shot glass full of Pabst Blue Ribbon to calm herself.

"And all those bills coming in, Lord have mercy," she said.

There was a long silence on the phone, which was not atypical of their conversations. They could each hear the other breathing.

"Well, what you want us to do?" asked her mother.

"I don't know," Pearl responded. "Do you think he's okay?"

"Oh, Mary."

The conversation continued in this way for some time, neither saying much that would fully communicate the depth of their feeling, yet the sighing and the breathing conveying it all. Pearl could imagine her father sitting in his lounge chair, the TV tuned to a Saturday afternoon football game, the volume turned down so he could listen to the play-by-play over the radio. He would wait for his wife to tell him.

When her mother was sure that everything would be okay—that is, when she had convinced herself that Manuel would in fact come back—she told her daughter she would pray for her and that she shouldn't worry too much, that maybe she should come and stay with them until it was over. Pearl refused, less because of pride and more because she was simply too exhausted to imagine walking to the bus station and buying a ticket.

Hanging up the phone she realized how nice her mother had been not to mention so many things. Her younger brother, Louis, was getting married the following week, and Pearl was supposed to be in the wedding. Surely by now her mother had received the letter asking for more money. And then there was her marriage. She had moved to Lafayette and then Rayne with nothing more than the prospect of being a waitress—and really just to get away from that boy who had broken her heart. What had her mother thought of that?

She turned off the water (it had been emptying into the overflow drain) and put the phone on top of the toilet. Taking off her dress and her bra habitually, she thought of nothing. No steam clouded the mirror and the water wasn't hot, though it never had been. She pretended that it was and let out a sigh of fake indulgence. In fact, it was only stuffy, and soon it dawned on her that she needed to get out of the house.

It was the Saturday of the Frog Festival, and there was much going on that could distract her. After the bath she put on a tattered white dress and made her way to the fairgrounds, the opposite direction Manuel had walked to work for the first and last time nearly a week before. The fairgrounds were near the interstate, no more than a five minute walk from their house. Before she could see anything she could hear the music and the laughing and the talking.

Turning a corner, it all came into view. An old lady at the front entrance collected the one dollar entry fee, and beyond her Pearl saw a few amusement rides for kids. Near the front there stood a group of belles, chosen by a panel of judges to participate in a frog jumping contest, in which each would dress their frog up in pretty dresses and ladies' hats and ceremonially begin the race by tapping their frog on the rump. They stood out among the afros and bellbottoms that surrounded them. Along the dirt path that led from one end of the festival to the other, there were booths set up where homemade crafts were being sold. She walked through them and on toward the echoing of amplifiers off in the distance.

An acoustic band played folk songs on a homemade wooden stage toward the back of the festival grounds. She made her way to the sound and took a seat beside a couple that was drinking beer. Others danced. Everyone was waiting for Clifton Chenier, but rumor had it he wouldn't show until later that afternoon.

She heard someone call out the name Harry, and her eyes immediately went in search of a face. When she saw a man put on his business grin and turn at the sound of it, she knew that it was Harry from Acadiana State Bank, and she watched the scene from a distance, wishing she could make out the words. He shook hands with someone. They were each drinking beer and pointing to the stage. They didn't notice her, not only for her quiet, but because they'd never met her.

She had felt a stranger in Rayne before—in the grocery buying food for their special dinner, walking a letter to the post office—but at that moment she became acutely aware of her aloneness. There had been little time in her months in Rayne for her to meet anyone. She hadn't felt the need. Looking at the man who'd turned down her Manuel's loan, Pearl realized then that she wanted to talk to someone, and it was this that caused her to forget the music for a moment and fold her arms about her waist.

She found herself strolling aimlessly about the walkway, where she browsed through craft exhibits. On either side there were booths set up by local businesses: the Baskin-Robbins man was selling a special green "frog" flavor, a local restaurant owner served fried frog legs, and there were others, too, who weren't from Rayne. They were selling everything from frog gumbo to fried frog po'boys to any and every kind of frog souvenir. One woman was even selling mirrors decorated with colorful glass shards placed against one another to resemble frogs.

"These are nice," Pearl said to the woman.

"Thanks. My boyfriend and I make them by hand."

"They're very pretty." Pearl smiled at the woman.

Pearl continued to look at all the artwork. The mirrors themselves were hardly big enough for her to see her own face, but with the colored glass patterns that surrounded them, each one became something sizable enough to place on a wall, like an art print. One used a deep, coal-black glass for the eyes of a lime-green frog sitting on a Santa Fe–colored lily pad. An abstract one had been arranged with different green shards held together by a river-blue caulking. Many of them looked to Pearl like they could be murals on a stained glass window at Saint Joseph's. There were no price tags on any of them.

"Have you had much luck today?" asked Pearl.

"We've sold a few, but we're still waiting for the big crowd to show for the music later on," she replied.

"My husband is an artist," said Pearl.

"Is that right? Where is he?"

"He's not doing real well right now."

"Oh, I'm sorry to hear it. Is he sick?"

"He doesn't feel right."

"Well, I hope he gets better soon. Not even able to make the festival, was he?"

Pearl said no. "I'm Pearl," she added.

The woman smiled as she took Pearl's hand. "Geena. My boyfriend is around somewhere. I think he's listening to the band."

"Where are y'all from?"

"California. Above Napa. In the redwoods. Have you heard of Humboldt? Anyway, we've been on the road now for three months. This really is a nice festival. We haven't ever seen anything like it. It almost makes us want to stay."

A thought came to Pearl: "You could stay with me. I live right around the corner."

Geena was taken aback. "That's so nice of you. You would really do that for us?"

"If you would like to stay."

"This *is* the kind of small place that Irv and I prefer, but we'd like to get to Washington by next weekend. Thanks so much, though. That's really sweet of you. Say, would you like a discount on one of these mirrors? We usually sell them for $15 to $20, but why don't you have this one for $5?"

She held up the abstract one, the lily pad–green and river-blue one. The small mirror was set off to the side of the shards so she could see herself only partially in the smooth reflection. Most of her was fragmented in the greens of the shards. It was very beautiful, but Pearl only had a few dollars in her purse.

"Oh, what's it worth, anyway?" Geena said. "Why don't you just take it as a gift."

"Oh, I—"

"Sure. You were willing to put us up and you haven't even met Irv yet."

"But this is too much. This must have taken so much work."

"But we love what we do."

"Well, why don't you come for a late dinner tonight after the music is over, and then I'll feel better about it."

They agreed to it, and Pearl took the mirror. Irv came up on them, just as they might have begun to talk about their men.

"Found one you like?" he asked Pearl.

"They're all so nice," she said.

"How've you been, love?" he asked Geena.

"How do you feel about dinner later with Pearl?" she replied.

Irv seemed pleased with the idea. He looked at Pearl and smiled. "Pearl, do you know who you look like?"

"My husband says I look like Janis Joplin."

"So you know. That's right, man."

"Nothing left to lose," she replied. Pearl fell into their way of talking quickly. It made her feel good about herself to know that she'd had the foresight to invite such people to dinner. Perhaps her husband was right about how things work out. Of course, there was no guarantee that she would become friends with the couple, or that they would even come for dinner, but she thought how maybe it isn't so much seeing it work out, but believing.

The crowd grew larger as the festival stretched into the afternoon, and Pearl talked with Geena and Irv in between customers. They told her all about Humboldt and how there was nothing quite as spectacular as being surrounded by a forest of thousand-year-old redwoods, especially at dusk when it's quiet and you can see their shadows lengthen and overlap one another. That was it, Irv said. Geena smiled.

You could say, they admitted, that the Grand Canyon gave you a similar feeling. There is no way you can imagine its vastness. It's a high desert that extends in every direction as far as you can see, the earth painted browns and reds and the shimmering sun blurring tiny Joshua trees at the horizon. You believe you can walk or even drive for days with your eyes closed and nothing will change, but then, almost before you can see it, you're upon it. The gorge drops nearly straight down so that the river looks like a brown band of silk tossed from the sky, and as you look the length of the canyon walls in one direction, you realize that they extend beyond your sight. You turn around and notice the same thing, except that they curve around you and then continue out of sight again. There is everywhere to look. It's more than any one person can see at once.

Like the drive along Highway 1. You have to manage the curves, avoid the edges of the cliffs that lead to the deadly beauty below. For brief, anxious moments, you can take your eye off the road and see a wave crash into a rock below, or see the cliffs rise tall out of the water, or see the mountains fill up the sky to the east. But you will always want more because your fear of falling off always brings you back to the blur of the road. Ultimately, you see the beauty only peripherally.

Pearl, who had listened to them so intently that she had even ignored the customers who had interrupted the descriptions with questions about the mirrors, couldn't reciprocate, for she had no similar stories to share. Every year her parents had taken her and all the kids to Waveland, Mississippi, to play in the polluted Gulf of Mexico. There were mosquitos on the beach and jellyfish, and you had to watch so that you didn't step on beer cans sticking through the sand. It was really nothing. She would have liked to have had a story to tell them about some place, but she was content to listen to theirs, and instead of making her jealous, their stories led her to picture herself in those places, and it made her happy to think of herself in some far off, idyllic landscape.

An accordion sounded and much of the gathered crowd immediately recognized it as Clifton Chenier's. A loud cheer went up and soon the booths were empty and the open area in front of the stage filled with people. He began with "I'm the Zydeco Man," and a few couples got up and started Cajun dancing. Mothers held their babies on their shoulders, and men in T-shirts and blue jeans held beers and talked to each other beneath the music. The belles stood near the front and showed their white smiles. A few black men and women stood apart, near the front and back of the audience, talking and eating and clapping. Nearly everyone bent their knees in rhythm at least for a couple of beats, especially when they didn't know what else to do, whom else to look at, what else to say.

Pearl, who had followed Irv and Geena from the crafts exhibits, went to the concession stand and bought a draft beer and a fried frog leg, thinking how this would be a nice time. It had not occurred to her that she might be a third wheel, for they had addressed her as they would each other, but when she returned, they were talking to themselves, and she noted the difference in tone.

"There's a festival in Mobile next weekend," Geena was saying.

"What's the theme?" Irv replied.

"Not sure, but it's a beach town."

"You know what that means," said Irv.

"Time for the sand-and-sun models."

Pearl sipped her beer and held her frog leg and mirror awkwardly without announcing her return. Clifton Chenier was good, after all. Given the crowd and the weather and the success of the day so far, it was a pleasant afternoon for her in the City of Murals.

"It was a good day," continued Geena.

"How good?"

She quoted a figure, and to Pearl it seemed unfathomably high.

"Good thing you ran into that guy," she said. "What was his name?"

"I don't remember. I don't think he ever told me."

"Well, we can thank him for today."

Just as Pearl was going to ask about the man, the band began another number, a quick-moving, catchy Cajun tune with a waltz beat, and Geena grabbed Irv and then they were dancing. Suddenly, people were dancing all around Pearl, bumping into her and excusing themselves. "That's okay, that's okay," she kept saying, putting on a smile as she tried to make her way out of the dance area. Someone bumped into her arm and she spilled most of her beer. "I'm sorry," she said.

As she made it out of the way, the number ended and the dancing stopped, and Pearl was left with an empty cup, the colored mirror, and a pair of muddy shoes that had been stepped on by anonymous feet. She was trying to stay positive. Everyone put their hands in the air and clapped and cheered, and so she did too, but she wouldn't have convinced anyone of her appreciation, except that, as it had seemed to her the whole day, no one was looking at her anyway.

It would be getting dark soon, and the atmosphere was already changing. Mothers left with their children. The sun relented. The sky yawned and showed the pink back of its mouth. Teens lounged at the side of the stage like alley cats, waiting for night. The band played an instrumental, a song fit for coming and leaving. There were very few people in the crowd who could find ways to enjoy both the day and the night, and while it would've been clear to Pearl had she seen them that Irv and Geena were among these few, she didn't think to question herself, whether in fact she was a person who, at this point in her life, could enjoy either.

The band began its first set in earnest after an introduction from the mayor. Clifton Chenier was a light-skinned black man who had all the trappings of a regional star. He was wearing a cape and a crown, and when he belted out the blues and opened his mouth, you could see a row of gold teeth shining back at you. They played zydeco, and he was backed by a band that supported the rhythm and blues sound. The way he squeezed his accordion, you would think it should have been painted in psychedelic colors. It was enough to distract Pearl from herself, anyway, and that was saying a lot.

Over the next few tunes, Pearl caught sight of Irv and Geena dancing, and it made her consider her proposal. She realized that she would have to confront the question of Manuel's absence and she didn't know what she would say. Still, she looked forward to their company. The music carried on and it seemed that it might last all night.

She felt a hand on her shoulder and turned.

"Hey there."

It was a boy, probably in his late teens. He had a charming smile and he seemed innocent enough.

"Hi," she replied.

"Would you like to dance?"

"I'm sorry, I'm waiting for someone," she said, and then immediately regretted it.

"Oh. Well, are you sure you wouldn't want to just dance?"

"No thanks." She smiled at him.

"Okay," he said and went off to report to his buddies. She could see them laughing at him. He took it good-naturedly, laughing and throwing back comments at them that she couldn't hear.

Geena saw her then. She whispered into Irv's ear and came to visit.

"I'm sorry we lost you," she said. "I thought you might have left."

"It's okay. I was just watching the band."

"Have you seen this guy before? What a sound! I've never heard anything like it."

"He is something in his outfit, isn't he? We have one of his albums at the house, if you'd like to listen to it."

"I bet it's wonderful, but I just talked to Irv, and he says we should get back to New Orleans tonight. Our friend—the one whose apartment we've been staying in—he's coming in tonight on a Greyhound from Jackson, and he needs us to pick him up. I'm sorry. I didn't realize it earlier when I said we could come."

Pearl thought how Geena genuinely looked disappointed.

"We don't have a phone number, or even an address right now, but why don't I take your info, and next time we pass through, I'll be sure to call."

Pearl wrote down her address and phone number and handed them to Geena. Clifton Chenier was singing his latest tune, "Louisiana Blues."

"It was nice to meet you," said Pearl. She could see Irv in the crowd, waiting for Geena to return, and she thought it impolite to keep her from him. She said goodbye, and Geena offered a hug. Pearl walked out of the fairgrounds, away from the singing and the dancing, the revelry fading as she moved toward home.

It was not until the following week that Irv, sitting in the passenger's seat of the Nova as Geena drove through the foothills of the Appalachians on their way to Washington, reached into his wallet for a quarter to pay a toll and found the phone number of the man he'd driven to New Orleans. *That would be wise,* he remembered him saying. Not finding the money, he searched through Geena's purse and instead came across Pearl's number, noticing then that they were the same. As the engine idled in front of the tollbooth and Geena waited, it all came to him suddenly. Thinking back to that drive from Rayne and the soft-spoken man who had seemed so easy, so gentle, so calm, he took a coin from the purse and put it in his girlfriend's hand, wondering if that man—what was his name?—had ever come back; or if he hadn't, if he ever would.

How to Live Domestically as an Artist

STASH THE UNFLATTERING portraits of your wife in the closet and clamp a lock on the drawer where she keeps the .44. Shift the armchair so the view angles down to the mountain road, so you can see her coming home from work in the afternoons as you read the newspapers' account of the latest gallery openings. Feed your infant child twice after she leaves in the morning and carve out time near noon to walk across the calle with little Emi to see Ma and Pa, who've bank-rolled this apartment, this life. Cuernavaca is an art town, remember, and there is still a chance, after so many failures, to finally make something work. Remember that Mexico is your home. Forget the States. Forget your first wife. Forget your first child—well, don't forget them, but stash them in the back of your mind, for this current situation, de repente, requires constant vigil. Forget that whole diversion that was the Caribbean.

When the baby cries, pick her up and put her on your shoulder. Whisper to her in the Veracruzano accent of your youth and let her get used to your soft scent, your soft voice. Learn what puts her to sleep— the humming of the motor on the window unit, the running of water from the bathroom sink but not the kitchen, that faint sigh you emit when you're near sleep yourself. Commit these to muscle memory. Say her name aloud: Emi, mi Emi, no mames, mi Emi, calmate mija porfa mi Emi, and know that this time, with this child, it will be different. Show her the paintings of her that you've been working on. The one projecting her in pigtails in five years' time, walking on the surface of a chlorine-blue pool like Jesus. The one of her flying over the ravine behind your parents' house across the street. The one of butternut squash in a field of vetiver in the background, Emi hovering over it with her freckled face and a look of complaint, a hand outstretched for the tamarind-red candy of your youth. Smile as she watches you work.

In the afternoons at your parents', let your mother coddle Emi on the porch while you put together a swing set. Resist the urge to chafe at how your father oversees your work. Ignore his mumbles about how the top bar isn't level, how you're not bolting the chains correctly to the anchor, how he wishes he still had the strength so he could do it. Let him smoke at a distance and complain and do not respond. Think of the times when he punched you out as a child because you asked por qué too many times, when he told you that you needed to stop being such a faggot with your art and grow the fuck up. That will remind you to laugh at his benign mumbles now. Things are much better today.

Return to the apartment in the late afternoon to give Emi a nap. When your wife's motorcycle pulls into the drive, hurry to the kitchen and put on a pot of water to boil for tea. As her heels click up the concrete stairs to the apartment's entrance, turn on the Mozart she likes, but play it low for Emi's sake. Take out the loose-leaf tea and tie an apron round your waist. Put on a smile when the door swings open. Be prepared for the best. Be prepared for the worst. Have the recipe book out, and for Christ's sake, make sure you've already bought the ingredients you need. When she walks in, smile and walk gracefully into her arms. Take the cues. When she ends the hug, you'll know what's next. If the mood is right, then pour you each a glass of tequila. If it's not, then wait for the kettle to whine and pour her tea. Either way, return to the kitchen and begin to shuck the corn for the elote. You learned in your last marriage the power that resides in being the cook. With the other wife, you hadn't been, and that had been bad. Besides, cooking provides a sense of pride if things are good, and a needed distraction if they're not. Slice the zucchini and tomato exactingly. Toss them in a bowl with the authority of a dictator, and your new wife will respond with a respect you've always thought you deserved.

When she blithely chides your cooking technique at the too-loud sizzle of the pan at the introduction of vegetables, whatever you do, do not pick a fight. And after you've picked a fight, whatever you do, do not escalate it by calling her out for her drinking (as if you're not a drinker yourself). And after you've called her out, whatever you do, do not explain how, in the limo on the way to the church, your father pled with you to reconsider this marriage, how he said this second woman, this second wife, this second marriage, this would all go nowhere. And after you've blurted all that out, don't be surprised when the tequila comes out and she takes the knife out of your hands and starts to prep the calabacitas con rajas in her own way, which is to say, with a certain amount of vinegar. And don't be surprised if she keeps drinking through the process. Don't be surprised if you do, too. Keep your seething, false sense of self-righteousness at bay.

And when Emi wakes at the sound of the raised voices, be the bigger one and go take care of her without the first hint of an accusatory glance. And when you fail and give the glance, let her go by herself to take care of the baby. And while she's nursing, don't return to cooking, for she has reasserted control in that domain, and her preparation methods do not resemble yours. And when she returns to the kitchen, whatever you do, do not instigate further. Do not say anything about how hard it is being a stay-at-home artist and father. And when she laughs, do not denigrate her job. And after that escalation, allow her to approach, but keep your hands up. When she calls you out for sleeping with the neighbor, don't deflect like you always have. Don't deny it. And when you respond by telling her that she's crazy, understand that what happens next is out of your control. There's a part of you that deserves it, you know, and a part of you that says that no one deserves anything remotely like this.

As she heads for the bedroom with that steely look, know that she is going for the .44. Know that the lock will only give you a head start, for there is nothing that will keep her from it in this state. Walk silently to the open door and take to the steps. When you hear the crashing sound of the drawer being forced open, sprint to her motorcycle. When she fires the .44 out the window and hits the handlebars as you churn the thing into gear, punch the accelerator and don't look back. Don't look back. Don't look back.

Strangers

I AM CALLING MY father today for the first time in I don't know
when. A woman (his sister? his girlfriend? his new wife?) answers the
phone in Spanish, and I can tell she is wading through my words until
I come to my name. Then there is a pause, and she speaks out into a
house that I can't picture: "Manuel. Su hijo."

I guess he would call himself my papa, the Spanish term of endear-
ment. As a child I always thought I would call him Daddy, but now that
I'm twenty-four, I feel like maybe just Dad, or even Manuel, would be
more appropriate.

"Hello, son," he says cheerily, as though I call every day. It's time for
me to choose a name for him, and I go with Dad. If Mom were home,

maybe I would just say hello so she wouldn't know whom I'm talking to. But that's a lie. I wouldn't have even called.

"How are you?" he asks with a slight accent and a stress on the *you*. I am fine. I am doing very well. I've been at a master's for a while and I just landed a position teaching at the local college. It starts in three weeks, and I'm back living with Mom until an apartment opens up.

He wishes me happy birthday (it was a month ago), and it makes me wonder how old he is. Fortysomething? I know that he's younger than Mom.

"I tried to call but the area code was mixed up." The area code changed four years ago, but I just say I'm sorry I missed him.

There are so many things I want to find out that I don't know where to start or what to ask, so he talks instead.

"I'm glad you caught me here now. I am leaving tonight for Mexico City."

"Really?"

He explains how he now lives in Brownsville on a tourist visa (he's not a US citizen or even a permanent resident), and that it will expire soon. Even with a new one, he'll have to continue to border-hop every ninety days. He has no official home in the States, and no actual home in Mexico.

"So I have to go down to the capital and renew my papers," he's explaining. This bureaucracy, he says, it is thick. I get caught up in these details and my mind goes blank for a moment, but then, as his words echo and I try to think of what to say, a question emerges from somewhere inside me: "Could I become a Mexican citizen?"

"Well, yes, son"—the word hits me—"you just need a few documents. Let's see"—and I can tell he's really thinking about it and that it hasn't even occurred to him to ask why I would want this, not that I could give him an answer—"you will need your birth certificate, my birth certificate, maybe some other papers. Do you want me to check for you? I'll be at the office in Mexico City tomorrow. You'd have to set up some kind of residence in Mexico, but that is nothing. You could use my old address in Veracruz. You could even stay there if you like. My sister, your aunt, I think it's her place now. Anyway, how does that sound?"

It's all happening so quickly, I don't even know why I asked or if I'm certain I'd go through with it, but I'm shaking and smiling. Picture it: two exiles in Veracruz, sitting at a restaurant, looking out over the blue Gulf, talking about where we'll go next. With a single phone call, it seems as though all this might work out like a dream, as if it had been aligned so that it could happen with the slightest of effort, the faintest of pressure placed against the buttons of a telephone.

I hear a car that sounds like Mom's pull in the driveway and I get nervous, but then I look out the window and see it's just someone lost who's turning around. She's only gone to the grocery though, and she could be back any minute. We're making supper together, and I'm supposed to be boiling and deboning chicken.

She's never really said much about him. But every once in a while she drops the strangest of lines. Once, when we were on the phone while I was away in college, she asked me if I'd been cooking lately, and when I told her about a shrimp soup I'd made, she responded that the best shrimp soup she'd ever had was in Veracruz with Manuel. And then she asked about my classes. I didn't say anything, but you can't forget something like that, nor can you really imagine anymore that your mother is just your mother and wasn't also, at least at some point in time, a wife.

"Son? How does that sound?"

"Sorry."

"I'd like to see you sometime," he says. And then, in a single swooping sentence, he invites me to visit him.

The silence seizes me again, but this time I'm smiling through it. There's lots for me to do here. I only have three weeks before I start to teach at the college here in town, and I have to make lesson plans, order books, fill out paperwork, find a place to rent, and, of course, I'd have to tell Mom, an unwritten rule of living at home.

"When could I come?"

"I'll be in Mexico City tomorrow, and then I'll go to Veracruz for three weeks. Just call me when you want to come and I'll give you directions."

Would he always have been like this if I had called? When I was at a pool party at fourteen and a girl put my hand between her legs and I wanted to tell someone but not Mom, or when I shaved for the first time and broke out in a rash from using soap as shaving cream, or when I wanted to know how it was when I was a baby after he'd already left us once and somehow we were all living together in the Virgin Islands, or when I wanted to know why he left after that to go back to Mexico for good, or when I wanted to know why it had been so strange when I'd seen him that one, dreamlike time in Chiapas on that basketball trip for college, could I have just called him? Should I have? Would it have been like this? He's always seemed so far away, but maybe that's just fear. We've always had a phone number for him.

"Son?" He hits me again with it.

"Sorry."

"That's okay," he says softly, laughing.

"When would be good?"

"Oh, whenever you have time," he says.

"Sounds good," I reply immediately, as if to one of my friends, and for the first time I realize how much I am like him, and that I really should meet him for real, whether it's in a cabana or a bar or even a plain old house. How strange, to recognize myself so clearly in a phantom figure over the phone; to picture him, me, as a twentysomething leaving home and coming to a foreign land, crisp dreams exploding through sleepless nights in shrieks of ecstasy and excitement like firecrackers; to imagine myself in another twenty or so years and wonder: Will there be someone calling me?

I hear the car pull in the driveway and hate that I have to end it.

"I better go," I say, and he doesn't ask why. Mom would ask, but he doesn't have to know. Or is it that he doesn't care?

"Goodbye, son," he says softly, with his accent. I know now. I know I have to go.

"Goodbye," I say, and hang up hurriedly, putting down the phone before I can hear the keys rattling the lock. But looking out the window I see that it's only the stranger again, who still hasn't found his way, who is turning around again the same as before, who is still looking for someone's home.

A Family, with Death Snakes

THE ODYSSEY SPLIT open to the sirens, the sophomore read beside the hotel's pool. He ignored his teammates, who lounged beneath palapas like seals at La Jolla, their oversized haunches spilling over the thatched armrests of rattan chaise lounges. Not expecting to play in the exhibition game that night, Tommy, the sophomore, didn't worry over studying game film. Instead, he submerged himself in the ancient voyage home to Greece, a reading assignment due in his honors ancient literature course upon their return to New Orleans. On every page, Odysseus arrogantly avoided peril. He told tall tales like the hero he was. Witnessing all that chicanery and bravado, Tommy hardly felt the cool, blue water on his toes.

Two things made reading difficult. First, teenaged gunmen walked the borders of their Chiapas resort. While he hadn't pieced together the entire scope, newspapers reported violence nearby, in a place called Acteal. Pacifists shot praying at a church. Pregnant mothers knifed in the abdomen. Had this news broken before they'd left, the university probably would've canceled the trip. Anyway, it seemed the killings had been alarming enough for the Mexican federal government to guard the hotel with these armed boys. Dressed in green. Younger than him. Stoic. Theirs, a life that might've been his, had he grown up with his father in this country. From this distance, they looked like toy soldiers, pacing back and forth along the razor-thin edge of his book's spine.

The second distraction: his asshole teammates. They were a loud, intimidating pack of man-children. In his sixteen months of college, he'd gathered that three of them had fathered sons, one had once drunk more beer in a single afternoon than Tommy had in his entire life, and they all routinely felt the power of Wu-Tang's message. *RZA speaks the truth*, Caramel once said at a bar, stroking his chin, seeming to make a political point. Everyone else had nodded drunkenly in assent except Tommy, who didn't know what they were talking about.

He'd gathered that he couldn't live up to their hedonism. Better, perhaps, to keep his nose in the books like Coach Lynch hollowly urged them to do, as if that man cared about anything but their eligibility. But how to ignore all this intimidating joviality? In the pool, bigs played chicken. Point guards yapped about sorority girls back home. Even the managers squirted each other with water guns. At a certain point, reading became impossible.

"Hey, yo T! Put that fucking book down, dog."

It was Caramel, so nicknamed because he'd been a stripper who went by Caramel Cobra. He played a swingman at this Division III level, though he stood only six-three. He called out to Tommy from the diving board: "You in your motherland, homie. Soak this shit up." He dove off, crunched himself into a ball, and hit the water hard, sending a spray that dotted Tommy's Homer. If he could've responded, Tommy would've said that he *wasn't* from Mexico. His father was, but he'd never known the man. He'd grown up in Louisiana with his Cajun mother, whiteness written on his cherubic face, in his blond hair. His ignorance of Mexico ran deep, but always and everywhere he went, there was his name: Tomás.

As he struggled to maintain focus on the Achaeans, he watched Coach Lynch and an assistant approach, talking about the matchups tonight against the Fighting Death Snakes. Whether they'd face any zone. The rotation. As they walked by the pool, Caramel called out.

"Coach! What you know about that reception after the game? They gonna be some girls there or what?" A round of jock-deep laughter echoed off the chlorinated water.

"Cool it, Romeo," Coach replied. "It's a big fucking deal. The governor of this state is gonna be there. You have no clue what these kids you're playing against have been through this week. I hate to break it to you, boys, but you gotta act like decent humans tonight."

General chuckles ensued. Caramel absorbed Coach's jab begrudgingly. His eyes landed on Tommy. "Damn, T. Give that shit a rest," he said. He sent a playful splash Tommy's way. Wiping chlorine out of his eyes, Tommy looked poolside for validation. A teammate looked back at him and laughed. Maybe everyone was right. Maybe life was for living. Tommy flung aside the ancient Greeks. Feigning surrender to the moment, he dove in to do whatever it was that looked like what playing with teammates in a pool should look like.

. . .

Silvia clutched a cigarette carton filled with chicken feed. She carried it to the edge of her dead parents' yard and dumped it there for the rooster, Charlie. As if weary of paramilitary outfits, Charlie glanced around a moment before lowering his head down to peck. Silvia looked, too. The hills remained quiet. She saw only her mother's patch of bougainvillea. "Coma," she urged the bird, as she plucked a bunch of flowers from their stems. Inside, she placed them in a vase beside the laminated memorial to her parents and a votive to the Virgin. At the top of the hour, she observed the clunky movements of her parents' cuckoo clock, a gift handmade by an uncle long ago disappeared from the village. She listened to its internal gears churning as a wooden sparrow emerged from a tiny door and the bells chimed. Beneath those mechanical whorls and chirps, Silvia arranged the flowers as her mother would've—her mother, who once gazed on them from the sink while washing dishes, a guardian of beauty. She would shoo Charlie if he ventured too near that patch of color, as if she'd been more concerned with the preservation of that small splendor than with men in the hills with guns. As the cuckoo retreated, Silvia moved to the sink to wash her hands.

Her aunt would arrive tomorrow from San Cristóbal to overtake her care, and Silvia wanted to establish a routine of her own first. Thinking of what her parents had consumed weekly, she made a trip to the pharmacy in town to buy necessities. "See, Auntie," she wanted to be able to say, "I can take care of myself."

Near the village center, she passed over a concrete basketball court cracked and besotted with weeds. No nets hung from the rims, and militants had graffitied the Coca-Cola ads of the sunbaked backboards. Once, her father had coached local boys on this court. Now, drunks used it as a place to pass out somewhere near the foul line. Just after the massacre, the federal government landed helicopters here to empty troops out onto the scene in an unconvincing show of official concern. By then, it was too late. The soldiers, it was said, had taken to washing blood off the church walls to hide evidence of the brutality before reporters arrived.

In springs of her past, the court held a pre-Lenten festival. Local vendors unfolded wooden chairs and dangled wares from their backs: trinkets and beads, palm fronds and incense, toy windmills and roses made of tin painted the color of blood. And always, basketball games at the heart of it. As winners advanced, more vendors descended, replete with the sweetest candied powders and elixirs Silvia could imagine. Lime sodas the color of lizards. Cherry candies a shameful shade of lipstick. All of it plastic-tasting and perfect. Silvia would gorge herself as her father coached a game from the sidelines.

Inside the pharmacy, the clerk nodded as Silvia entered. In this town, the gesture passed for sympathy. Silvia didn't give her the satisfaction of a nod back. The old woman might be sorry now, but where had she been yesterday for the funerals? Scared of retaliation for mourning, probably, but still. Silvia scanned the aisles for items she recognized from her parents' pantry, but a jigsaw puzzle caught her eye. Its box depicted Michael Jordan clad in red and white, a gold chain around his neck as he cradled a brown ball in midair. Her father had loved Jordan. She brought the puzzle to the front.

"¿Este?" the woman asked.

"Sí."

"Diez."

Silvia laid a coin on the glass and slid it toward the woman, who considered her. "Mira," she said, "¿Sabes del juego partido esta noche? En Palenque. Con un equipo de Los Yunaites." A basketball game. Tonight. Your father would've liked it, she concluded.

Of course, she knew about the game in Palenque. And this vieja was right: not only would her father have loved it, he would've been instrumental in its planning. In his twenties, he'd played for a regional team that made it to the finals of a few statewide torneos relámpagos, lightning-round tournaments popular in Chiapas. Two straight years, his team won the crown with him as the most valuable player. This was in the late 80s, when Silvia was just a toddler. The way he told it, he'd been humbly specific about his attributes: "I was never the fastest defender, but I had good footwork," he would say. "I had passable anticipation. I knew where everyone stood on the court at any given time. Where they would be as I drove the lane."

His success had caught the eye of a government official, who, after the second championship, offered him a job coaching youth in Chenalhó. Near Acteal. Paz a través del básquet. *Peace through basketball.* That was the government's tagline for the program, and it became her father's philosophy. Was the reason he'd been at the church that fateful day last week. Government offer in hand, he'd moved his family to Chenalhó, where Silvia grew up in the shadow of this basketball goal.

"¿De veras?" Silvia responded to the clerk.

"Ándale, pues."

But she had no way of getting to Palenque. Anyway, the sun was high in the sky, and what was the use of remembering her father that way when, anytime she wanted, she could return to this court? She walked outside and sat down in the baking sun at the top of the key, where she dumped the puzzle pieces onto the whitewashed concrete.

. . .

Because of the US drug war, the roads leading south from Coatzacoalcos promised less terror than the roads north. Still, as Manuel crossed from Veracruz into Chiapas, he knew better than to drive any but the busiest highways.

A signed contract from Sami Hayek at Pemex Oil rested on the passenger seat. Its presence confirmed the promise of a new life. Yes, his second marriage had failed. Yes, he was leaving behind another child, a daughter this time, Emi. But the promise of a stable income and career in waste oil incineration foretold a bright future. He and Sami Hayek had just penned the deal that morning, assuring him work and a paycheck for six months. Manuel was ecstatic. He considered what his son, the basketball player, might know about Sami's daughter, the actress, Salma. Could this be the kind of aside he might drop in conversation after the game? A way to obliterate, with one choice reference, the awkwardness of having only met Tomás the one time a decade before, at his parents' estate in Cuernavaca?

Passing through a small village, he stopped to stretch and smoke. Beside the town's basketball court, he lit a cigarette. On the baking concrete, a girl sorted the pieces of a puzzle. He walked to her. Looked over her shoulder and watched. In the half-formed puzzle, the face of a famous black athlete was coming into focus. He'd never been a basketball fan—soccer was Manuel's game—but he recognized Michael Jordan. On that one visit a decade before, his son had spoken of the player like a god.

"¿Te gustan los Bulls?" he asked the girl. She did not look up, instead tried piece after piece to fill the void where Jordan's chest should be.

"My son plays basketball," Manuel said. "He's playing tonight. In Palenque. I'm headed there now."

The girl dropped a puzzle piece to the concrete and looked up at him. She looked thirteen, at most. A beautiful, sad girl. Manuel read her plaintive eyes: she did not have to ask.

• • •

Coach pulled Tommy aside to tell him he'd be starting. He explained that Caramel, their starting two-guard, had been vomiting and shitting all over himself in pregame. "Don't go thinking this is some kind of feel-good, emotional decision," he said, unaware that Tommy didn't know his father would attend.

"And don't be nervous," he added. "This is just a jamboree. It's December. There's no pressure, but you've been pushing Caramel in practice. You show you can hold your own in a game situation, I might think about a shift in the rotation."

Caramel was a junior and a mainstay on the wing. Team lore had it that, in his inaugural practice, he'd supplanted his predecessor. First, he'd manhandled the guy on defense, then quick-posted him on a break, drop-stepped him off the block, and dunked on the poor sap with no sense of impropriety. "I'm the greatest of all time!" he was purported to have said, mimicking a Muhammad Ali gesture. Caramel and his predecessor had never spoken after that. Having heard the story, the sophomore knew what it meant that Caramel felt so free and easy talking to him: it meant that he hadn't felt threatened.

Maybe there's a place for me after all, Tommy thought. Though he'd held his own in practice, he hadn't dramatically upstaged the junior at any turn, and so he hadn't thought anyone had noticed his work.

A buzzer sounded through the locker room's thin walls. Players gathered to listen to Coach's final, uninspiring words. This game was a chance, he said, to work out the kinks in their full-court press. To experiment with the new defensive rotation for bigs on penetrations from the wing. It'd be an up-and-down affair, he added, and they shouldn't take their foot off the gas. The more they pushed in this heat and climate, the more prepared they'd be for conference play. The sophomore nodded as he'd become accustomed to, but he received these words differently. This time, they weren't just clichés. This time, they were specific mandates he'd have to carry out. He felt their importance as if they'd come from his father, whom he'd never known, but whose sway over his consciousness had held across the whole of his childhood.

"One more thing, guys," Coach added. "These people, they've been through some hard times. Let's remember that, okay? Now go out and kick some ass."

. . .

Silvia and Manuel arrived at the gym just after tip-off. They snuck in beside a vendor selling roasted corn and sat on wooden bleachers behind Tommy's team's bench. Tommy stood on court guarding a Death Snakes power forward on a weakside switch. The boy, nearly close enough for Manuel to reach out and touch, seemed farther away because he was playing. Tomás, Manuel knew, wouldn't see him.

The action shifted to the other end of the court. Manuel asked Silvia if she wanted anything. She shook her head no and glanced outward. He studied her poker face as she observed not the action of the game but the fans opposite them. Was she looking for someone specific? Was she paranoid about the possibility of violence? Did she recognize anyone from some past he couldn't glimpse? She'd been silent on the ride from Chenalhó, but something in her devout attention to the rain forest beside the road had revealed the depth of her trauma. He'd understood he shouldn't ask questions. Instead, he'd scanned the radio. When he landed on a station playing American punk and she turned her head like a prisoner to a dinner bell, he left it there. "Die, Die My Darling," by The Misfits. He'd never heard it, but he knew English well enough to follow the words, a demented man commanding his lover to die. He couldn't fathom why such a song would speak to her, but as he watched her parrot the macabre lyrics, he smiled and let her keep the mystery of their importance to herself. As his son streaked down the court to defend a fast break, he told the girl he'd buy her an ear of corn. At a time-out, the American players trotted to their bench. Manuel watched his son sweating as he sat down and leaned forward to listen to his coach. The little man yelled at them, but his voice was too shrill and the language too basketball-specific for Manuel to follow. He saw how Tomás nodded in the face of the spit-filled vitriol. The boy understood the dictates. Seemed unfazed by the invective. Manuel turned to Silvia and pointed him out to her.

. . .

Silvia followed Manuel's finger. In the forward slump of the sopho-more's shoulders to listen to his coach, she saw the form of dozens of players who'd listened to her father. Her gaze carried to the coach, who looked nothing like her own father. This man scorned his players. This man was a chafa, a fake. A man not able to see the court clearly, her father might have said. She wondered whether any of these players had yet rebelled. She was no basketball player herself—she'd spent her dad's practices on the sidelines imitating his coaching stance—but she'd hung around those teams enough to know the ways of the secretly mutinous.

When the time-out ended, Silvia watched as Manuel's son remained on the bench. A manager offered him a bottle of water. As he turned to accept it, Silvia saw him catch sight of Manuel and freeze. Manuel gave the boy soft eyes. She could see that the sophomore had no idea Manuel would be here. A teammate nudged Tommy, and he turned quickly back toward the court. She noticed how, at the perceived slight, Manuel winced, deepening the creases beside his eyes. In that moment, Silvia gathered the truth of their estrangement. The rest of the game, she watched the action like a diehard.

. . .

At the postgame reception, the sophomore accepted compliments from his teammates. "I see how you doing it," one offered. But Tommy was scanning the crowd for his father. "Fifteen and seven. Not bad, boy. Caramel better watch out."

Tommy focused on the governor, a dark man with a gray beard who wore a tan suit and bolo tie, who prowled the grounds like a jungle cat. He squinted at those he felt superior to, which was everyone. Lynch and his assistant stood in garish tropical attire by the nut plate, rehashing the close loss. A white-linen table boasted a spread of fried plantains and empanadas, beans and rice, and pitchers of margaritas served by indigenous waitresses the color of the Mississippi River. Tommy noted their deference. Wondered at their lives. They wore full-length dresses cinched at the waist with embroidered white belts. Caramel, still ghostly from diarrhea, held court in his warm-ups with a Death Snake who spoke passable English and gestured grandly, making big eyes as he told stories of recent brushes with militants. The difference between the Zapatistas and the paramilitaries. The role of the federal government in allowing the violence to happen. Tommy eavesdropped, wanting to discover what stories might have been his.

• • •

Manuel and Silvia assessed the reception, each from their own vantage. To Manuel, it evoked memories of schmooze fests he'd endured to procure funds for his new business. The spread, similar. Clusters of small-talkers eyeing a chance to move to a more socially advantageous crowd. The only difference was the height of these featured guests. And, of course, his son's presence.

To Silvia, the reception looked like a grander celebration of the type prepared in her village for the championship teams her father coached. Yes, this was more elaborate. And yes, the governor loomed here. But as the coach of the Fighting Death Snakes shook hands with the sophomore to congratulate him on a game well played, she didn't see the coach's face. Instead, she saw the face of her own father. This was not just sentimentality: they truly resembled each other. The face, worn and rough like a stone; and the body, too: boxy shoulders, sturdy build, hardly the build of a basketball player. No one could've gleaned from this man, or her father, that they were any good at a sport that valued length and litheness. They must've been similar players. She extrapolated from his physicality a series of movements—a pass on the fly without looking, a pointing of a finger in praise of a teammate—and allowed herself to envision this coach as if he were her father.

. . .

Manuel nudged her toward the food. He made her a plate and poured himself a margarita. He scanned the crowd first for his son, and then for someone to talk to. Coach Lynch, alone, gathered cashews in his fist, and Manuel took his opportunity.

"Mr. Lynch," he said.

"Yes, sir," the coach responded.

"My name is Manuel. I contacted you before your trip. I am father to Tomás."

"Tommy! Of course! Welcome. Say, your boy had a great game. Looked like a senior out there."

"It was a joy to watch him play."

Lynch looked down at Silvia.

"And what's your name, little girl? I didn't know Tommy had a sister."

Manuel thought of his Emi. Coach Lynch searched him for a response. He hadn't known until the moment of leaving Emi's mother that he would never return. He'd masked that guilt with the glimmer of Sami Hayek's promise. Siren song of the new. "Silvia here, she doesn't speak English," Manuel said. He looked down at her. She looked up at the coach, who waved at her stupidly. Manuel could hardly bear it. "Silvia," he said to her in Spanish. "This man thinks you are my daughter. Do you want to play along?"

. . .

She considered. First, it seemed like a betrayal—and worse, dangerous in these times. What would it mean, to accept this illusion? Here, she was surrounded by things that defined her father—coaches, players, talk of games—but all of it now without him. All this, to say nothing of her mother. The proud way she'd stand by in the postgame wash of congratulations. The tamales spiced with hoja santa and chipilín she would cook to celebrate victories. But that was over now. None of that existed anymore, even if the remains of that life had lain around her all day: man-children in warm-ups clowning around, the particular smell of a sweaty gym, how a crowd rose to crescendo at a thunderous dunk on a fast break. Silvia clasped her hands to Manuel's forearm and looked up at the American coach with a smile of belonging.

"How about that," Lynch said. "Why don't I go get Tommy? I can snap a picture of the three of you. One sec." Before Manuel could say anything, Lynch ran off to retrieve the sophomore.

. . .

In how Lynch framed it on the walk over, Tommy gathered that his father had contacted Coach before this trip. That Coach had assumed Tommy knew the whole time. It *had* occurred to Tommy to track the old man down, but he'd tried that before without success. After visiting his father in Cuernavaca at age seven, he wrote letters expressing a primal yearning to know that distant father from this other country. He'd written of his interest in basketball, how he hoped his father might see him on the court one day. After sending them, he'd retreat to his backyard goal beside Mom's flower garden of azaleas, call out the play-by-play as he acted out a Final Four, final-seconds scenario. In those moments, he'd imagine his father watching, listening to the dramatic narration. And then—"Four! Three! Two! One!"—Tommy would let fly a winning shot. After it fell through the net, the ball bounced on the dirt in an echo of solitude. His father never responded to his letters.

And so, as the sophomore walked to greet the mythic man and pose for a photo, he convinced himself he felt pleased that he hadn't made contact. He prepared himself to say something polished, something to indicate a casual indifference. Still, he had no way of preparing for the presence of the girl. This girl Coach was now calling his sister.

"How about a family photo? What do you say?"

What could he say?

Lynch directed the shot like it was practice. *Control freak,* Tommy thought. Coach ordered Tommy to stand with arms outstretched around Silvia and Manuel. Silvia to his left, her arm grazing his side (he recalled, as a child, asking Santa for a sibling). His father stood to his right. He felt the soft touch of Manuel's hands against his shoulder, caught his cigarette scent. The smell evoked a moment in Cuernavaca in a pool with his father. Manuel had waded to him, smoking, and asked what he was reading. It was *The Little Prince.* Manuel had nudged the spine down to the poolside concrete. "Why always so serious?" he whispered. And smiled, as if that togetherness were permanent.

It had not been. Neither was this one. In the electricity of his father's giddy grip, he felt Manuel relishing this false moment—reading had sensitized Tommy to such subtleties—and decided then and there that he would never return to Mexico. Years later, Tommy was to remember that moment—innocent nonsister to his left, affected father to his right, a reporter scribbling notes nearby—as the moment when he first considered life as a journalist. Eventually, he would team up on a piece about black life in New Orleans with Caramel, who, having talked that night with a Death Snake about the boy's recent horrors, found himself on track to a political life of his own.

• • •

Looking beyond Lynch, Silvia watched waitresses gather plates smeared with residue of guacamole, crumb of tortilla. Their movements so crisp; their gestures so decisive. As a younger child, she longed to play that role after tournaments. These perfectly dressed girls, they moved with such authority. She'd once envisioned costuming herself in that gleaming white outfit of responsibility. Holding a plate of food, bowing at the waist in acknowledgment of a favor granted. Catching winks her father sent her as she stood by, ready to serve. But those yearnings were gone now.

The American coach's command interrupted her hypnosis. He gestured for her to wrap her arm around Tommy. She looked up at the sophomore. In his hesitant gaze, she saw a young face she trusted. She couldn't name the good she felt at his nearness. Perhaps it was simply in the eyes. That soft, exotic gaze. He couldn't be more than five years older. And in how he was looking at Manuel, she perceived a sense of loss that she was coming from the opposite side of: he was only now seeing what it meant to have a father, while she was just learning what it meant to live without one. She imagined then returning with him to the United States—no notion of foreign domesticity beyond that, just the trip itself. This was someone she could feel strong on a journey with. Someone she could be happily silent next to. He would never do anything but keep his arm around her. Like this. In any event, she decided in that moment to make of her life someday a moving thing, regardless of her aunt's impending care. She did not yet know that basketball would carry her on that journey, that she would coach a team in San Cristóbal, a role that would take her to faraway countries; but in that moment, she felt certain for the first time that she wanted basketball to define her.

· · ·

Teammates gathered to watch the photo shoot. The governor meandered over, told Coach they should get a basketball in the picture. Maybe a couple of Death Snakes, too. An assistant sprinted off to do the important man's bidding. He booked for the hotel lobby, and gunmen on the resort's borders turned at the quick-moving body. Silvia watched them. As they gripped their AKs, she clutched Tommy's waist tight. The aid returned with a basketball. Both teams watched and laughed at his desperate, sycophantic gait. He brought the ball to the governor, who walked it to Coach Lynch. The token Death Snakes—whom Silvia recognized, whose parents, she knew, were also now dead—stood still in the wash of the politician's notoriety. By then, even the waitresses were watching the scene unfold.

In the picture that made the local paper, the one meant to show how bonds had been forged across cultures, a pair of Death Snakes photobomb the shot while Tommy smiles awkwardly, as if he's not in on the joke. Manuel stands silently by, never having had a moment to say the first word about his own new life, or Emi, and if you know the story, you can see that unrequited urgency in his face. Silvia leans her head against Tommy's side, her expression a bougainvillea trembling in the heat. Her posture is uncertain, and you can note the fierceness with which she clings to the sophomore. Below the photo, falsely attributed to the governor, a caption reads: Después del juego partido, una familia, con Los Death Snakes. *After the game, a family, with Death Snakes.*

Blood Summons

DURING MY FIRST year as a salaried citizen, I resolved to pay for my own trip to meet my father for real. He was in Veracruz again, though, and I couldn't just make a call and buy a ticket. There was a language to be learned, a border to cross. I'd need a good traveling companion.

My first choice: my girlfriend, an Austrian woman eight years my senior I'd met in grad school who spoke perfect Spanish and found me beautiful largely because of my awkward and earnest yearning for my father. Problem was, she'd moved to San Francisco, and I'd moved back to Baton Rouge, my hometown, and everyone knew that her ex-boyfriend had recently doubled down on a dot-com startup backed with VC money. This was the early aughts, just after the tech bubble crash, and that he'd managed to keep his business afloat under those circumstances gave me the intimidating impression that he was a titan of digital circuits. At the very least, I knew he lived where she'd just moved. He was fifteen years older than me, established as a Stanford grad and a success in Silicon Valley, and I was nothing more than a failed writer turned comp teacher lost in the shuffle of the state university all my friends had been funneled to straight from high school. When Sophia told me over the phone that she wouldn't come with me to Mexico, I knew I'd have to ask Sean.

Sean: short son of a Connecticut doctor, gregarious knower of many wondrous things, redheaded crew-cut captain in the Marine Corps. During a peacetime lull after the rush of post-9/11 calls to the Middle East, he'd been stationed in South Bend. He'd soon be discharged, and his big plans for postmarine life involved taking the GRE and applying for grad school programs in English. That's how we'd met, by taking a grad-level English class together at Notre Dame on the Victorian novel. I know: it doesn't sound like this would suit a marine, and in the end, it didn't. He landed at Yale in American studies, and from what I hear, he's now an advisor to the South Sudanese ambassador on military matters. Point being, he's an ambitious dude, and he had high expectations for himself even then. He knew a lot about traveling to weird places in weird situations, and so he'd make a good companion. When I called him, he didn't hesitate.

"Let's make it happen," he said.

I didn't say, "Yes, sir," but it felt like I should. That June, he drove his blue '91 Sentra to Baton Rouge from South Bend to pick me up. We got his tires checked at the local Firestone where my mom's father had taken his Chevrolets for years. The mechanic gave us the thumbs-up, and off we went.

I discovered a major problem right away. Sean drove a standard, and I hadn't learned on one. I told him so an hour into the drive, and we pulled over so he could teach me. "You're gonna need to take over at some point. I got a bad back on a mission to El Salvador. I can't go more than a few hours straight."

Beside a crawfish pond tepid with still water, I took control of the foreign car. It lurched and stopped as I tried and failed to put it into gear. Sean took pride in training marines, and he stayed patient. "It's a give and take of pressure," he said. "As you release the clutch, you're pressing down on the accelerator." After seventeen kills of the engine, I satisfied him when I got to third gear without a stall, and once more, we accelerated toward unknown lands.

Through staticky phone calls to distant Mexican relatives and some sleuthing, I'd discovered that my father lived in a town called Poza Rica, in the state of Veracruz. He said he worked for the oil industry. I had some notion of that life since I'd grown up in Cancer Alley, surrounded by refineries and raised in part by a grandfather who'd worked forty years for DuPont Chemical. He was a good man, and his daughter, my mother, was a good woman, and so I hoped for the best. My father had heard through relatives that I'd be coming, and in the one phone exchange we'd shared, he hadn't been exactly enthusiastic. That was enough for me to arrange separate accommodations for Sean and me. I'd arranged for us to stay in a town called Xalapa, about a four-hour bus ride from Poza Rica. We'd read about it online. It seemed like the kind of fun-loving place that would cater to our weird, artistic sensibilities. That way, if things went bad with my dad, we could avoid any long-term awkwardness.

But first things first: we'd head for Poza Rica so I could meet the man and feel things out. On the drive south, Sean asked direct questions about my relationship with my dad. I was no great communicator of my origins, but over Texan prairie and borderland palm, over Tamaulipan highway and Tampico oil plant, I fumbled in fits and starts through various basics of the story as I knew it: how my father had come to the States in his twenties to stay with distant relatives in a small Louisiana town called Rayne; how he'd started an airbrushing shop there at the time my mother had moved to the area after college at LSU; how they'd courted over a week and then married; how they'd fought one night and he'd hitchhiked to New Orleans, then used the last of his credit to buy a flight to the Virgin Islands; how my mother discovered this through his mother, who ushered the news along to her; how my mother arranged her own flight there, packing everything she owned; how, when she arrived at the Saint Thomas airport, my father picked her up, and his mouth had dropped at the sight of all (and I mean ALL) her things passing by on the baggage claim conveyer belt; how he had arranged, through his boss at a dairy that supplied milk and cream to cruise ships, to live rent-free for a time in an abandoned trailer home in a field of cows near the sea; how I'd been conceived and born there; how my mother had slowly learned that her devotion to being a good Catholic wife was not as strong as her distaste for the island; how she had flown back to Baton Rouge with me when I was eighteen months old; how we hadn't heard anything from my father then for eight years until he wrote us a letter the summer of my tenth birthday, inviting us to visit him in Cuernavaca; how we'd answered his call and taken a flight; how I'd felt so at home there in that other world; how I'd witnessed my parents' affections and cried at the sight; how I'd bawled at the airport, refusing to let go of my father until my mother pulled us apart to board the flight home; how I hadn't seen him since except for that half hour in Chiapas that I won't get into; and how I was, maybe, you know, kind of a little nervous about how this visit would go.

Dusk of our second night, we reached Poza Rica, but my father's directions had been imprecise. We stopped at a Mini-Super, where, in broken Spanish, I asked the clerk if I could use her phone. My father answered right away, speaking his slightly accented English with a gentility that reassured me that this trip had not been a terrible idea. He asked me to describe the street outside the store, and I relayed that request to Sean. Like the marine he was, Sean scanned the road and reported back with a rigid litany: laundromat, tin roof shack, tin roof shack, restaurant with white plastic chairs, tin roof shack, this Mini-Super. I repeated the list over the phone. The lady behind the counter watched me silently.

"Okay," my dad said. "I know where you are. I'll meet you there."

Fifteen minutes later, a man with gray-black hair drove up in a blue

Town Car with Texas plates and a teenage girl in the passenger seat. He drove past Sean and me, and then doubled back. He got out and looked at us. The girl stayed in his car. He walked toward me like he was tumbling and his eyes squinted his visage into a nervous pucker. He looked vaguely foreign, though he had a face that could pass for an American of indeterminate ethnicity. He drew me in for a hug and I caught a waft of cigarettes, and then something strangely sweet in the smell of his neck.

"I'm so glad you're here," he said. "Follow me to our house, and we'll have dinner. In the car is Silvia, and I will explain to you who she is while we eat."

In the Sentra, Sean dropped all pretense of being a marine captain. "Dude, you have a sister," he said. I hadn't gotten a good look at the girl, but as we followed them, I tried to make her out through the back of the Town Car. No dice: my dad drove so fast that Sean could hardly keep up. Every time we came to a stoplight, an army of window-washers accosted us and obscured my view.

With Sean's tracking skills, we kept up. My father led us to a small apartment just a few blocks off a main drag. As we parked, a woman emerged from the door, and Silvia got out of the Town Car. She looked about twelve. She was a little shy and she didn't walk right up to me but instead to the woman at the door. I discovered soon that she wasn't my half sister but my stepsister, daughter to this woman my father seemed now to be married to. My father introduced me to both of them, and they smiled and took me in politely. Inside, my father's mother sat at the kitchen table playing solitaire. I had no idea she lived here, too. I hadn't seen her since Cuernavaca. The house was packed to the gills, and I saw that it'd be difficult for all of us to stay here even that night, much less any longer.

The six of us ate a dinner of tortillas and beans at the tiny card table. At bedtime, my father, whose name is Manuel, which is also my first name though no one calls me that, offered me the couch and Sean a mat he placed on the floor. Once the two of us were alone in the living room buzzing with box fans to stave off the heat, Sean whispered to me, "You all right?"

"I think so," I said. "But we can't stay here."

"Good thing about Xalapa. You wanna stay here while I drive ahead tomorrow and figure that scene out?"

"No," I said. "I'll spend plenty of time here eventually."

. . .

The next morning, they saw us off. Dad had given us directions, and Sean followed them precisely. We passed over rusted-out bridges and through the jungles of Veracruz until we came into the mountainous town of Xalapa, where our little apartment waited. We arrived at the gated compound of a rich engineer in the middle of the afternoon and stopped the car in front of a brick wall lined with broken glass across its top. We pushed a button, and when a voice responded with "Bueno?" I explained that we were the visitors slated to stay for the summer.

"Claro. Entonces, pasen," the voice said flatly through the intercom. The gate buzzed and swung open. We made our way down a cobblestone path lined with bougainvillea until a short bald man in a collared shirt and slacks met us with a smile and a businesslike handshake. He led us to the guesthouse. Inside, it looked smaller than the pictures: there was a small entryway with a bench just barely big enough to sleep on, and just enough wall space to set up our Coleman stove if we wanted to cook anything. There was a shelf, too, for Sean to line with the books he'd brought to study for the GRE. To the left stood the tiny bathroom, and off the entryway lay the bedroom. The man spoke with polish as he gave us the tour, pointing to objects and naming them. "El baño," he said. "Bathroom," I said. "Así es," he'd reply. "La mesa," he said. "The table," I said. "Así es," he replied. It was very formal, and the exchange gave me a sense of dread about the little time we figured to spend on his property.

After he left, we spoke freely. "We'll rotate who sleeps in the bedroom," Sean said. "Although, if you're going to be going back to Poza Rica, maybe you should get the bed on days you come back."

"Let's see how it plays out," I said.

. . .

It played out this way: I spent those first few days in Xalapa with Sean exploring. A seasoned traveler, he'd hiked the Appalachian Trail and backpacked across France. He had an adventurous spirit and a daring bravado for talking to strangers despite hardly speaking Spanish. That first afternoon, we walked the city for five hours, getting the lay of the Xalapeño land and trying not to get lost. Even then, he tried out the language like some kind of conquistador. To a group of fruit vendors at a market we passed, he tried to tell this basic story where all he wanted to say was that "I went to the bus station, something-something happened, and it was very funny." Except, instead of saying "estación de camiones" for bus station, he said "estación de camarones," meaning, if it meant anything, *shrimp station*. And instead of saying "muy chistoso" for *very funny,* he said "muy chichotes," which, if it means anything, loosely translates as *very big breasts.* In other words, he had said, with classic American pomp, "So, ladies, I went to the shrimp station, and this incredibly cool thing happened. Very big breasts!"

And yet, because of his charm and uncanny ability not to be embarrassed, we had a great time interacting that way with strangers and walking around. I made note of the bus station when we passed it, and when the walking got tiresome, we slipped into a bar on a narrow street that sloped dramatically down to a park. La Chiva, it was called. *The Goat.*

Inside, a man in his thirties and a girl my age were pushed against a dark wall, singing songs and playing guitar beneath a dim spotlight. Their voices were flawless and the young woman was beautiful. The man, much older, sang with a bluster that Sean immediately admired. We sat down and ordered beers. When the two of them arrived at a set break, Sean leapt immediately into gushing applause and invited them, in English, to join us. I translated shoddily, and unnecessarily, since they'd already understood the basics of his gesture. Soon enough we were all sitting around the small table, Sean and the couple exchanging stories. They understood enough English for Sean to hold the table with his way. Me, I couldn't have carried that off, both because of my limited Spanish and my natural inclination to be a wallflower. I had no ability to tell a tall tale. But Sean, he boasted about our grand adventure to find my father, making requisite mention of the wonder of the experience for me. I listened with a kind of removed awe, only then understanding the gravity of what I'd set in motion. The couple followed with great interest and started asking me questions: When was the last time I'd heard from my father? What had it been like, to meet him yesterday? When was I thinking of taking the bus back to visit him once more?

They cut the conversation short, but only because they had to go back up onstage. "Do you think they're together?" Sean asked me. They each wore a wedding ring, and I mentioned this. "That's too bad," he said. "She's fucking gorgeous." It was true.

When their set ended, Sean offered to help them carry their gear. The husband accepted with a pleasure that seemed to come from having white kids offer a brown man assistance. As we dragged their amp outside, they asked us where we were staying. We told them about the little guesthouse, about the polished man who'd deposited us inside the room and then disappeared.

"That is caca," the man said. "How much are you paying for that?" We told him. He and his wife gasped audibly.

"Manuel," the man said to me, for again, that was my real name, and here in Mexico I'd decided to go by that name, that name that no one had ever called me back in Baton Rouge, where I'd grown up to "Tommy," the diminutive version of my middle name, Tomás. "Manuel," he said in exasperation, "that is too much. You two, you must come and stay with us."

And so, in that way, we freed ourselves of the weird vibe of the engineer's guesthouse. The next morning, we moved our things to Enrique and Gabby's two-story quarters, near the city's university. It stood not far from a lazy river, in an area teeming with lights in the trees and young students—Mexicans and study-abroad Americans, too—strolling the shops and bars all hours of the day and night. They welcomed us so unabashedly and so warmly that I passed full hours in those first days imagining my entire life playing out infinitely in this dream world. The thought of my father in that strange oil town down the road faded so completely from my mind that I hardly thought it possible that I'd ever wondered about the man at all.

But those times were fleeting, and at night, as Sean snored and the sounds of the bars across the street rattled inside my head, I kept circling back to my father. I'd pined and ached for him for hours at a time as a child. I'd gone so far as to pretend that, like the Catholic God I'd been raised to believe in, he was always watching me like some kind of omniscient overseer. On the public basketball court near my home in Baton Rouge, I'd call out my moves like an announcer, imagining myself at the Final Four in Dallas playing for LSU, the school where I was now teaching writing, crossing someone over and sinking a floater in the lane as Brent Musburger narrated the moment. In my head, my dad would be watching on TV, but also, I imagined, he'd be watching even *then*—on that decrepit little backyard court as I invented the scenario. It would please him to see how dedicated I was to becoming such a driven and successful person. Things hadn't panned out that way, but at least I had a job now. Of course, I doubted I was any good at it, for talking in front of strangers didn't come naturally. Still, I could at least envision a way to spin it into something impressive sounding for my age. As I summoned sleep in Enrique and Gabby's apartment, I murmured to myself in different cadences, practicing ways to narrate my tiny new life to my outsized dream of a father.

· · ·

It didn't take but two weeks for a pattern to emerge. Wednesday afternoons, I'd walk to the bus station, buy a bus ticket for Poza Rica, and say goodbye to Sean and Gabriela. My father would pick me up a few hours later, and for the next few days, I'd stay with him and his family. There, I learned to expect a head-spinning combination of, on the one hand, tedious day-to-day boredom, and on the other, melodramatic revelations and nightly confessions. Then, I'd return to Xalapa on a Saturday afternoon bus, my heart filled to the brim, yearning to tell

Sean and Gabriela the latest news, but unsure how to distill the chaos down to its essence. There were the stories my father told me about his time as an art student during the Olympic massacres in Mexico City, showing work beside David Siqueiros and editing a weekly with Alejandro Jodorowsky; the hard-drinking locals he'd befriended in the Virgin Islands while the baby version of me learned the words for *cat* and *water*; how he'd charmed his way into the dairy job on the island. Sean and I, we'd go out to La Chiva and sit around drinking while I tried to tell all these things in Spanish to Gabriela and Enrique. When I failed, Gabriela would ask me questions in English and then translate for our new circle. By then, Sean had befriended a group that included an American couple backpacking through the region, a Brazilian river guide who wanted to climb a nearby mountain called Orizaba, and a group of Enrique's local musical friends who were nightly fixtures at their house. All of them called Sean "el rojo" for his hair, and he took to it with blatant ecstasy. I want to say that their house felt like the late-night salons of Frida Kahlo and Diego Rivera, but none of us were famous, and we had no politics and only the immediacy of our lives to hold us together. Still, I loved that I'd found a group of people to listen to that seemed to genuinely care for me, even if they couldn't always understand my every word. I liked that, through Sean and Gabriela, they knew my story, and that they cared to ask about it when I'd return from Poza Rica. And maybe, most of all, though I didn't realize it at the time, I liked that they were strangers, that I could speak freely with them about my life and not worry whether the things I shared would get back to my friends back home in Baton Rouge. I was a new person here. Here, I was my father's son, in my father's country, but I was also my own man for the first time, staking out my own claims in a weird city that he held no title to, and the freedoms this afforded me vaulted me into a new kind of adulthood, one that graduate school had never let me glimpse.

· · ·

One story I learned to tell was about the night my father took me to a strip club in Poza Rica. I'd arrived to his tiny house late on a Wednesday, and as I'd come to expect, nothing much was happening. My grandmother sat in front of the TV playing solitaire and watching telenovelas, and my stepmother sat at the white plastic kitchen table smoking cigarettes and looking out the back window. Sweating and bored, my father asked me if I'd like to go out. Like always, this meant we'd be going to La Herradura, a tiny bar where the oilmen and roughnecks of the shitty town met after hours to ogle the waitresses and talk shop over carne asada and glasses of beer. Going there had become our routine. On one trip back to Xalapa, as I told the gang that part of it, Sean had explained how this was a ritual to be cherished—that is, getting fucked up with your dad for the first time—and it was usually at those outings at La Herradura that, after he'd had enough to drink, my father would tell me about the time when he met my mother, or the time when we were all in the Virgin Islands, or some other wonder that astounded me. When he got drunk, he'd harp on the true fact that I'd taken my first steps on the beaches at Magens Bay, a postcard-perfect place pined after by half the world, which was just a short walk from our trailer home in the cow field.

But that night, he was feeling frisky. Maybe something was going on with his wife, or maybe he enjoyed that we'd found lots in common and had begun connecting. More likely, though, it was just that his friend Sergio, a business associate, suggested the lewd outing. Whatever it was, we left La Herradura that night earlier than usual. The three of us, my dad, Sergio, and me, piled into Sergio's car and headed for the place, called La Bomba. We arrived already drunk, and when the giant tattooed bouncer saw we'd come with Sergio, he let us in. I saw how passively my dad shuffled in and I realized then that that's where I must have gotten it. I followed him, and we took a row of stools against the wall. I was the only white person, a foot taller than anyone else. My light hair attracted the strippers, who must've smelled American dollars, for within minutes, Sergio was offering me high fives as a string of beautiful, sad women removed their clothes for us and gyrated without shame on the disgusting table before us filled with cigarette butts and spilled drinks. As a perverted kind of thank-you to me for attracting them over, Sergio spoke in whispers to one of the girls and summoned her to my lap. She sat on my thigh, fully naked, and started rubbing up against me. Within moments, she took my hand off my drink and put it on her body, stared deep into my eyes from a place I'd never know, as if she understood just who I was and how I'd gotten here. She moved my hand down her body, all the way down to her thighs. Out of the corner of my eye, I saw Sergio making the exact face of a stock sexual criminal, complete with snarled lips and leering eyes as he licked his lips. The girl took two of my fingers and put them inside her, never once averting her gaze. I let out a gasp, glimpsed my father turning away. I didn't want to push any farther in, didn't want to pull away. She held me there for an extended moment. She rolled her eyes up into her head and shut her lids, then leaned back enough so that my fingers slid out. A terrifying wave of applause rose up around me. The woman smiled the smile of an athlete fully in command of the fans, like she was celebrating a last-second shot in the Final Four.

Next thing I remembered, we were back in the car. My father drove us drunk toward Sergio's. He seemed nearly as stunned by the goings-on as me. All the while, Sergio kept blabbering about the girl. When we got to his house, Manuel unlocked his door and Sergio tumbled out, ranting about the pussy he wanted and the pussy he had and why was it that he'd ever stayed with his wife in the first place. Sophia came bubbling up into the clear air of my head then, and I longed to talk to her, to try to explain any of this at all, but she hadn't given me her Bay Area phone number.

In the overwhelming silence of Sergio's exit, my father motioned me up to the passenger seat from the back. There we sat, his mother's Town Car idling in the Poza Rican night. We were surrounded by the exhaust of oil refineries, their dim haze floating up and hiding the starlight in the weary Mexican night.

"I don't know what to say," he said. He put the car in gear. I had no idea where we were. The road lines blurred like melting neon as he swerved and slalomed. Just when I thought that silence would rule, he managed a few meager words.

"Son," he said. "I have something to tell you," he said. His eyes closed as he idled forward at a few kilometers per hour.

"What is it?" I asked, mainly to keep him awake. "You can tell me anything."

"You have a sister," he said.

"You mean Silvia?"

"No," he said. "Her name is Emi. She lives with her aunt in Mexico City."

Our tires were grating against the curb, ricocheting us back into the middle of the road. What could I say? What more could he have said? I started crying. As a child in Catholic school, teachers sent home flyers advertising events, but they only gave them to the oldest child of a family or, in the sadder cases, to the only child. To me. "Oldest and Only! Oldest and Only!" they would cry out at the end of the day like warmongers. I'd always wanted to be the oldest, and not just the only. And here it turned out, all this time, I'd been both.

The next day, I bussed to Mexico City. My father told me to send Emi his well wishes. She'd be very excited to meet me, he assured. He promised to set me up with his brother's family, who lived in DF. Not far, he said, from the last place he'd known my sister to be living. She'd be about seventeen now, he said. I was twenty-three.

My cousin Julio picked me up from the Mexico City bus station. He stood about my height, and like many of my new Mexican family, he seemed to have been informed about the fact that I had played college basketball. He wanted to talk to me about Hakeem Olajuwon and Kenny Smith. Vernon Maxwell, the Rockets. As he drove us to his parents' house, I answered his questions about the players I'd played against and the teams we'd played. He looked at me like I was some kind of celebrity. I wasn't. I'd only ever played NAIA ball, but it didn't matter. I wanted to sneak in questions about Emi, but he gave me no shot.

That night, after meeting Julio's mother and father—my aunt and uncle—and sharing an awkward meal and a one-way heart-to-heart with Julio in which he revealed his obsession with Silvia Saint the porn star and urged me against my will to watch *Faces of Death*, he agreed to take me over to Emi's house. He spoke about her in casual tones that suggested he'd known about her all his life and that her place in the family was not assured, that she'd been an outsider to that strange grouping of us, the León kids, that unincorporated collection of us so called because of the royal-sounding name we all shared. "You never knew about her?" he asked me, surprised. "Well, anyway," he said, "here we are. Go up these stairs and buzz the apartment for #3. When you're done, have her give me a call, and I'll pick you up."

As I climbed the stairs to the apartment building, I listened to the sound of his tires on the asphalt turning around. At the top of the landing, a metal box encased buzzers to different units. I pressed number three. Soon, a teenage girl with a face that reminded me of my own answered the door and smiled at me like an old friend. She pulled me into her embrace before I got a look at her eyes. She held me tight and real. We stayed like that forever. Swaying. She didn't want to let me go. I didn't want her to. I closed my eyes and thought of nothing and everything that I had been, everything that I had ever wanted. After a few moments, I started to feel like I understood something, and I hugged back fiercely. Eventually I opened my eyes and saw a woman in the hallway crying. Emi's aunt.

"Bienvenidos," she said. She motioned us into the apartment.

It was a small place with a cramped living room overstuffed with uncomfortable furniture and a couple of serene-looking cats. My sister took my hand and led me to her room. There on the wall, framed and dusted, hung pictures from the Baton Rouge newspaper, pictures of me playing for the state championship six years earlier. I looked at myself in the frame: I'm leaping in the air, high above two defenders, having just caught an alley-oop. From the angle the picture had been taken, it looked like I might dunk it. I was only six-two, though, and white, with no leaping ability. I remembered the play. I'd laid the ball in, simply, just as my grandfather had taught me. It had been a fluke that none of the defenders had seen the pass, and so it looked like I was soaring when really it was just that they were flat-footed and the picture had been taken from a worm's-eye view. You could see the outline of my body plainly, the grayscale *5* on my white jersey, but you couldn't see my face. "I've known about you my whole life," Emi said. "Even though I've never met you, I've always known that I love you."

· · ·

At La Chiva that next weekend, Sean and I sat at our usual seats. Gabriela and Enrique joined us, and I told them the story straight. For once, I didn't need prompting. I had something to say. Phrases occurred to me—phrases like "squalid refineries in the dusk" and "like something out of a Márquez novel," phrases I'd never used before. No one spoke as I narrated, and for the first time in my short and suddenly remarkable life, I felt the magic that comes from telling a story and telling it well. The hush of my audience invigorated me, offered me a sense of myself not as someone who had experienced wondrous things, though I realized then that that was true, too, but rather the sense that I was a person with the capacity to sing those songs and make them pleasing to the ear. There was a new woman in my little audience that night, a woman I'd sleep with eventually, awkwardly—my first and only one-night stand, a woman who walked me through the experience like a mother guiding a child—but that hadn't happened yet. A lot hadn't happened yet: I hadn't yet been told that I'd need to take my grandmother and her Town Car back across the border to her homeland in south Louisiana, leaving Sean to climb Mount Orizaba with his new Brazilian friend and return north later; hadn't yet confirmed my girlfriend's affair in the Bay Area; hadn't yet flown out to beg for her hand in marriage on a cloudy day on Half Moon Caye; hadn't yet been followed north by Gabriela; hadn't yet been told her story, how she'd been strong-armed into marrying Enrique at the tender age of fourteen; hadn't yet heard from Sean, heading back from Mexico to Baton Rouge with her in the car; hadn't yet heard him say that she was coming to stay with me to try out America; hadn't yet discovered all the strange and beautiful turns my father's pathetic life had taken.

But I had met my sister. And now, I'd told the story of our meeting. And these castaways had listened. In the din of expat conversation in the tiny goat bar, a childhood-Christmas calm was rising up through the blood of my family, that Louisiana family that raised me to be good, and when I finished telling my story, I put down my glass of beer, trembling. They sat silent in the wake of my words, and I accepted their gestures of empathy and compassion as a sacred offering I'd earned, as if the broken, raging world were finally now in order.

Cazones, 2016

MY DYING FATHER and his friend, the former mayor, told me that if it was stories of the massacre I wanted, then there was this old farmer living in a seaside village we should track down. So, we lowered ourselves into the mayor's old green Volkswagen Beetle—the two of them in front and myself in back—and made for La Costa Esmeralda.

From what I gathered on the road, this farmer we were after, he'd been a riot policeman at La Noche de Tlatelolco, the 1968 massacre in Mexico City at the time of the Olympics. "Sin duda," the mayor said, "he killed many people that day. He is a farmer now, my uncle. A very old man."

My father turned to me, smirked, and raised an eyebrow. Was he actually excited by this news? Since losing his last job, he was homeless now—and yet, as his mischievous expression declared, up for an adventure. I was, too. Across all the years that I'd been raised by my mother and then afterward working in Louisiana, I'd hardly known him, and yet I'd been told often about this spirit of adventure he possessed. It was the one thing I'd hoped might have bonded us, even if it never had.

Near the coast, the forest spit us out and we came upon a tiny town called Cazones. Stray dogs lay in the road, ribs showing. Crumbling cinder block houses slumped under the simple weight of their tin roofs. Women in full-length dresses held baskets and looked at us with practiced indifference. Barefoot children stopped kicking a soccer ball to watch us pass like we were a funeral procession carrying some famous dead. One of them raised his hand at the sight of Vicente, the mayor, who waved back. Potholes dotted the dirt road, and the brown sea washed up against rocks beside us. It was a cold December day, and the clouds made it feel even chillier.

Vicente banked a hard right just as it seemed we'd tumble into the surf. Looking between their heads and out the windshield, I saw the gray of the sky and a hill rising green and rocky beside the shoreline. We passed an abandoned hotel, beautiful in its decayed splendor, somehow gaunt seeming with its courtyard of plastic chairs and tables. Beyond, we came upon a cattle guard and a homemade gate. Vicente braked and got out to unlatch it. My father turned to ask me what I was thinking about all this, and I liked how this made our little operation feel like a collusion.

"We won't tell this old man you're a journalist," he said. "We'll just invite him to lunch and get him drunk. Then he'll start talking."

Vicente drove us through the open gate. The path rose up a muddy incline. Behind us, the gray sea became vaster with our heightened vista, and when I turned to face the front, I saw an open field and an old man wearing work boots and a jump suit. He was brandishing a shovel, spearing the dirt to dig a hole for a fence post. He didn't hear our Beetle, but when Vicente parked and we slammed the car doors shut, he turned to size us up. He stood like a bull, his expression impenetrable, and I had my first inkling of the obvious, that this was a bad idea. Vicente waved. "Tío!" he shouted.

The old man walked over, still holding the shovel. His eyes became legible. He had a full head of gray hair, wrinkles in his face that cut to the bone. They etched him into a constant expression of mild frustration. He was a hard worker, that much was plain.

"Tío Héctor!" Vicente said. They hugged. Héctor eyed my father and me. "Excuse me, uncle," Vicente said. "This is Manuel, my friend. He was a protestor at La Noche de Tlatelolco. Isn't that something? And this is his son. Also Manuel. He's a journalist, and he wants to ask you some questions about the old days. You know, the massacre. The riots. The ones you worked as a granadero. That was another lifetime ago, wasn't it?"

I knew better than to look at my father. Héctor stared at me and said nothing. His eyes said everything. "Mucho gusto," I offered. "Lo que pasa es que—" But Héctor cut me short. He whispered to his nephew. Vicente whispered back. Old Héctor excused himself. He said he wanted to check on his hens, but we all knew he was making a decision. When he moved out of view behind his farmhouse, I looked at my father for some sense of the moment. He was looking at Vicente. The two of them set themselves on the verge of laughing gravely, but they absolutely didn't.

"He knows he has sinned," Vicente said, as if this were simply a joke.

"Maybe we should leave before he comes back." I said.

"No!" Vicente replied. "We will do it like you said, Manuel: we will take him to lunch, get him drunk, and he will start talking. It's nothing, Manuel. No pasa nada."

"Well," my dad said, "that wasn't exactly the pl—"

Héctor returned donning a Dallas Cowboys cap, having removed his work gloves. He looked at me. "So, you want to hear about the massacre? Let's eat."

As he walked toward the car, Vicente opened the door for him. He got in back with me. We sat shoulder to shoulder, this killer and I, my father and the mayor in front again. We coasted the hill, cold sea frothing white before us, and then passed through the open gate. Vicente got out to close it, but he couldn't figure out the latch. My father got out to help, to no avail. They fumbled with it while I remained shoulder to shoulder with Héctor, who turned to watch them struggle. He smelled of sweat and fowl and manure, and I became aware of my own clean smell in his midst. My soap smell felt like an affront to his life's work, whatever it had been, and I hoped he wouldn't hold this against me, whatever that might mean. My father and Vicente yet fiddled with the latch, and I felt I had to break the terrifying silence. "They're no farmers," I said in my simple Spanish. To my relief, he laughed.

"No. Vicente, he was always like his mother. Very smart, that one, but very weak."

Still, more time to fill. "How many cows do you have?" I asked the murderer.

"Three," he said. "There is one you cannot see behind the house. She is the prettiest one."

"What is the weather like this time of year?"

Before he could answer, the bumbling duo returned. "We got it," Vicente said.

"Nice job," Héctor replied, then turned to me and winked.

As we rode on, his farm faded in the rearview. Vicente cruised along to the abandoned hotel, only it wasn't abandoned. We pulled up a gravel drive beside the courtyard, where an old woman appeared. She waved at Vicente, and he waved back. As we got out of the car, she came over to hug Héctor. Vicente introduced my father and me, and we took our seats at the plastic chairs. We sat less than a stone's throw from the roaring sea. Because it was so cold, the woman disappeared and returned with jackets for us all—except Héctor, who remained sleeveless. "I'll make some food and put on coffee," she said. Shortly, she returned with shrimp tostadas and coffee and took a seat beside Héctor.

"What's the occasion?" she asked.

"Well," Vicente started. We each settled into distinct roles: Vicente was the touchstone, the excuse for the gathering, the nephew who turned conversation to family when things got touchy. The old woman—Héctor's sister, it turned out—played the dutiful cook who would leave to fetch coffee and snacks. My father was the gracious and curious interviewer, the eloquent family friend with a different take on the old days who, as I'd been told he could always manage with anyone, quickly established a rapport with Héctor. I was the listener, the one for whose benefit my father's questions were being asked. And Héctor, he was the storyteller.

He told many stories, any one of which a writer would happily stake his reputation on: of prostitutes holding court with Octavio Paz in a giant mansion off the Paseo de Malecon in Veracruz, of grenades hidden in a middle school classroom in the jungles of Guerrero during a stand-off between agitators and the military, of secret orders given behind the scenes of the massacre I'd made the trip to Mexico to write about. He told the kinds of stories you don't forget. The kind I'd dedicated my life to pursuing. The kind I'd so far failed to find in my middling career. The kind you ache for in times when you want to wish your own life away. The kind you wish were your own, if only you could have them without the lived experience and pain beneath them.

There was one story he told at my father's precise prodding, one I know my father and I both cherished in the same way, though we never talked about it and I never saw him again after that trip. It was a story that helped me see that, at least in accidental moments, Manuel really could be the man I'd always dreamed he was.

In 1956, Héctor was eight years old. This was in Tuxpan, where he was raised, just a few kilometers from where we were sitting. In those days, Héctor and his friends would play guitar and sing songs at the bridge passing into town. Sometimes, beachgoing tourists would stop and ask for son jarocho. The kids would play a song in that style, and maybe get a peso or two in return. Héctor was all right on the guitar, and the money added up.

One day, a strange man crossed the bridge on foot. They didn't see where he'd come from. His Spanish was touched with a foreign accent. "Do you kids want to make some money?" he asked. "Sure," they said. "Okay, then. Come next week at exactly this time. If you're here, I will know you are serious, and I will ask you again."

They thought nothing of it. A lot of crazy travelers came through. Still, they made sure to play the bridge the next week at the same time. And again, this same man came by, this time driving a car. A Cadillac. He was dressed in linen. He wore dark sunglasses and a pressed shirt. He smiled like a fox and he seemed to know what he was doing. "Do you still want to make some money?" he asked. "Sure," they said again. "Okay, then. Not far from here, there is an open field, a triangular cow pasture bordered on two sides by the sea, on the other by the road. Follow this path beside the bridge for two kilometers, and look to your right. That is the field. Do you know it?"

They nodded.

"Okay, then. Meet me in that field next Saturday, and if you do what I tell you, I'll give you each 8,000 pesos."

The stranger left them at the bridge, and they leapt in excitement. This was 1956, and 8,000 pesos would have been—"Well," Héctor said, "think of what we could have done with that money!" They were going to be rich. They spent that week immersed in the dream of eloping from Tuxpan forever, of leaving their families behind for great adventures.

The following Saturday, they walked to the field. The stranger was there. "Okay," he said. "Here is what will happen. In thirty minutes, planes will fly overhead, very low to the ground. Very loud. They will drop boxes from their cargo holds. The boxes will be wooden crates with parachutes. They will land in this field. When the crates land, pick them up. They will be heavy. Carry them to the house at the top of the hill." And the stranger pointed to the top of the hill. Héctor recognized the house then, the one with the boat beside it. "When you finish bringing all of the crates to the top of the hill, meet me by the—" But Héctor stopped listening once he saw the house. The boat gave it away. Everyone in town knew it. It was headquarters for Fidel, the house from which he'd been planning and preparing. And these crates, they would be filled with the guns and ammo he would use once he landed in Cuba.

These children, including Héctor, they did not stop to say "no thank you," and they did not stop running until they were in their homes with their mothers and their fathers. They hid inside for a month, and then for longer—until that boat was gone, and with it Fidel, until it was safe to go back to being the children they'd been before: children playing at being grown-ups whose parents still worried for them, children who played guitar at the side of a bridge, happy to think that the people who passed through their lives were nothing but benign strangers who were also mothers and fathers, the kind of people who might take pity on local boys with only innocent songs and no whiff of revolution, no hint of violence or mischief yet in their eyes.

Héctor fell silent. He was as shocked that he'd told the story as any of us—except my father. My homeless wreck of an emphysemic father, who would die only weeks later. He'd known what to ask. When to stay quiet. What expression to offer at what moments of the telling. When to give that subtlest of laughs that is simply an exhalation through the nose. In the wash of the surf and the quiet of the table by the sea, the very sea that Castro had braved sixty years before, he had stolen a glance at me as the old man gestured and held court. I'd caught it, too. It didn't last longer than half a second. His eyebrow had raised. Hint of a smile, soft as rain. "Here," he was saying, "this is for you."

ACKNOWLEDGMENTS

THIS BOOK WAS twenty years in the making. So many people contributed to it. In early years, Paul Kelly and John Biguenet lit the fire. In graduate school, Valerie Sayers provided wit and wisdom and guidance. She and John Crawford have remained true over decades. Tony D'Souza showed the way.

In conference workshops, many insightful and kindhearted supporters nudged me toward better stories—Luis Urrea, Mona Simpson, Gregory Spatz, Elizabeth Kostova, and Matt Bondurant helped me with those appearing here. Beth Staples and Rus Bradburd published two of these stories when no one else would. Special thanks to *Ecotone*, *American Short Fiction*, *Fifth Wednesday Journal*, *Cosmonauts Avenue*, *Puerto del Sol*, *Xavier Review*, and *Ellipsis*, journals that published works appearing in this collection.

At the University of Iowa Press, many hardworking, passionate people helped bring this book to life: Jim McCoy, Karen Copp, Allison Means, Sara Hales-Brittain, and Susan Hill Newton, thank you. Thanks also to Elizabeth Sheridan, copyeditor extraordinaire, and to Julia Borcherts, Hailey Dezort, Jordan Brown, Nicole Leimbach, and Dana Kaye, who helped immensely with publicity.

Many organizations provided hope in moments when it felt like I should find something else to do. Bread Loaf, Squaw Valley, the Sozopol

Fiction Seminars, Lighthouse Writers in Denver, and Aspen Summer Words were places of inspiration.

A host of friends and intimates kept me afloat through this process in different times, in ways mysterious and life-affirming: Amanda Bourgeois, David J. Daniels, Jay Baus, Marion Rohrleitner, Jeremy Sparks, Scott Losavio, Aaron O'Connell, Erica Martz, Robert LeBlanc, Anna Blundy, Mike Toups, Andrea Sanz, Sarah Hoffman. You believed, even when I didn't.

For fifteen years, my boss, Doug Hesse, encouraged me regularly, never once questioning if maybe I should dedicate a little more time to committee work. I probably should've.

Dad, I'm grateful that our story hasn't ended in quite the way this collection does.

There's too much to say, Mom. We'll talk. I love you.

Brandon Taylor, you changed my life by choosing this collection.

THE IOWA SHORT FICTION AWARD AND THE
JOHN SIMMONS SHORT FICTION AWARD WINNERS,
1970–2021

Lee Abbott
Wet Places at Noon
Cara Blue Adams
You Never Get It Back
Donald Anderson
Fire Road
Dianne Benedict
Shiny Objects
Marie-Helene Bertino
Safe as Houses
Will Boast
Power Ballads
David Borofka
Hints of His Mortality
Robert Boswell
Dancing in the Movies
Mark Brazaitis
*The River of Lost Voices:
Stories from Guatemala*
Jack Cady
The Burning and Other Stories

Jennine Capó Crucet
How to Leave Hialeah
Pat Carr
The Women in the Mirror
Kathryn Chetkovich
Friendly Fire
Cyrus Colter
The Beach Umbrella
Marian Crotty
What Counts as Love
Jennifer S. Davis
Her Kind of Want
Janet Desaulniers
What You've Been Missing
Sharon Dilworth
The Long White
Susan M. Dodd
Old Wives' Tales
Merrill Feitell
*Here Beneath Low-Flying
Planes*

Douglas Trevor
*The Thin Tear in the Fabric
of Space*
Laura Valeri
The Kind of Things Saints Do
Anthony Varallo
This Day in History
Ruvanee Pietersz Vilhauer
*The Water Diviner and
Other Stories*
Don Waters
Desert Gothic
Lex Williford
Macauley's Thumb

Miles Wilson
Line of Fall
Russell Working
Resurrectionists
Emily Wortman-Wunder
Not a Thing to Comfort You
Ashley Wurzbacher
Happy Like This
Charles Wyatt
Listening to Mozart
Don Zancanella
Western Electric